# PUMMEL IN THE TUNNEL

I first noticed that something was definitely wrong when somebody hit me in the back of the head with a club.

I went flying down on my knees and elbows, slapped the ground, yelled, and came up on the bounce, smashing someone's testicles in the process.

A whole platoon of thugs was pouring out of a small doorway in the side of the tunnel. I caught a wall with one hand while swinging with the other. Then there were other things there, and I was surrounded by dozens of them.

In the movies, the hero always beats the crowd of bad guys because the stupid bad guys always come at him one at a time, giving him the chance to take out one opponent at a time. In real life, if your enemies have any brains and coordination at all, they will mob you, all of them at once, and then you will go down, no matter how good you are. At best, you might take out one or two before you are deleted.

My opponents seemed to have neither brains nor coordination, but they did have enthusiasm, and there were an awful lot of them. Also, even waiting in line takes a certain amount of coordination, and for these idiots, fighting seemed to be a series of random events. Once, apparently by accident, four of them came at me at once, and I had to drop and roll. Fortunately, they weren't bright enough to know what to do to me once I was down. I was up again in a hurry, and dancing around.

I swear that there were at least fifteen of them on me alone. Against odds like that, you fight to win, without thinking about the damage, jail time, or lawsuits you might be generating. I've always been partial to knees. Knees are low and easy to get to without the flashy, dangerous, high kicks that some of the other good targets require. Also, knees break easily, they put your opponent down fast, and barring modern surgery, they generally don't heal properly for years, if they heal at all.

I guess I broke a lot of knees that night.

# BAEN BOOKS by LEO A. FRANKOWSKI

*A Boy and His Tank*

*The Fata Morgana*

# THE
# FATA
# MORGANA

## LEO FRANKOWSKI

THE FATA MORGANA

Copyright © 1999 by Leo A. Frankowski

A Baen Book

Baen Publishing Enterprises
P.O. Box 1403
Riverdale, NY 10471

ISBN: 0-671-57876-6

Cover art by Gary Ruddell

First paperback printing, July 2000

Library of Congress Catalog Number 99-27089

Distributed by Simon & Schuster
1230 Avenue of the Americas
New York, NY 10020

Production by Windhaven Press, Auburn, NH
Printed in the United States of America

## ACKNOWLEDGMENTS

A lot of good people helped me out by proofreading this book, and by giving me many valuable suggestions. Special thanks go to L. Warren Douglas, Alan G. Greenberg, Gilbert Parker, Tom and Jane Devlin, and Mike Hubble, who has a habit of quoting my books back at me, chapter and verse.

# ONE

The boat was dismasted, and in parting company the mast had knocked a hole in the bottom of the ferrocrete hull.

We were sinking in a Force Ten gale, with gusts of up to seventy, but it was debatable whether she would sink to the bottom of the East Pacific Basin, or wreck herself on the rocky shores of an island that couldn't possibly be where it obviously was.

We had already done everything we could think of, which wasn't nearly enough. We had stuffed a mattress into the hole, and wedged and blocked it in as best we could with the sea water slapping to and fro on the lower deck. Tons of stuff were awash down there. Plugging the hole seemed to help only a little. The water in the hold wasn't getting any deeper, but it wasn't getting noticeably shallower, either.

The engines had flooded out early on, taking the big pumps west with them, and the electric pumps were losing ground as the batteries slowly died. Adam was valiantly working the manual bailer, but he was only postponing the inevitable.

The automatic distress beacon was ready to be switched on and the life raft was inflated, loaded and in the water. Back in the cockpit, all I could do was wait and see if our navigation was really five hundred miles off, and I was staring at one of the Line Islands, or if the solid looking thing in front of me was really a mirage, the Fata Morgana, as Adam had twice called it.

A sad ending for a pair of good engineers, I suppose, but perhaps a better way to go than some of the alternatives. I've read that drowning beats the hell out of, say, death by fire, but I don't know where the writer got his information.

# TWO

I guess it all really started because of a problem that exists in the Special Machinery business.

Special Machines are designed and built one at a time, in accordance with your customer's needs and specifications. If he manufactures widgets, you might make him a machine that assembles widgets, or maybe paints them, or wraps them in plastic film for shipment.

Each special machine is specially designed, you could even say invented, to do only one thing, but to do that one thing extremely well. Such a machine can be very productive, but it is generally of use to only one company. Thus, our industry is one of the last bastions of craftsmanship in this increasingly automated, mass production world.

To be sure, our machines are largely responsible for all that bland mass production, since they can turn out identical products at a fraction of the cost of any other method known, but there is nonetheless a great deal of personal satisfaction in designing something, building it, and then watching it work as you had planned. It is a rare joy that the operators of our machines can never have. When there *is* an operator, that is, and the whole system is not completely automated.

❖        ❖        ❖

I've always liked workshops and factories. Some people—my ex-wife, for example—claim that the industrial environment is alien, unnatural, and inhuman, but for me it is the most natural thing in the world.

I am a man, and as such I am as much a part of nature as any tree or beaver or bee. The machines that I build are as natural as any beaver lodge or bee hive. If there is any fundamental difference, it is that, being a man, I use the mind nature gave me to direct my efforts, rather than depending on my instincts alone. Even then, I don't think that I can claim that a beaver never thought about her work, or that she never sat back to admire a well built dam.

In Special Machines, our sort of craftsmanship entails a whole set of problems of its own, problems that the rest of the world rarely perceives.

You see, in order to get new business for your company, you have to have competent people ready to start on your customer's job. No purchasing agent in his right mind would trust an important order to someone who had nothing but a vacant shop.

And in order to get competent people, you have to have interesting work for them to do. Even if you could afford to pay them to sit and do nothing while you were waiting for the next job to come in, the best workers would all quit within days, leaving you with no one but the sort of people who would be better off working for the government. When you start paying people to not work, you are automatically selecting for incompetence.

It's a shame, but the only sane course of action is when the work is gone, you have to lay almost everybody off. It hurts, but there's nothing else you can do.

It then becomes a matter of "If we had some eggs, we could have some ham and eggs, if we had some

ham." I've seen a few companies that never were able
to get started up again. Oh, in an ideal world, there
would always be a fresh job to get into whenever the
last job was winding down, but if I ever began to notice
that happening to me on a regular basis, I'd start
believing in Santa Claus, or maybe even God.

So when a big (for us) Chrysler welding line was
getting ready to be shipped, and nothing new was
in the offing, most of my best engineers had their
computers in word processing mode. They were
updating their resumes on company time, and I knew
that I was in trouble.

Oh, I had plenty of money. The previous three jobs
had been profitable, the company bank account was
flush, and I hadn't even been paid yet for the last
one. The trouble was, looking for work, I'd called
on everybody I knew (and many that I didn't) and
I hadn't been able to find anything, anywhere, that
was ready to shake loose in less than two months.

By which time I would have to hire a whole new
bunch of strangers, assuming that I could find such
people. Then I would likely end up having to fire
half of them for incompetence, after gracing each such
bumble fingered fool with a month's pay in return
for his efforts at screwing things up. And then I would
have to waste yet another month teaching those with
some small bit of ability the proper way to get things
done. That is to say, *my* way.

All with the net result of an ungodly amount of
personal aggravation, late deliveries, and cost over-
runs that, in this industry, you generally have to eat
on your own. It's not like doing "cost plus" work
for the government. Starting with a new crew, my
next job would run at a loss, not only to my bank
account, but also to my reputation, which—in the long
run—is the only really important thing that any
company has ever got. Once you have the right reputation, you can *buy* everything else you need.

# THREE

I sat alone in my office wondering what I would do next, after I fired everybody, when the room darkened and I noticed that my chief engineer was filling the doorway into my office.

Adam Kulczyinski is the biggest man I've ever met, standing six foot five, and so wide that, from a distance, he looks squat. He's powerful, not like a bodybuilder, but like a big time wrestler who's going to seed. He has thick legs, thicker arms, and a big, hanging gut. When you add thinning, unruly hair, bushy eyebrows, and a huge beak of a nose, you have a remarkable looking individual.

He walked in with a yellow legal pad filled with numbers and sketches, sat down in the chair across from me, and put his feet up on my desk. His shoes were very expensive Italian jobs, since with what I had to pay to keep him, he could afford anything he wanted. But the soles were worn through because he never got enough time off work to either have them fixed or buy a new pair.

His suit was crumpled, of course, since his suit was *always* crumpled. On business trips, I've seen Adam put on a good suit fresh from the cleaners, and watched it crumple as he stood there. It was just one of his many magical talents.

Another of his peculiarities was that he always wore both a belt and suspenders. I'd asked him about that, and he'd said, "A good engineer, he don't take no chances."

Now, most people would get fired for putting heel marks on their boss's desk, but I'll put up with a lot from a man who really knows what he's doing.

Hell, once I went into engineering to find Adam winning a *farting* contest with a Japanese customer. Three detailers were acting as judges, holding up scorecard numbers for volume, odor, and tonal quality. When I mentioned his conduct to him later, all he would allow was that, "Yeah, well, it probably woudda shown more class if I'd 'a let da customer win. I just got carried away wit da spirit of da competition, is all."

Adam was one of the few people left in the world who still spoke with a Hamtramck (pronounced hamTRAMik) accent. Hamtramck is a small city that is completely surrounded by the city of Detroit, like a tough little amoeba that a bigger amoeba could swallow but couldn't quite digest. Any place else in the world, the larger city would simply have absorbed the smaller one, but here, for fairly good reasons, the city fathers involved were just plain scared to try it.

You see, early in the century, Hamtramck had been populated by Poles who had abandoned Europe in favor of the American car factories. For many years, it was actually the largest Polish-speaking city on earth. Thus, those who "came over on the boat" never had to learn English at all, and the second generation developed something that was almost a creole of English and Polish. It involved substituting a "T" sound for an unvoiced "TH", and a "D" for the one that was voiced. The word order used was half way between the two parent languages, and its other unwritten rules were beyond my understanding. Furthermore, while I have never been able to get

Adam to admit it, I am positive that he has a lot
of fun making his statements as deliberately ambigu-
ous as possible, and just filled with internal contra-
dictions.

In writing this history, I have found that I am completely unable to do justice (or rather to do proper
injustice) to his strange accent. Nothing that I am
capable of putting on paper sounds exactly like
whatever it is that Adam actually does. I regret to
say that even when I am quoting him, you must take
it for granted that what I am actually doing is para-
phrasing his statements into something closer to a
civilized tongue.

Yet while Adam's accent was probably authentic,
to the extent that it really was what he grew up
with, it was more than a little bit phony as well.
I say this because sometimes, when he was tired
or distracted, he would start speaking pure, Midwest Standard English, the language of Walter
Cronkite, until he caught himself and went back to
his Hamtramck accent.

His constant use of an illiterate creole convinced
some people that he was a "regular" sort of guy, and
others, who didn't know him well, that he was a fool.
He liked people thinking both of those things. Very
few of his associates realized that he had graduated
*summa cum laude* from Michigan Tech, an engineering
school that is second only to Cal Tech and MIT. He
never mentioned it. In fact, I've heard him denying
that he'd even graduated from high school. The only
reasons I knew about his education were because I'd
seen his resume when I'd hired him, and because I
went to the same school that he had. Oh, he'd been
a senior when I was a freshman, and we'd never
actually met during that year, but it was not easy
to miss a man as big as Adam in a crowd.

Even then, I'd phoned our old school, not so much
to verify his technical skills, but to see if he'd actually

passed an English course. He had. Indeed, he'd minored in English Literature, and pulled straight A's doing it.

But whether it was because of or in spite of his various peculiarities, when Adam designed a machine, the machine performed flawlessly. What's more, it generally worked perfectly the first time it was turned on.

Therefore, if Adam wanted to talk with his feet on my desk, I was willing to listen with my feet on the rug.

"I take it that that's not your resume," I said, pointing to his pad of yellow notes.

"Nah, I do dose on one of da draftin plotters, on dat nice cotton bond what I had you pay for."

"I wondered why you wanted that stuff."

"Well, if you woudda axed me, I woudda told youse."

"Maybe I just didn't want to know. So what's your idea?"

"So sales has screwed up again, and we're looking at some serious layoffs."

From Adam, this was a remarkably tactful statement, seeing as how I did most of the actual sales work myself. Not out of choice, you understand, but because I have yet to find a sales engineer who was both good at his job and willing to work for somebody else once he'd learned the ropes. You have to be a good engineer to be able to talk to other engineers, and once you have the sales contacts besides, the temptation to "buy your own cannon," and run a company the way one ought to be run is just too strong.

I'm very familiar with the process, since that's how I got my company started twelve years ago, and that's how I lost my first (and last) four sales engineers. And so although I suppose that it represents a monumental case of hypocrisy on my part, well, let's just say that I'd gotten tired of training my own future competitors a long ways back.

"Look, I've gotten solid promises for two big lines in a couple of months. Most of the guys and girls have been working sixty, seventy hours a week for over a year now. By the time they come back from a long, deserved, company-paid vacation, there will be plenty of work for them to do," I said.

"Nah, you know better den dat. Dees guys, dey been pulling down twice deir regular wages for so long dat dey tink forty hours' pay is like bein' on welfare. Dere's udder outfits around wit plenty of work dat'ud snap up our best people in a hurry. But me, I figure dat if we could give dem sometin fun to do, we could keep our best ones, anyway. Say ten from engineering and maybe a dozen from da shop. Da other tirty-five, well, dey're not so bad, but we could live without 'em, and anyway, dey're the ones dat will still be dere without a job when we need 'em back again."

"There's money in the bank to pay for it, but what's your plan?"

"I figure dat you've always wanted a yacht." He pronounced it with the "ch" sound left in. "You never said nuttin about it, but everybody else wants one, and you always looked pretty normal. So. Did you know dat you can buy da materials for da hull of a one-hundred-foot-long yacht for around ten tousand dollars, if you build it out of ferrocrete?"

"Now wait a minute. A hundred footer, new, has to go for something like a couple of million bucks, at least, and the hull has to be the major expense item of any ship. There has to be a catch, somewhere!"

"Dere is! Ferrocrete is pretty labor intensive to make, but keeping people busy is exactly what you want to do just now."

"Even so, the gap between ten thousand and two million is still too fantastic."

"You got to look at da economics of da yacht-makin business. Dose tings are built for people who got too much money an' don't know what else to do wit it. Did you know dat half da production cost of one of dose big babies goes into teak wood decking an' cherry cabinet work on da insides? You're talkin a coupla hundred bucks a board foot for some of dat stuff! Now, you don't own no teak in your office or your car or your house, so why should you want any on your boat?"

"Okay, so we keep it sensible and Spartan, but you're still a long way from saving two million bucks."

"You got to look at deir sales expenses too, boss. All dose fancy showrooms. All dose magazines wit all dose slick photos, an' all dose good-lookin girls in dose string bikinis, or dose better-lookin girls not in dose string bikinis. I've heard dat da total weight of all da books an' magazines about yachting produced each year outweighs da actual boats produced each year by a factor of more den tree to one."

"That's hard to believe. But anyway, say we get our best people involved in building this boat. Why, a hundred footer will absolutely fill the big assembly bay. If a customer walks in and sees it, he'll know that we don't have any serious work under way, and he'll drive the price down to the point where we couldn't make a profit, knowing how hard up we are. And when we *do* get a real job in, what do we do with the half finished boat? Scrap it?"

"Not to worry. I got dat all figured out. We rent da warehouse across da alley from da shop. It's been empty for a year an should oughta come cheap. Den if a customer comes over unexpected, you or Shirley holds him up in da front office for a few minutes while da rest of us runs back to da shop and looks busy. An' when we get real work in, we just leave da boat sittin dere until we hit another slow spot. I figure dat just having it dere will make da guys an' girls feel a lot more secure."

"Okay, say we do this thing. Just what am I going to do with a yacht once we get it done? I haven't had time to work out with my Karate master for months. I haven't had time for a vacation in eight years!"

"So dat's da udder beauty of my plan, boss. Once we get it done, when we hit a slow spot like now, we all go for a boat ride! Wit a boat dat big, we got room for all our people an' deir wives an' kids an' husbands. Or, if da season's wrong, from what I hear, dere's always more work you can do on a boat. Like dey say, 'a boat is a hole in da water dat you pours your money into.' Or in our case, our man-hours."

"I doubt if they say it quite the way you do, but okay, okay. You've sold me to the extent that I'll seriously explore the idea with you."

"I figured dat you'd come around." Adam turned to the open door past which our accountant-secretary-receptionist sat. "Hey, Shirley! It's a go!"

"Dammit! I didn't say that!"

"Yeah, but you will."

Shirley brought in a roll of drawings, smiled and left. I gritted my teeth. Among my best people, I believe in running a loose ship, but I also believe in getting a little respect now and then, too.

"So this is something you've designed, Adam?"

"Nah, da Coast Guard dey wouldn't let me do it. Seems dat you got to be a la-ti-da Naval Architect before you can draw a rowboat, an' us lowly Professional Engineers just ain't good enough. Dis is a standard plan, wit maybe a dozen built like it in da last ten years or so. I got maybe forty or fifty little changes I want to make in it, but I figure I can sell da brass on 'em okay."

What he showed me were the plans for a huge sloop, with a single mast reaching to a hundred and forty feet above the water line. Her beam was twenty-eight feet. Drawing eighteen feet, she displaced over a hundred tons of water. The ballast alone weighed almost forty-five tons, and she carried over five thousand square feet of Dacron in her two sails.

"Big."

"Look, boss, we gotta have room for forty people. If da guys an' girls tought dat dey was buildin dis ting just for you, well, deir hearts wouldn't be in it and dey'd start tinkin dat gettin back into da machinery business somewheres else wasn't such a bad idea. Even like it is, dere ain't much spare space. Half da people will be sleeping in a bunk room, and da married couples only get an enclosed half of a queen-sized bunk bed. You, however, get a spacious owner's cabin in da stern."

"It doesn't look very spacious. What's more, it's right above the engines. It'll be as noisy as hell in there."

"It won't be dat bad, boss. Lots of soundproofin. Anyway, we won't be using da engines except when we're going in or out of port, or in an emergency, and you'd want to be on deck dose times anyway."

"Grumble. I take it that you plan on getting this big cabin in the front of the boat for yourself?"

"And give myself a bigger stateroom dan my boss's? Never would I be so crass! No, dat's for nobody in particular. It's just sort of a social room. I mean, you know, sometimes a guy has to spend a little time alone wit his girl, an' I figure dat if we don't give 'em someplace to do it, dey'll be sneakin around an' messin up da sail locker all da time."

"Oh. Here you had me thinking that you'd finally found the right woman to settle down with. I still say you ought to try married life. I mean, we all joke about it, and a bachelor like you only hears about the down side of marriage, when your friends are in the doghouse, but use your couch instead. But I can testify that a wife and maybe someday kids are what really makes life worth while."

"Yeah? Well, if your home life is so great, why don't you spend more of your life in your home? As often as you get dere, I'm surprised dat your wife remembers who you are. I saw you sleep in your office for a week straight, when we was late gettin dat Chevy Tonawanda job out."

"A necessary temporary expedient. Find yourself a good woman, Adam."

"Lookit, boss. I got restaurants to do my cookin, customers to bitch at me, and a government to take away all my money. What da hell do I need wit a wife?"

"If you say so," I sighed. "Another thing. These are damn big sails. Putting them up and taking them down will be a hell of a job."

"You're way behind da times, boss. We got hydraulic roller reefin' on bote da sails, and hydraulic winches on everyting else. Dere's an onboard computer dat can keep her on course no matter what, an' a satellite navigation an' guidance system dat knows where it is to witin ten meters, anywheres on Eart. Dis baby can be sailed by one person alone, an' even den you only got to check on tings every so ofen."

"We both know just how unreliable automatic machines can be. Murphy's Law rules the universe."

"Right. An' when tings *do* get screwed up, like you know dey will, we'll have plenty of manpower on board to set tings right."

"This boat's going to be fast, huh?"

"Fast enough. It won't win no races, but where's da sense in buildin a superfast boat? You want to get somewheres in a hurry, you book a flight on a jet. Dis boat's for gettin dere wit style!"

"Uh-huh. You are sure that all our best people will go along with this plan?"

"Natch. I've already talked it over wit each one of dem, sort of on da sly, you know?"

My thought was, *What the hell. It will probably keep most of my key people happy, and it just might turn out to be fun.*

"Okay, let's do it. But if I hear one single joke about boat anchors, the whole deal is off." In the Special Machinery business, a boat anchor is a machine that never did work properly.

As he got up to leave, I said, "Say, have you given any further thought to that offer I made you the other day? You know, about being a partner here."

"Nope. Don't have to tink about it. Da answer's da same as it was last week an' last munt an' last year. I don't want nuttin to do wit da headaches o' being a boss. Da way it is now, I do what I like to do an' I got nuttin to worry about. An' I still figure dat in da long run, I make more money gettin a paycheck den you do gettin to keep whatever's left over after da bills is paid."

"Well, perhaps true, but there are some great benefits to running your own show."

"Bennies? What do I need wit more bennies? I got a big new company car, a company parkin spot wit my name on it, an' a company expense account in case I feel like takin a cab to work. Shit, now I'm even gonna get a company *yacht*!"

# FOUR

I got home almost early that night and took my wife, Helen, out to dinner. We ate out often, since cooking was one of the things she didn't like to do, and she wasn't much good at it when she did do it. She made up for it in other ways. Even now, after a messy divorce, I still think that she is one of the most beautiful women I've ever met.

She was tall, or at least taller than I was, with a slender set of geometrically perfect curves that she carried with an inborn, aristocratic poise. She had long, straight blond hair that framed a face that was almost too perfect to be real. I don't think that I ever looked at her without being amazed anew that such a vision of loveliness could be mine.

We'd gone to high school together, where she had been a rhythmic gymnast, a cheerleader, and the homecoming queen. Not that I was the homecoming king, far from it. And my only sport was karate, which in my neighborhood was more a matter of survival than something you did for fun. Actually, we didn't have much to do with each other back then. I just admired from afar, knowing that I would never get a chance to get any closer to her. I doubt if she noticed me at all.

I went off to college, graduated, and went to work in the machinery business. All told, I've been fairly successful.

Helen spent a summer in charm school, something she didn't need, and then went on to Michigan State University. Washing out in her freshman year, she came home and married her high-school sweetheart. A big fellow, he had been the quarterback of the our high-school football team, and was as handsome as she was beautiful.

His only big problems were that he was a thief, an alcoholic, and a worthless bum. The marriage broke up, and someone told me that for a time, Helen worked in Detroit as a topless dancer. I've tried not to find out much about that.

I met her again just after I'd started up my own company here in our home town. I was on a winning streak, and Helen seemed to be a part of all the good things that were happening to me.

Now, I was by then a long way from being a starry-eyed pup in high school. Yes, I noticed the small signs of drug addiction, just as I guessed that she was early in the second trimester of pregnancy. But I also knew that she was the loveliest woman I'd ever seen, and that one such as I was lucky to get her any way I could. With enough tender, loving care, we could work her through her problems.

Maybe, if I'd had a father to advise me . . . But I hadn't seen my parents for fifteen years. And anyway, for the first few years after we were married, things worked out pretty well for Helen and me. If there really had been a drug problem, she licked it. Well, in later years she got to drinking a bit much, but that's something else, entirely. In the same way, her stomach bulge disappeared, and she was no longer sick in the morning.

Yes, I was making a lot of money, and yes, she liked having lots of money. Well, I liked money, too.

Hell, who doesn't? I tell you that for a lot of years, being married to Helen was good.

By the time we started working on the boat, our marriage was starting to get less good. Quickly.

Inside of a week, the old warehouse had been leased, our big plotter had turned out full-scale drawings of the ribs, and our plumbers and electricians were bending three-inch black iron pipe into the flowing curves that would form the hull. More pipe and re-rod went into framing out the bulkheads, which were then wrapped with hundreds of yards of chicken wire and plasterer's lath. Then it was all sewn tightly together with steel wire to form a dense mat, and by the third week these bulkheads were being welded to the massive I beam that formed her keel and stem.

Twenty layers of chicken wire and lath were stretched over the ribs and bulkheads, followed by three more layers of re-rod, and then even more chicken wire and lath. All this was stitched together by pairs of people with pliers, passing steel wire through the hull to pull it all together.

When this dense steel fabric was completed—hull, deck, and bulkheads—Adam handed out big rubber mallets to all and sundry, and we spent three days 'fairing' the hull, making it as smooth and hydrodynamic as chicken wire and lath can get. My wife Helen even showed up one day and actually did over an hour's worth of manual labor.

We stood back and admired.

She was huge. Even though she was belly up and not yet infused with concrete, she was a thing of beauty.

Directing the work was Adam's job, since I had to spend most of my time on the road, trying to find some real work for my young company. Still, it made my sales job easier, being able to show to potential customers a full crew working back at the shop.

Three times during the construction of the hull, we had VIPs over. Shirley would press a button on the underside of her desk that connected to an alarm bell in our boat shop, and then flutter about with charming, feigned inefficiency, getting the customer a coffee that he really didn't want.

Meanwhile, Adam would be yelling "SHOWTIME!" and hustling our crew back across the alley to our special machinery factory. They'd turn on the machines, pick up the tools they kept laid out, and look as industrious as hell, while the customer was still getting past Shirley's smile. I don't think that any of our guests ever caught on to what we were pulling. Or if they did, they had class enough to not mention it.

While we were involved with boat construction, there was an ongoing debate as to what we should name her. Dozens of names were batted about and discarded. For a while there, it looked as though the consensus would settle on calling her *The Wind-Lass*, and the auxiliary boat *The Wench*, but in the end she became *The Brick Royal*, and the tender was *The Concrete Canoe*. I don't know who thought up the names, but I liked them.

With the metal frames and mesh reinforcement completed, it was time to plaster on the concrete. Adam divided our people up into three shifts, since he insisted that the plastering be done in one continuous "pour." Apparently, wet cement does not stick all that well to cured concrete, and he meant our hull to be perfect. Adam called it a "carbon-alloy reinforced composite ceramic monolith", one time when he was really tired. Cement mixers and plastering machines that squirted the mixture through long hoses were rented, two of each so that in case of a breakdown, our work could continue uninterrupted.

Adam himself carefully measured out all of the

ingredients beforehand. The hydraulic grade cement, the sifted sand with its carefully measured moisture content, the pozzolana and other arcane chemicals, and a precisely measured amount of water. And God help the poor soul who dared add a single spittle's worth of moisture over what Adam had allowed.

Work started at the bow, and in a continuous helical strip a few inches wide, the crew forced the cement mixture into the matted steel wire, rod and pipe, always careful to leave not the tiniest void in the material. Inside and out, with vibrators and trowels, every bit of hull, deck and bulkheads was plastered such that the new concrete never went against previously laid concrete that was more than a half an hour old.

Following closely behind them was a crew whose task was to trowel the wet cement to smooth perfection. At the end of each shift, the sections completed were carefully covered with plastic sheeting, so that the concrete would cure slowly and not dry out.

We were three days completing the task, and I don't think Adam slept once during the whole process. I'm glad that it didn't take longer than that because just after we started plastering, we got a rush job in from Saginaw Steering Gear.

Adam flatly refused to start on the new work himself, or to let anyone else leave off working on the boat until the task at hand was completed. I shouted and ranted and screamed for half an hour, but to no avail. Not one of my workers would obey me! Adam had the whole damn crew brainwashed! As I was swearing, shaking my head, and leaving, one of my Bridgeport operators came to me and said that they were sorry, but that the best they could do was to punch out and work for free until the hull was done. And then they all went and did just that!

I actually had to hire a dozen minimum-wage types

from Kelly Services to sit at the computers in engineering and look professional, just so the GM rep
would think that we were working at his job! I mean,
wasn't this what the whole exercise was intended to
prevent? But Adam had everybody so hyped up that
they would have quit the company before they let
that hull be ruined. I couldn't fire them all, so I did
what I had to do, trying to keep my customer satisfied.

Just don't let anybody tell you that being the boss
is all roses!

Business was good for the next year. The hull just
sat there, but that was okay. The longer concrete has
to cure unmolested, the better and stronger it gets.

Then I saw another dry spell coming, and I figured that it was time to get working on the boat
again. I hadn't been in the warehouse since we had
wrapped her in plastic, and when I checked on her
one Sunday around noon I was surprised to see that
major changes had taken place.

*The Brick Royal* was now sitting upright in a huge
wooden cradle. The rudder, prop shaft, and propeller had been installed. Nearby was a huge cast-iron
keel, resting upright on its horizontal wings. She had
been beautifully painted in red and blue, and while
her design was completely modern, there was a lot
of antique gold-covered scrollwork at both the bow
and the stern. It looked like it was heavily embossed
in the concrete, and must have been painstakingly
sculpted in when the hull was being "poured."

Adam's head stuck up from inside the boat. "I
*tought* I heard somebody out here."

"Hi. What are you doing here? It's Sunday morning. Why aren't you in church?" Another of Adam's
strange quirks was that he was a staunch Catholic,
something I'd given up on when I was twelve.

"I went to da early mass."

It's never wise to discuss religion with anybody who actually believes in the stuff. That wasn't what I wanted to bitch about anyway. "Adam, all this fancy scrollwork pisses me off! It's formed right into the hull! That means that while I was paying the Kelly Services people to do nothing, and sweating blood for fear that the GM rep would find out about it, you and your people were out here farting around with nonessentials! I'm about ready to kill somebody!"

"Cool down, boss. You neva hoid of an applique? I made all dat fancy stuff one Sunday a few munts ago, and glued it on wit epoxy."

I just grumbled, since I couldn't tell if he was lying or not. "So how did you get the boat turned over?" I asked.

"Easy. You know when we had to hire a crane to get dat big Ford Flatrock job on da railroad car? Well, when da crane and crew was here, it only took dem a coupla minutes extra to flip da boat for us, so dey did it, no charge."

"I'll bet. What about that cast-iron keel? Where did it come from?"

"Well, da guys at Chevy Grey Iron, dey needed a hardness tester, but dey didn't have no budget for it, an we needed an iron keel, an we had a little extra time left over on a job, so we bote did da obvious ting."

"And the rest of this work?"

"Da paint, you mean? Well, you know when we had to buy all dat weird paint for dat Brazilian job? Well, I just ordered some udder kinds of weird paint at da same time an nobody noticed."

"Dammit, Adam, I meant to pay for the paint in any event, but as an employee, you shouldn't pull shit like that! It sets a bad example! I mean, if you want some real authority around here, you should take me up on that partnership." I went up a long, shaky ladder and climbed into the boat.

"Nah. Like I told you before, boss, I like bein a lowly peon. No worries, no hassles."

"You'll have lots of worries and hassles once I call the police and have you charged with theft. Where did this hydraulic power unit and all these valves come from? I mean, those are *Vickers* valves, worth hundreds of bucks each!"

"Well, you know. Sometimes you get trough wit a job, you got a lot of parts left over. Da distributors, dey charge you a hefty restockin fee if you send 'em back, so I figured, what the heck. An you ain't gonna have me arrested. You tink any judge would believe it, dat I stole your stuff, just so's I could come over here on my own time an mount it in your boat? Anyway, look at da bright side, boss. Doing tings my way, you're saving a lot of money on your taxes. I mean dis way, dese valves an stuff came out as a straight business deduction. Your way, after dat restockin fee, you'd have to pay company taxes on your business profits before you got da money for yourself, personally. Den you'd have to pay personal income taxes on dat before you could spend what was left on dese here same valves. I'm savin you a fortune."

"You're putting me in jail if the IRS ever hears about all this."

"And how're dey goin to do dat? Dere's not a ting on paper anywhere dat shows you got anyting to do wit dis boat, let alone ownin it."

"You've got a point there. But next time, let me know what you're doing, okay?"

"Boss, you got no sense of adventure."

"You've made some changes that weren't on the plans. What's this glass thing on the deck?"

"Dat's a solar still. Dey was knocking down some old stores downtown, an I picked up da big plate-glass windows almost for free. It's only tree inches high and it's strong enough to walk on. It don't weigh all dat much and under ideal conditions, it should make about tirty gallons of fresh water a day. A nice backup, hey?"

"I suppose so, as long as we're just distilling water. If I find a barrel of corn mash back here, somebody besides me is going to jail! What about that thing just forward of the still?"

"Dose are solar cells. Just another backup for all da udder generators."

"All what generators?"

"Well, dere's da generator on da engine, right? Just like on a car? But most of da time we won't be usin the big engine, we'll be sailin, so dere's a genset, wit a small diesel engine dat powers nuttin but a big generator. But dat uses fuel, too, so dere's anudder generator dat works trough a clutch off da prop shaft, to give us juice like durin a storm or sometin. And of course da solar cells, because it's free power, so what da heck."

"What? No windmill?" I said facetiously.

"I looked at dat, but a windmill would have to go on top of da mast, an a generator up dere puts too much weight right where you don't want it. We got backups enough, for power, anyway."

"Weren't the solar cells expensive?"

"Nah, dey were free. Dere was dis Air Force satellite dat got canceled, an we sort of got da solar panels donated to us."

"We 'sort of got donated' government property? You're sure it wasn't stolen?"

"Stolen? Boss, you use such naughty words! How about 'was put to da highest an da best civilian use'? Anyway, dose guys, dey owed me a couple of favors and dis was da payoff."

I shook my head and went away with visions of prison dancing in my head.

# FIVE

The crew only spent three weeks working on the boat that time, but during those weeks I spent very little on materials. Adam had been squirreling away all sorts of parts for use on the *Brick Royal*. Some—tubing, fittings, wiring and connectors—came out of our own bench stocks, and others—valves, motors, cylinders and drives—were identical to parts that had been shipped to our customers with the machines we built them. I expect that Adam designed the boat's fittings around the parts he could scrounge. Then again, he might have designed our customer's machines so they needed the same parts he wanted for the boat.

A big old marine diesel engine was being completely rebuilt in our shop, but that I understood. I'd managed to pick it up myself a few months ago, along with the transmission, shaft and packing box, all at scrap-metal prices.

But the radios, the radar, the satellite dish, the forward-looking sonar, the Global Positioning System, and the electronic navigating machine stumped me. I was afraid to ask, and put it off for a week, but eventually my curiosity got the best of me.

"Oh, dat stuff. Well, you see, boss, da guys over at Nautical Micrologic needed some material handlin'

25

stuff—just some conveyors an tings—and we needed some of deir stuff, so we made a deal. No big ting."

"No big thing, is it? Well, where did the materials and labor for the conveyors come from?"

"It was dat Brazilian job again. I mean, we was way ahead on dat one, and it don't look too good to da customer if you make too big a profit on dem. Dis way, everybody's happy."

"Everybody but me and the IRS." I walked away, shaking my head as usual.

One thing I did pay for, and plenty, was the carbon fiber and epoxy needed for the mast. The cost of these materials was about the same as the price of a custom-made aluminum mast, but it would weigh almost half a ton less. Weight way up there you don't need. Also, the composite mast would be a lot stronger. Too strong, as it turned out later. An aluminum mast might not have been strong enough to punch a hole in the bottom of the boat.

The *Brick Royal* was beginning to look almost finished when we started back on our next real job. The car companies were still a bit slow, but it was looking as though we had a first-class customer in a certain Brazilian auto aftermarket manufacturer.

The first machine that we did for them remachined used water pump housings. They were very pleased with what we designed and built, and they paid for it before the due date. Now they had another, much larger project for us if we could start immediately, and of course, we could.

The new job was a variable remachining line for engine camshafts that would take just about any used camshaft ever made and put it back to the original specs. You could throw in old parts in any order, and have them come out just like brand new, as long as the programmable controller was informed of the proper part number.

When the camshaft machine was about half

completed, their rep came by and asked us to quote on five more lines, for engine blocks, engine heads, crankshafts, brake drums, and rotors. We got the crankshaft job within the week.

Most machinery companies end up spending between two weeks and two months debugging a tool before it's fit to be seen in public. All of the sins of misinformation, improper assumptions, and outright incompetence come out in final assembly and debug.

It's a trial, but it's not like trying to convince a jury you didn't break the laws of man. You're on trial with Mother Nature herself sitting in judgment on whether you tried to break her very strict rules.

Rudyard Kipling had it down pat. Machines are not built to comprehend a lie. They can neither love, nor pity, nor forgive. If you make a slip in handling them, you die.

Or at the very least, you can lose your shirt. It's the expenses that you incur during debugging that can make the difference between an almost embarrassingly high profit and a dead loss.

Indeed, my fledgling company had been forced to lose a few not-so-small fortunes, until I hired Adam. It was his fantastic record of ultrasmooth startups that made him so valuable to me. Before long, his startups made him and our company both famous throughout the machinery industry.

And whenever anyone asked him about it, he would invariably say, "Of course it woiks! I got God on my side!"

Super Spooks in the Sky had nothing to do with it. Machines designed and built by Adam always worked because he was incredibly competent. He was one of those rare individuals who was both remarkably creative and absolutely anal when it came to checking every single tiny detail.

As time went on, I got to scheduling less and less time for Tender Loving Care, at least on our own shop schedules, but being a chicken at heart, I left it at three weeks as far as what I told the customer was concerned, just in case.

There is a ceremony in the special machine business called "The Buyoff." Representatives from the purchasing company, usually one senior plant engineer and a couple of juniors, come to the builder's shop. They inspect the machine and the parts it makes, they watch it function, and they sometimes run it themselves while it produces a certain number of parts within a specified period of time. If all is well, they approve the machine for shipment and payment. If Mother Nature doesn't accept excuses, neither does the purchaser's plant engineer.

Only this time, the Brazilian company's President, the Chairman of the Board and the Chief Engineer showed up, in addition to the usual plant engineers. And they came three weeks early. When the Brazilians arrived unannounced, and asked to see their machine immediately, I was a more than a bit flustered.

"Gentlemen! Of course, you may see anything that you wish. But surely you realize that you are here three weeks early."

A very distinguished-looking gentleman, who turned out to be their Chairman of the Board, spoke through their interpreter. "Of course, we realize this, and it is not our intention to make you anxious. We are totally confident of your ability to ship us an outstanding machine at the proper time. However, we have come north from Bela Horizonte a few weeks early to see for ourselves the truth about the remarkable stories that circulate concerning your Chief Engineer."

*Omigod!* I thought, *Somebody's told them about the*

*shit Adam pulled, padding the account on that last
machine we sold them! They know about* The Brick
Royal!

"My Chief Engineer? He's extremely competent, sir,
or, uh, señor, but of course, what a man does on
his own time is none of my business, you see."

The reply, after a few layers of translation, and a fair
amount of extra conversation in Portuguese, came back,
"I am not sure of what you speak, my friend, and perhaps it is best that I do not know. What I was discussing was his remarkable ability to design a totally
new machine, build it, and have it work perfectly the
very first time it was turned on. You will understand
that you are not the first tool-building company that
we have dealt with. Always before, they were months
late in their deliveries, and never had we purchased
a machine that worked to absolute perfection until we
received your last excellent effort on our behalf. Therefore, we have come early in order to watch the machine
being completed, and to observe the startup."

Vastly relieved, I took the delegation back to the
assembly bay, where the electricians and painters were
putting on the finishing touches.

"Ah, it will be completed soon, yes?"

"Oh, yes, sir. Perhaps by noon today. We are slightly
ahead of schedule."

"Then we will watch."

It wasn't until one-thirty that Adam had finished
his own final inspection of the line, and would permit
electrical power, compressed air, and coolants to be
turned on. With a bit of a flourish, he pressed the
start button for the first time, and all of the proper
indicator lights turned on.

Adam went over to a stack of old camshafts that
we'd bought at the junkyard, selected one at random,
and scanned its part number into the machine. He
placed the camshaft on the input rack and pressed
the palm buttons.

The machine started, handing the part automatically from work station to work station. The cam was washed, its oil cavities were blown out clean, and every machined surface was measured at many different places. The part was magnafluxed, and since it was within allowable tolerances, our machine decreed it to be salvageable.

Those bearings and other surfaces that were worn down or otherwise undersized were MIG welded back up until they were oversized and then ground down precisely to specification. The oil cavities were again blown out clean, the camshaft was pressure washed again, dried, and then lightly oiled for shipment. Finally, it was placed on a storage rack reserved for parts of its type.

And at every step of the line, our machine had worked perfectly, the first time that it had ever operated. Adam had done it again. The VIPs were all excited, and wads of brightly colored Brazilian money changed hands among them. There must have been some hefty bets going.

Then the Brazilians had to play with their new toy themselves, like a bunch of teenagers who had just invented sex.

When they finally ran out of old camshafts to fix, the chairman not only handed me a cashier's check for the full amount owed on the tool, he also gave me a purchase order for all four of the other new lines that I had quoted them.

I could see now where I was going to get the money to buy the sails for *The Brick Royal*. Dacron was no longer good enough, and the Kevlar sails that Adam insisted on were going to cost me three times what the hull did. One of those little catches that I had known would be there all along. There would be enough money left over to take Helen on a cruise, or even buy her that new house she'd been hinting about. Not to mention retiring for life, if the mood struck me.

While I stood there with visions of untold wealth dancing before my eyes, Adam publicly hit me up for a new company car. He wanted a big new Chrysler convertible. And with the Brazilian's check still in my sweaty hand and all of them watching, well, I had to agree to it.

But still they didn't go home. Adam took them across the alleyway and showed them our boat. I cringed, and stayed behind. I shortly heard a series of loud "BONGs," and knew that Adam was showing off his ferrocrete again. He'd hand you a big sledge hammer and challenge you to knock a hole in the hull. Nobody could do it, and the hull would ring like a cathedral bell. Remarkable stuff, ferrocrete.

The chairman came back in an hour to tell me that the old engine I had purchased was entirely too inferior for so noble a vessel. He announced that he would be sending us one that was only three years old, that had been rebuilt in his own plant and which incorporated all of the most modern new developments, and complete with transmission, propshaft and propeller. All this as a free gift, in thanks for our excellent workmanship.

Then they all drove over to the Tri-County Airport and hopped a jet for Disneyworld.

# SIX

In six weeks, a beautifully rebuilt, late model diesel engine arrived with the freight prepaid. Far more importantly, for the first time in the life of my young company, I could see clear sailing far into the future. With this much business spaced out over two years, I could afford to pick and choose among the other work I took on, with no more dangerous underbidding just to keep my people busy. Also, I was now flush enough so that I didn't have to go begging to the bank for every machine I built.

You see, nobody builds a machine more complicated than a hammer completely by himself. For example, almost every machine bigger than a hand tool has a programmable controller, a small computer, to run it. These are built by companies like Allen-Bradley or Westinghouse, who have spent years and megabucks developing them. It would be absolutely absurd for a tool builder to try and make one of his own unless he was designing a standard machine that he figured he could sell a few thousand copies of. Furthermore, the customer wouldn't want anything that they couldn't buy a replacement for in a hurry. Machines break down, and down time is deadly expensive. The same goes for bearings, motors, hydraulic parts, drives, spindles, cutters, gears, belts and the thousands of other things that go into a machine tool. Often, more than half the selling price of a tool is spent on purchased parts and assemblies.

Thus, to build a machine, you must not only pay your people's salaries and benefits, as well as your overhead, you must also lay out a very substantial slug of cash for purchased parts. This makes you a slave to the bankers, a bland, polished and thoroughly despicable brand of quasihumanity. But now I was free, free at last, or so I thought.

I told Helen that from then on, I would be spending a lot more time with her, and asked her to pick out a cruise that we could go on together, sort of like a second honeymoon. I was sure that our relationship was on the upswing.

I was then contacted again by the Brazilians, who had yet another profitable order for me, and also a desperate request to speed up the previously agreed on delivery schedule. They offered some nice bonuses for it, but they wanted all of their machines delivered by yesterday, if not the day before.

Well, you try to keep your customers satisfied. We went over our schedules, and by building all of the lines in parallel rather than sequentially, by not accepting any other new work, by temporarily renting more factory space, by hiring a lot more new people, by farming out a lot of the parts to my friendly competitors, and by floating a bodacious loan with the bank, we could get all of their work out in six months.

Of course, I wouldn't be likely to get home much during that time, but I thought that my wife was used to that sort of thing by now. Even so, I spent a whole evening with her explaining exactly why I was doing what I was doing, and how it would be so much better for us in the future.

So for six months, it was "interesting times," as they say the Chinese say, but the work got done.

Sometimes I hardly got home from one week to the next, and when I did, I found that Helen usually didn't want to talk to me. She preferred screaming. We got into a fight damn near every time I got home, which sure took the incentive out of getting there in the first place.

Building the machines in parallel instead of in series was more work than we had thought it would be. Normally, the engineers and designers would have designed the first machine, and then started in on the second while the controls designers and the mechanical checkers were doing their thing on the first. By the time the mechanical designers were working on machine number six, the controls people would be on number five, the machinists would be building the parts on number four, the purchasing people would be getting in the purchased parts on number three, the assemblers would be putting number two together in Assembly Bay A, and the electricians and the pipe fitters would be working on machine number one in Assembly Bay B. That is to say, a production line, of sorts, would be in operation.

As it was, everything had to be designed at first and at once, at a time when the electricians and Bridgeport operators had nothing to do. Despite the different names that various skilled workers had, the truth is that specialization is for insects, and good people can do anything they put their mind to. Working outside his usual trade is good for a worker, it's broadening, and a lot of our people volunteered for strange jobs. We had electricians designing controls and machinists designing what they usually build. In a few months, the engineers would be working with milling machines and arc welders.

And they were all having fun, doing unusual things, but of course they weren't as efficient as someone who had been doing it for years. Costs were going way up, and worse, serious mistakes were occasionally

made. Some things had to be done twice and even
three times, and still weren't being done as well as
we usually did things.

On top of it all, we were working in four buildings scattered around the city, and an ungodly number
of man-hours were being wasted just running between
them.

Coordinating all of this was a major headache, and
I spent long hours at my desk. Somewhere through
all of this, late one night, I must have confused a
process server with one of the runners who were
circulating between our various shops. As best as I
was able to figure out much later, I must have just
said that yes, I was me, and thrown what he handed
me into the "IN" basket.

A few hours later, I was hungry when Helen walked
into my office, carrying a big bag of McDonald's stuff.
It was after nine at night, and I hadn't had time for
lunch, yet. It was an unusual event, since Helen didn't
like the factory. She came to my office maybe once
a year, if that. I was used to it, and it no longer
bothered me. Since the night before had ended in
another yelling match, her actions struck me as being
a peace offering. I took it as such. She was as beautiful as ever, and I never could stay mad at her for
long.

She sat on my desk and smiled while I ate a Big
Mac and admired her. It must have been then that
she swiped the divorce papers from my "IN" basket
before I even knew that they were there. Or that Helen
was divorcing me.

Before I found out what was happening, Adam
reported that his new Chrysler convertible was gone.
"It was in my driveway last night and it wasn't dere
in da morning."

I had Shirley file the paperwork with the leasing
company, and got him a replacement. Only this time

he got a cheap compact, and I told him to take better care of it.

In the end we were victorious. The Brazilians happily "bought off" all six lines in one single day, and promised to send me a whopping big check shortly. All the machinery was loaded onto the same container ship bound for Rio de Janeiro. I thought that when all the checks cleared the bank and all the bills were paid, I would be a multimillionaire.

It was time to make up with Helen. I bought some flowers for her on the way home, but the clerk at the shop said that my check wouldn't clear. She said that the computer said that my account was empty.

I said that there was some mistake somewhere, but I'd worry about it later. I paid her with a company credit card and went home.

To find that I didn't have one.

The furniture was gone, along with everything else that wasn't nailed down. Even my dog Boner was missing, along with his doghouse and his water dish. A thief couldn't have taken Boner, not without leaving somebody's blood around, and who'd want to steal an old water dish?

Having no idea at all what I should do next, I sat down on the front steps. After a bit, a process server came up, handed me a folder of divorce papers, and went silently on his way. I was so shocked that I didn't know what to do, so I didn't do anything for about an hour.

Eventually, I got up, drove downtown, and checked into a hotel. Then I spent most of the night in the hotel bar. I had long known that Helen was less than totally pleased with me, but I had been sure that she would eventually see that what I was doing was a good thing for both of us. I mean, she knew that when I wasn't at home, I was working. I wasn't out with another woman.

I knew that she really wanted to be filthy rich, and

I had finally gotten us up to that Great Mud Puddle in the Sky! At no time did I ever imagine that she would leave me at the very moment of our victory.

Now that she was gone, I didn't know where she was, and I could think of no way to contact her. Her mother wouldn't even talk to me, and I didn't see anything that I could do about that, either.

Sometimes, booze is the only answer.

Booze stayed the only answer for about a week and a half, until Adam showed up about noon one day and half carried me over to his place. After a few days of drying out, he and Shirley let me back into my office.

Things were up and running, in a quiet sort of way. All of the temporary people had been let go, along with the rented factory space. The permanent crew was working on a traveling hoist or crane, the sort that they use to lift big boats out of the water and drive them over to their cradles. It was half built in the big assembly bay.

"You don't really want to ask," Adam said, and I nodded yes. "Boss, why don't you go back to your office and administrate something. Or better still, go out and find us some more work. Me and Shirley'll take care of everything else."

And they did. Shirley even refurnished my house. It was mostly done in K-Mart modern, but at least I had a place to sleep. She was looking for a housekeeper for me when the other trouble hit.

I hadn't had any luck with new work, some of my old customers being a little miffed at the way I'd been sending "No Bid" notes to them for the last six months in reply to their requests for quotes.

I was getting ready to go to divorce court when a certified letter arrived from Brazil. It said that my good friends south of the border were declaring bankruptcy. They wouldn't be paying me for the machines I'd sent them.

❖     ❖     ❖

The thing about special machines is that they are
special. They're built for one specific customer to do
one specific job. It is most unlikely that anybody else
would want a special machine secondhand, except
at scrap metal prices. Even if I could get my machines
back, it wouldn't do me any good. I was in absolute trouble.

A Brazilian lawyer wrote that if I appointed him
to be my attorney, with a suitable retainer fee, he
might be able get me ten, or even twenty cents back
on the dollar. Of course, between the bank and my
other creditors, I owed about sixty-five cents on the
dollar for those machines, and my company bank
account was running on fumes.

At the divorce court, my lawyer, Alan Greenberg,
wanted to fight, but I told him to just agree with
anything Helen and her lawyer wanted. It didn't make
any difference. I was wiped out in any event. I figured I might as well let Helen feel good for a little
while, anyhow. And so her lawyer and the limp-
wristed little judge gave my wife more of my nonexistent money each month than I had ever made
even in good times, not that she had any chance of
collecting any of it. They simply had no real com-
prehension as to what the universe was about to
dump on all of us.

Finally, Alan insisted on doing *something* for me,
and got the judge to agree that if Helen remarried,
or cohabited with a male, all of my obligations toward
her would cease. I didn't much care, or see how it
would make any difference, but it seemed to make
my lawyer happy.

A week after that my creditors pounced on me and
I found myself sitting in bankruptcy court, with the
same damn judge. My lawyer said that it was illegal, but the judge didn't agree. I also thought that
more time would be given me to sort things out, but

within three weeks, my factory was empty, padlocked and sold. So was my house, but the money there went to Helen and her lawyer.

My car was leased, so they had to let me keep that, and I had always kept a set of credit cards separate from my wife's, so they were paid up, but when I went across the alleyway to look at *The Brick Royal*, she was gone.

I had abandoned the Catholic Church along with the whole idea of God when I was in my early teens, and my family had abandoned me a few years later after we had one final knockdown dispute concerning religion, or rather my lack of it. For many years, my whole life had wound around—had actually consisted entirely of—my fine little company and my magnificent wife.

With both of these two foundations brutally ripped away by the power of law, government, and a woman that I still couldn't help loving, I found that I had nothing left out in the world, and nothing left inside of me either. I was a hollow man, empty, and without hope. I was devoid of everything, even hate.

I was back in the bar when Adam found me again. He sat down beside me and ordered a beer. "You know, boss, it wasn't really da Brazilian's fault. At da courthouse, I heard dat dey got knocked flat because *deir* biggest customer went belly-up."

"Just like a line of dominoes," I said.

"An dey are still fallin. It's lookin like Delta Distribution might crash and burn because of what we didn't pay them. A coupla udders might go, too."

"Shit. They say misery loves company, but I sure never meant that to happen. Not that I feel all that charitable after what they did to me at the bankruptcy court. I don't know what I'll do now. Probably spend a week getting properly drunk, and then go out and really tie one on. What about you? You got any plans?"

"Me? Why, I'm stickin wit you, boss. So are most o' da udder guys an' girls."

"Adam, you are out of your frigging gourd. For one thing, I'm not your boss. I'm nobody's boss, because I don't have a company anymore. I made my last payroll, but that cleaned me out, so show some sense and go find a soft place to land. And tell any of the other people you see to do the same thing."

"Nah, don't talk like dat, boss. We still got fait in you. You always pulled it all togedder before. Anyway, it's time we all took dat boat ride you promised us."

"Boat ride? Adam, they took the boat along with everything else. Anyway, we never got it finished, and equipping it would have taken even more money than you've got squirreled away."

"Boss, dey never took da boat. *I* took da boat. Well, me an some of da guys, an half of da Bay City Police Department. You know dat big travelin hoist we was buildin? Well, dat was for da guys at da marina. See, dey needed a new boat hoist, and dey didn't have one big enough to handle *Da Brick Royal* anyway. We needed some sails, life preservers, safety equipment, some kitchen stuff, an, oh, a list about as long as your arm. So, as usual, we cut a deal."

"I'd already ordered the sails, though I never had a chance to pick them up and pay for them."

"I know. Which was anudder reason why dey was so eager to deal. Dose sails was all custom made, an dey woulda been stuck wit a very expensive white elephant witout you to take it off their hands."

"So you're saying you stole the boat? How, for God's sake?"

"We had a brand new traveling hoist, didn't we? An you was always good about donating to da Policeman's Benevolent Fund, wasn't you? So at two o'clock on a Tuesday morning, we just picked da ting up and drove down da streets to da marina, wit a nice police escort, even."

"There has to be something illegal about this. The law says that a bankrupt's property gets divided up between his creditors."

"Nah. Dere is nutin nowheres written down dat says dat you own da boat, except for dis, of course."

He handed me an envelope that contained a bill of sale and the registration for *The Brick Royal*.

"You see, dere was da Coast Guard certification, da registration, an all dat stuff, an you was udderwise occupied, so I just sort of put it all in my name. But once everyting settles down, you file dat registration, an she's yours again."

I fought to keep tears from rushing to my eyes.

"Adam, I don't know what to say."

"Den yous don't have to say it. Come on. Drink up. Da guys an girls are down at da marina, puttin da finishin' touches on da boat. It'ud be nice if you let dem all know dat you was still alive an all."

Adam insisted on stopping at the doctor's office on the way to the marina, and I got nine shots in my arms and butt to update the medical records on my passport.

Then he drove me to see Alan G. Greenberg, our lawyer, where there were two Power of Attorney forms ready for us to sign, one for me and one for Adam. They would let Greenberg do whatever he felt was best with any legal problems that might come up while we were gone. I signed mostly because it seemed to make both of them happy. Personally, I didn't see where anything that might happen could possibly affect me anymore, except maybe for a bullet in the head, and I'd probably welcome that.

When we got to the marina, the "finishing touches" being handled was the unloading of a semi full of canned and dried food. Everything was being sorted out, logged, put into several layers of waterproof plastic garbage bags, and then carried into the spacious volumes below *The Brick Royal*'s lower deck.

"Dis one you *really* don't want to know about," Adam said, so I didn't ask.

I was a little shell-shocked by then, anyway. I went into the boat and sat down in the big center cockpit, which was little more than an outdoor living room, what they've been calling a conversation pit, although you could control the boat manually from there. Normally, the boat was controlled from the much smaller aft cockpit.

I looked back at it and was surprised to see that it had an automotive style convertible top! And the windshield looked suspiciously like it had come from a big, new Chrysler. On inspection, so did the padded steering wheel, the leather bucket seat and the electric windows. Oh, the single seat was now in the center, as was the steering wheel. The dashboard was like something out of a Hollywood spaceship, with five display screens along the front. On both sides of the driver were banks of switches and lights, and in back, once you swiveled the seat around, there was a chart table in case you wanted to do things the old-fashioned way. Yet it was obvious that most of this had to have been ripped out of the company car Adam had reported stolen! Damn his ass!

"I didn't steal nuttin. How could I? You can't steal what you already got. Da car was mine. I asked for it and you gave it to me!"

"I leased it for you, and you reported it stolen!"

"Well, how you got it was up to you, none of my business, really. And I didn't report it stolen. I just said dat it was in my driveway and da next morning it was gone. Nobody ever asked me if *I* was da one who drove it away."

"Adam, you're hopeless."

"Yeah. Don't you feel glad?"

"Shit. Are you sure that this top will stay in place during a gale?"

"Dat top didn't give me no trouble when I drove da car at a hundred and fifty. You ever heard of a hundred-and-fifty-mile-an-hour hurricane?"

"I don't think that it's quite the same thing."

"Have fait. You'll be glad about da top when we're cruisin under a tropical sun. Da air conditionin will be nice, too."

"What tropical sun? We're in Bay City, Michigan!"

"Right now, yeah, boss. But once we get our people shook down, we're going to take tree years and sail her all da way around da world!"

"Ridiculous! I can't take off for three years."

"Oh, yeah? Why not? You got sometin else better to do?"

And you know? I really didn't have an answer for that one.

# SEVEN

Adam and the gang had the whole trip planned out, and I didn't see any point in changing anything.

About a half dozen of them, including Adam, had studied seamanship very seriously, taking all the courses in it they could find, and sailing rented boats whenever they could find the time. A group of the girls had really gotten involved with the itinerary, and made sure that we could get to the right place at the right time to see everything that was worth seeing.

When everything and everybody was finally aboard, Adam came up, gave me a palm-forward British-style salute, and asked if I wanted to take her out now.

"Me? I don't know anything about driving a boat!"

"Dere's nuttin much to it. Come on. Everybody's waitin."

I was still in no mood to do anything in public, but sometimes you've got to keep the peasants happy. I went up on deck and shouted, *"All right! You all know what to do!"*

I gesticulated wildly, with my fist held high, but everybody just stood there. "It always worked when Errol Flynn yelled that," I said to Adam. "They climbed up on deck, killed the Spaniards, and pulled all the right ropes to make the boat go. They even got the words to the song right."

"You don't got no tights on," Adam said. "And you don't got no mustache, either. Try sometin different."

"Okay. *All right, you swabs! Let's shiver the scuppers and keelhaul the fo'c's'le, and do all the rest of that nautical stuff that gets this boat moving!*"

Those of the crew who had been working and studying for years in preparation for this event just stared at the sky and pretended not to know me.

*"Or better still, do what Adam tells you to do, and wake me up when we get there."* I went below again.

We spent two months sailing around the Great Lakes, shaking down the boat and the crew, seeing the sights. I was in a strange, empty mood, and spent a lot of time alone in my cabin. The double catastrophe that had befallen me at the very moment of triumph still had me hollow, empty and numb. No one asked me to stand a watch or help with the boat, and I never volunteered. I took to drinking pretty heavily, alone, until Adam came in one day, silently picked up my case of scotch and threw it over the side, a gift for some future aquatic archaeologist.

Every now and then, one of the single girls would come in and let it be known pretty plainly that if I wanted a little company, well, so did she, but Helen had messed me up so bad inside that I didn't want to trust another woman, not even for a one-night stand.

Everybody else seemed to be having a marvelous time. We had fifty-three people on board. Thirty-one of these were me and my former employees. I'd had quite a few husband and wife teams working for me. Five were spouses of employees, eleven were children, two were boyfriends of two of the girls, and four girls had been sort of communally invited aboard by nine of our male bachelors. None of my business, so I never said anything. That and there were two dogs and a cat. The cat went missing on the second night out and I felt a little better. I never could stand cats.

At first, I took my meals in the galley along with everybody else. We were so crowded that we were eating in shifts when the weather was bad and you couldn't eat on deck. But my presence seemed to throw a wet sleeping bag over any group I was with, and after a bit I took to eating alone in my room.

We hit a major storm on Lake Michigan. There was plenty of warning, not only from the weather services but also off a fax machine that was hooked directly to a satellite. Adam had furnished us up proud, communications-wise. Besides the satellite hookup and two fax machines, there were six separate radios and radio telephones. I mean, we could be in the middle of the Atlantic Ocean and place a collect phone call to somebody in Fiji, if we didn't care about getting the people there up in the middle of the night.

For me, the storm was just a lot of banging around in my cabin. It never occurred to me that I might drown, but if it had, I still wouldn't have much cared. For some of the other people, well, the storm got to them right where they lived. Shirley was the first person to tell me that she was leaving. She and her husband said that thinking about sailing for three years was wonderful, but the actual doing of it was more than they were cut out for. I really missed them.

We took down the mast and motored through a canal in Chicago, which put us on a tributary of the Mississippi River, and then spent six weeks playing Tom Sawyer heading south. I suppose that there were lots of pretty sights along the way, but inside I was still a dead man.

We lost six more couples, a single parent and all the kids and dogs at St. Louis. They had planned it that way all along. Summer was over, and the kids had to get back to school. They all promised to rejoin

the crew next summer once school was out, but
somehow none of them did. At least now there was
enough room on board so you could turn around
without rubbing someone's back.

Everybody loved New Orleans except me. I saw it
as just an overrated, overpriced, and overheated place
where all you could do is sit listening to octogenar-
ians playing music that nobody else would want to
listen to at all under normal circumstances. The
swamps just south of that city are nice, though, and
Cajuns are more fun than people. Eventually, gorged
on shrimp, crawdads, and hot sauce, we raised the
mast and headed into the Gulf of Mexico. Yet even
these infrequent moments of pleasure were just a
surface ripple over my inner feelings of nothingness.

For me, the Caribbean Islands were a mixture of
overpriced tourist traps and pitiful black children living
in shacks that would be condemned back home if
they were used to house chickens. The water itself
wasn't bad though, once you got away from the
people. Adam finally got me out of my cabin and
into a SCUBA rig, and that was beautiful. Fresh-caught
lobster is the food of the gods, and even picking up
some sort of infection from a coral I brushed against
didn't blacken my mood all that much. For a little
while I felt better, and then suddenly I was farther
down than ever in the depths of depression. Adam
bought a case of St. John's Wort, and made me start
taking it, but I didn't feel any difference.

Sea sickness got to some people, and nine more
of our crew left the boat at San Juan. We took on
four thirty-gallon barrels of rum there, since rum sold
for less than Coke, and Adam let me resume drinking, as long as I did it in public.

Slowly, I was starting to become a human being
once more. As the winter passed, I even started
noticing girls again. I wasn't quite to the point where
I wanted to get involved with one, but I was noticing.

Especially since most of them were in bathing suits, and the island fashions that year provided about the same coverage as two Band-Aids and a cork.

I got to noticing Dawn in particular. Now that the kids and older folks were gone, she let the exhibitionist side of her personality come out. Any time we got out of port, she got out of her bikini, which a guy just naturally couldn't help noticing. That, and it seemed as if every time I caught sight of her out of the corner of my eye, she was looking at me, and grinning. I figured her for a tease, albeit a pleasant one. Then one of the mechanical designers told me that it wasn't a tease at all. She was *ready,* and what was I doing, ignoring a nice girl like that? But Dawn was young enough to be my daughter, if I had one, and anyway, I wasn't quite ready for another woman yet.

Then we hit a hurricane, or vice versa. Normally, a storm isn't much of a problem with a good sailboat, as long as you have plenty of sea room, and we did. You just take in all the sails, hang a bit of sturdy canvas to the backstay, tie off the wheel, seal up all the hatches, and try your best to ignore it. The boat just automatically puts its nose into the wind and you do five or ten knots, backwards. Adam had a surplus parachute rigged to one of the anchor lines, as a sea anchor. If we ever got close to shore, he could throw it out and stop us dead in the water, but we never needed it. We were even going in the direction that we wanted. Toward Panama, and the Canal.

Maybe the reason that bad weather and such never bothered me was because, deep down, I still didn't much care if I was alive or not. It bothered most of the other people a whole lot. As soon as we docked at Colón, ten more of our crew left the ship. They'd had all the sailing they wanted to do, thank you, and Bay City was actually a very nice place to live. We

tried to talk them out of leaving, but they were
adamant. This left us with a controls designer, a
Bridgeport operator, Adam and myself. And all four
of the bachelorettes that had joined up for kicks back
home. None of us were married, and it looked like
it could become a nicely balanced little group.

In fact, Adam bought some decent lumber in the
port of Colón, and the rest of them were busily converting the dormitory into two big staterooms, as we
motored our way through the Canal.

I was taking my turn at the wheel, now that we
were getting shorthanded, and naturally, given the
pairing off that was going on, Dawn was getting more
flirtatious than ever. I got to thinking that maybe I
should stop being such a grump, and come out of
my shell a little bit. She was twenty-four and I was
forty-two, but maybe that wouldn't be an insurmount-
able problem. She was certainly a fine-looking young
woman. She was down to the buff, lying on the glass
top of the solar still nine inches in front of my
windshield, and pretending not to notice me. A pleasant sight, but probably against the law in Panama.
I mean, she was also ignoring the people on other,
taller ships, though they weren't doing the same with
her. Then I got a radio phone call from a passing
freighter, thanking me for the scenery, but telling me
that Panama being a staunchly Catholic country, the
fines for doing what she was doing were huge.

"Get up!" I yelled to her, "Put some clothes on or
you'll get us a ticket!"

She gave me an "Aw, shucks!" look, stood up, and
her head exploded.

We were in Panama for three weeks while the
police tried to get things sorted out. It seems that
Dawn was hit by a .30 caliber hunting bullet. The
bullet was descending at a fifty degree angle when
it struck her, and from the direction it had to have
come from, there was no land higher than the boat

from which it could have been fired. No ship or
aircraft had been in the right position at the time.
The only conclusion that anybody could come to
was that somewhere off in the jungle, somebody had
just fired a shot into the air. A weird accident, and
a totally senseless death.

We humans like to think that we are somehow
important in the great scheme of things, that in some
way, our lives and our deaths have meaning. A certain
rational part of us tells us that this isn't true, that
the universe is a vast place, and quite indifferent to
us, but we don't like to listen to that annoying little
voice very often. And then something like the way
Dawn died throws it in our faces.

I was back in the bottom of my black mental hole
again, and now each of the other six people was also
living in his or her own private place of darkness.

When the police finally gave us permission to leave,
everyone but Adam and me decided to accompany
Dawn's body home, and each of them said that they
wouldn't be coming back. Adam tried hard to per-
suade them to stay, but Dawn's death just took the
wind out of the expedition.

I think that the only reason I stayed on was because
I was too numb to do anything else, or maybe
because, without Helen and my factory, Bay City
wasn't home any more.

I'm sure that it was his sense of duty that kept
Adam on board, though I don't know if it was his
duty to me or to the boat. After we saw the others
off at the airport, Adam looked at me and said, "'And
the weal of the crew was reduced down to two.'"

"That's from some sort of a song, isn't it?"

"Yah. Some sort."

"Adam, what are we going to do?"

"We're going to sail. Come on."

# EIGHT

We topped off our two thousand-gallon fuel tanks, picked up a few bags of fresh food, and left. We didn't need anything else. There was enough canned and dried food to last us for three years, even if we didn't do any fishing. That didn't count the "emergency" supplies, a ton of dried beans, Bay City being the Bean Capitol of the world. The solar still built into the deck produced ten gallons of pure water a day, and the osmotic water maker could pump out another hundred, at the price of running the generator set. We were as free as any human beings possibly could be, and yet I was living in my own private hell.

I had hardly known Dawn, yet somehow her death and the manner of it weighed on me more than my divorce and bankruptcy had done. It wasn't that I was berating myself with "if onlys," although it was true that if I'd just let her lie there, and not acted like a penny-pinching prude, she would still be alive. It was that an uncaring universe had blotted her out with no more concern than a truck driver has for a bug hitting the windshield.

The new cabins had been completed while we were in Panama, and Adam and I moved into them as soon as we were at sea. They were much larger than the other two, and being near the center of the ship, they bounced around less in the waves.

The rule on board had always been that at least one person had to be awake and in charge at all times. The boat could sail itself once it was away from port, but someone was still needed to keep an eye on things. There were Coast Guard regulations about having somebody there to answer the radio, and assist if someone else got into trouble. Then too, neither of us, being engineers, fully trusted anything automatic. We flipped a coin, and I got the noon-to-midnight shift. It wasn't as though we each had to work twelve hours straight, we just had to be awake in case anything came up. The schedule had the effect that each of us was alone most of the time, and having little to do but look out at the sea has a hypnotic effect that sneaks up on you.

The next stop on the itinerary was the Galapagos Islands. We got there, saw a turtle, and bought a basket of fresh fruit. We had a drink in the bar of another visiting boat, and left before sundown.

We headed out, sailing west.

A few weeks later, we hit another storm. The bouncing around wasn't as bad as it had been on our previous romps with nature. For one thing, we had a few square feet of the jib showing, and this put our tail to the wind. We were running with it, and in *The Brick Royal*, it made for a smoother ride. Sleeping near the boat's center of gravity helped out a lot, too. Adam had rigged up some hammocks that let you stay put while the boat rocked around you. They were slung fore and aft, which canceled the rolling of the boat, and ropes at the ends of the hammock went through pulleys at each bulkhead, near the ceiling, and connected together above you. This let the boat pitch while you stayed almost stationary. Adam said he was going to patent it, next time he got a chance.

In any event, Adam was in the cockpit and I was sound asleep when trouble happened. My first indication that something was wrong came when I was slammed awake. The hammock let the boat bounce around quite a bit without you noticing it, but when she rolled completely over on her side, I smashed into the ceiling.

The mast was built into the wall separating the two big staterooms. The noise was deafening, and I felt another strange bump. The emergency lights came on in time for me to see the mast pull loose from its socket, and then wrench sideways, shattering the new wooden wall into sharp splinters.

I was tangled up in the hammock, trying to get free when the boat suddenly righted itself, which naturally swung me into the swordlike remains of the wall. I managed to twist around so that I was looking where I'd been, and only a dozen or so sharp wooden shards got through the thick canvas and bedding and into my back. Painful.

The carbon-fiber mast, despite the stainless-steel shrouds and stays that held it in position, had somehow been pulled *three feet* above the lower deck. It slammed back down like a crossbow bolt, going through the deck, through four feet of assorted stores, and then right through the ferrocrete bottom of the boat.

A spray of wet lima beans blasted into me as I renewed my struggle to get out of the hammock. The boat went over again on its side, reacquainting me forcibly with the ceiling. The mast then pulled itself out of the hole it had made, and the next time the boat righted itself, the mast stayed horizontal. It cracked the upper deck, then pulled itself entirely free of the boat, snagging in the process the rope that connected the ends of my hammock. The hammock was thus pulled straight like the string of a discharging crossbow, and I was bounced off the ceiling yet a third time, this time catching it on the face and stomach.

The lights went out, either electrically or because of the way I lost consciousness. I awoke to find the cabin half full of water and Adam leaning over me.

"You okay?" he shouted.

"I respectfully request sick leave," I said.

"Request denied. We got work to do. Can you move at all?"

"I guess I have to, don't I. What the hell happened to us?" It was hard to talk in the wet, noise, and confusion of the dim emergency light, the slapping water, and the floating junk.

"We must have hit something. I don't know what. The boat broke. I don't know why. Get up."

"Help me up. Maybe we can get a mattress over that hole in the bottom. Unless you know of something worse that's happened to us."

Adam said, "You're bleeding from twenty places, but that shouldn't bother a determined engineer. The spars and rigging are dragging beside us, so we're in the trough of the waves. The engine won't start, so we can't use the big pumps, and the electrical pumps will run down the batteries in a few hours. But what the heck. You're the boss, so we'll fix the hole in the bottom first."

He was talking slowly, but moving fast, throwing foodstuffs out of the hold to clear the area around the hole. He had completely lost his accent, so I knew that he must be in pretty bad shape.

"That's Christian of you," I said while making my way to the forward cabin where we had stored the bunk beds when the boat was converted.

"Hey! Watch it! Coming from an Atheist like you, those are swear words, and now would *not* be a good time to have God mad at us."

With three mattresses, several dismembered bunk beds, ropes, bed sheets, and some hose clamps, we managed a lash-up that seemed to be holding. No mean feat considering the way we were waist deep in saltwater, with a few more feet of plastic garbage bags containing who knew what floating on top of it. The way everything was sloshing around, and slapping against the ceiling, didn't help any, either.

"The water is getting deeper," I said. "We'd better see about getting the engine started."

"*You* see what you can do about the engine. I'm going to go do something about the rigging," he said with a crescent wrench in one hand and a fire axe in the other.

"So much for the joys of a unified command. Okay. See you later."

After blundering around a bit in the engine compartment, I found the reason the engine hadn't started when Adam first tried it. The problem was that I had turned the fuel off at the stopcock a few weeks earlier. I hadn't figured that we'd be needing it until we got to the islands, and the fumes had been annoying. Now, however, the engine couldn't be started because the air intake was under water, as was most of the rest of the engine. The same was true with the genset, which was farther underwater than the big engine. I did manage to engage the manual clutch that started the prop-shaft generator turning. It couldn't put out enough power by itself to keep the electric pumps going, but it would stretch the time before the batteries went dead.

There was little more that I could accomplish down on the lower deck, so I went on deck to see if Adam needed some help. The wind topside during that gale was actually refreshing after slopping around in the chest-deep mess below. The boat, which had been broadside to the waves, was coming around with her stern pointed to the wind. Adam was coming back with the axe, his wrench having apparently gone adrift.

"Need any help?" I shouted.

"Nah. The shrouds parted company right from the beginning, and the forestay yielded to a little gentle persuasion," he shouted, gesturing to the axe. "Everything is now dangling from the backstay, and it's acting like a sea anchor."

"So we'll leave it be. There's no hope with the engine, at least not until the water level goes down a few feet."

"And it's likely to get worse without the engine pumps."

"Lovely. Adam, maybe my timing's bad, but we might not get a chance to talk about it later. Can you tell me what in the hell happened? Wasn't this boat supposed to be unsinkable?"

"Yeah, and the hull was supposed to be indestructible, but that's the way things go. Still, we got a lot of plastic foam between the ceiling and the upper deck, so we may go awash, but she'll stay afloat. The stuff we got in the garbage bags should help out with flotation, too. Still and all, it might be a good idea to get the inflatable life raft out and ready, and maybe *The Concrete Canoe*, too."

"You still haven't said what happened. I mean, it was your watch and all," I said.

"I'm not really sure. The wind was from astern, and we were holding our own, when suddenly a freak wind knocked us on our side. Then, at just that very instant, the tip of the mast hit something, hard. A whale, for all I know, or a submarine. Or maybe a submerged rock, or something that was barely floating."

"It couldn't have been a rock. We're four hundred miles from the nearest land."

"Yeah, that's what I thought. Except that a little while before all this happened, I fired up the radar just for something to do, and there was this island up ahead," Adam said.

"That's impossible. It must have been some kind of ghost, or reflection off the storm."

"Yeah, only it showed up on sonar, too."

"Our navigation can't be that far off. Besides all the different electronic stuff all agreeing with each other, you took a noon sighting with your sextant yesterday, and it agreed with everything else."

"I know. Look, we got other problems just now. You're still bleeding, so maybe you ought to do the light work and get the lifeboat out. I'm going to go down and work the manual pump."

The safety equipment was mostly stowed in and around the aft cockpit, where there was always supposed to be someone on duty, as things had been originally planned, at least. I got out the life raft, tied it securely to the boat with the rope provided, and popped the carbon dioxide cylinder. She inflated like a champ. The raft was covered with an inflatable roof, and had room and supplies for twenty.

*The Concrete Canoe* was big enough for thirty in a pinch, but it was an open boat. Furthermore, it took at least two men to launch it, so I left it in its compartment aft.

There was a combination Global Positioning System and satellite transceiver aboard the raft that was supposed to send a distress message to whatever ships were in the vicinity. I hesitated, and then decided not to turn it on for a while.

We weren't sunk yet, after all, and I wasn't ready to give up on *The Brick Royal* just yet.

Rescuers have been known to forcibly rescue people who really didn't need it. The feeling seems to be that if they had to go through all the bother of being heroic, then you had damn well better appreciate it and act humble. I once heard about a couple of mountain climbers who ran into a bad snowstorm while halfway up a slope. They were experienced men, well trained and well equipped. When the weather got impossible, they had pitched their tent, gotten into it, and then into their sleeping bags. They were quite comfortable, even though their tent was soon almost buried in the snow. As far as they were concerned, the snow was just more insulation. Their intent was to wait out the storm and then to proceed to the top of the mountain as they had originally planned.

Their rescuers, being much less well trained and prepared than the supposed 'victims,' and having had three of their members injured in the storm, had forced the recipients of their unwanted favors to abandon their equipment and to accompany them down off the mountain. The net result of this supposedly heroic rescue was that everyone concerned, victims and rescuers alike, became severely frostbitten. I had heard the story directly from one of the two unfortunate mountain climbers. A quarter inch of his nose was missing, along with all of the toes on his right foot.

Better to wait until we had abandoned ship ourselves, I thought, and were in the lifeboat before we called for help. If the Coast Guard arrived before we had abandoned ship, they might force us aboard their vessel, and then we'd likely lose *The Brick Royal*.

Our radar dome was mounted on its own mast, just in back of the cockpit. Despite the drain on the batteries, I turned it on, and by God, there really was something big dead ahead. I tried the forward-looking sonar, and it said the same thing. Switching both off to conserve juice, I tried the Global Positioning System, and it said we were four hundred miles east of the Line Islands. I tried our depth gauge, another kind of sonar, and it gave a depth consistent with where the navigation stuff said we should be. I turned everything off except the Chrysler windshield wipers and looked ahead. The clouds and spray to the west of us parted for an instant, and I saw what looked like a huge, multitiered city dead ahead.

"Adam!" I shouted over the intercom, "You'd better come up and look at this."

His head came up through the hatchway beside me.

"Sweet Jesus! You know, I read about something like that once. It was supposed to be an optical illusion. They called it the *Fata Morgana*, after the witch in the King Arthur legends. There was a big write-up in *Scientific American*, about how the different layers of calm air made it appear. It made a lot of sense at the time."

"There's nothing calm about the air out here. We've got gale winds going! This *optical illusion* is showing up on radar and sonar. I turned them on for a little while, and I saw the same thing you did earlier."

"Well, given the choice, I think I'd rather be marooned than sunk. But I'd rather be sailing than either of the above, so I'm going back to the pump. If you feel up to it, you might relieve me in a while, *Fata Morgana* or no *Fata Morgana*."

He went below and I went back to checking our emergency equipment. After a while, I had done everything I could think of, even reading the checklist, and went below to help Adam. Then, suddenly, the ladder wasn't where it was supposed to be, and I was knocked unconscious again.

# NINE

On the highest peak of the Western Isles, two figures stood watching as the storm winds blew their long capes high behind their backs. Aldrich Skybolt, journeyman wizard and Master of Radios, pointed due east into the wind.

"There! A ship! I told you it was coming!" He shouted above the wind in a language akin to ancient French.

"Yes, but it's an old one! Look, it has a mast. It's broken, but it's still a mast. That thing is a sailing ship. I was told that the outsiders stopped using such craft a century ago," cried Sister Joan of the Lyonnesse Nunnery.

"That's no ancient ship, sister! I have been hearing its many radios for hours. It may be powered by the wind, but its equipment is brand new."

"Believe what you want. How do you know that this ship is the one you heard? They stopped calling half an hour ago!"

"I tell you, I know! The law says that the Shire Reeve must be told immediately, as must the Council of Wizards and the Warlock!"

"Then you must tell them yourself, Master Aldrich, because I am going to alert the Archbishop of this ship's coming!"

"You're going to play politics when Christian lives are in

*danger? You know that I can't leave my post! Look! They're
sure to be shipwrecked on our shore, near the Point of
Avalon! The Shire Reeve there must be told first, so he can
call out the Sea Farmers and the Fishermen! Lives are at
stake!"*

*"All lives are in the hands of God, Aldrich, and God will
decide whether they live or die. And how do you know that
the people in that ship are Christians? Odds are that they
are Heathens, or even Atheists!"*

*"I warn you of the law, sister! When there is danger from
the sea, the Reeve must be told first. If you must suck up
to your superiors, and try to advance yourself at the expense
of innocent lives, do so and be damned! But you must go
to the Reeve first!"*

*"He's on my way, so I'll do it. But the Archbishop will
hear about this before your Warlock does!"*

*"Then so be it, but get moving, woman! There are lives
at stake!"*

*The nun ran down the long path to the shore. When she
was out of sight, the wizard hurried down to his cave,
unlocked a chest, picked up crude, handmade telephone and
said, "Warlock? Warlock? Are you there, master? A ship,
a strange new ship is about to wreck on the point of Avalon.
This may be the one we have waited for all these years!
Warlock, are you there?"*

❧

I awoke, naked and in pain, on a stiff, lumpy bed
with scratchy sheets. For some reason, this inferior
bed had been covered by a rich blue velvet bedspread
with a wide border that was heavily embroidered with
threads of at least a dozen colors. It portrayed some
sort of a medieval scene, a party of noble knights
and ladies with their dogs and horses on a field of
flowers. It looked to be done by hand, and if so, must
have taken thousands of man-hours, or more likely

woman-hours, to make. For a few moments, my back
and neck in pain, I couldn't help wishing that they
had spent more money on the mattress and less on
the decoration.

The ceiling was high above me, thirty feet at least,
and glancing about I saw that I was alone in a
sparsely furnished bedroom that was big enough to
be used for a game of professional basketball. Three
walls and the whole domed ceiling were heavily
carved, or maybe it was plaster work, but it was done
in a style that I had never seen before. It was partly
an elaborate floral decoration, but there were also bas
reliefs of men and women that gave the feeling of
being actual portraits rather than simple decoration.

One wall was made up of tall, thick Doric pillars,
beyond which was a small garden that looked out
on the sea, a few hundred feet below. There was no
glass in the windows thus formed, but the weather
was fair, and the temperature comfortable. The storm
was over, the sky was a cloudless blue with the
beginnings of a sunset, the sun being just a few
degrees above the horizon. Seagulls were flying above
a blue sea touched with pink by the occasional
breaking wave.

I rolled and sat up at the edge of the bed, and an
incredible pain shot through my head. I stayed there
a bit, groaning, and then let myself slowly back under
the covers. It seemed that I would live, but I was
far from well. My body was a mass of bruises, from
my lumpy head to my smashed toes. It felt as though
every tendon, ligament, and muscle I had was pulled.
Except for my eyeballs, all bodily motion was painful. The good news was that as best as I could tell,
my bones were reasonably sound, I could wiggle my
toes, so my spinal cord was all right, and the cuts
on my back were sewn up and bandaged.

My groans must have attracted the nurse, because
she came immediately. She wasn't the adolescent

dream that my ex-wife had been, but she was nonetheless a remarkably attractive woman. She looked
to be in her early thirties, with very fair skin and
long, blond hair, held back by a jeweled clasp. She
wore no makeup, but I caught a hint of a strange,
musky perfume. Her posture was very erect, and she
walked with a sort of flowing motion, almost as if
she were on wheels rather than legs.

I called her a nurse since somehow she acted that
way, but she certainly wasn't dressed like one. She
wore a floor-length vermilion dress held out by hoops.
The bodice was tight and was cut about as low as
it could go, actually exposing the upper parts of her
nipples. The entire dress, like my fabulous bedspread,
had been adorned with several thousand woman-hours
of embroidery.

She felt my forehead and then my pulse.

"Where am I?" I said. "What is this place?"

She answered me in something that was maybe
French, or even Latin, and I couldn't make out a word
of it.

"Is there anyone here who understands English?"
I said slowly, carefully, and a bit too loudly. I had
to find out about Adam, and *The Brick Royal*.

Again, her response meant nothing to me. I used
the few words I remembered from my high school
Latin, but got no response.

All I remembered from my college Russian was how
to say that I was going to go soon to the library,
but I was either not understood, or the nurse didn't
care about who went to Russian libraries. I tried the
limited Vietnamese that my parents had allowed me
to learn, but that too drew a blank.

Finally, resorting to sign language, I gesticulated that
I was thirsty and hungry, and at last met with some
success. Within minutes she was back with a bowl
of almost meatless stew in a porcelain bowl, a wooden
spoon, a clay cup, and a pottery pitcher of beer. That

is to say, I thought it might be beer, even though it was thin, flat, and strangely flavored. It definitely contained alcohol, which in my book put this place way ahead of the average American hospital.

After a cup of the beer, I felt the call of nature, and though it embarrassed me to do so, I had to gesticulate my needs. She handed me a chamber pot from under the bed, and discreetly left for a few minutes. I'd never used a chamber pot before, but I'd heard of them. It sufficed.

On returning, she talked a long while, and although I still could not understand a word of what she said, her tone and her bearing let me know that somehow I was in good hands, that all would be well. Later, she rolled me over and massaged my back, carefully avoiding the places where I had been cut.

The sun was setting. Contented and comfortable, I fell asleep. When I awoke, the thin grey light of morning was coming through the window wall. It was almost unpleasantly cool. My nose was cold, but the rest of me was warm enough under the thick covers, some of which must have been added while I was asleep. In a short while, the sun came up and shined directly in my eyes. I watched it for a long time, and it was definitely rising.

I knew that something was very wrong.

Last night I had lain in this same bed and watched the sun set out of that very same window. Only one wall had windows in it and that wall had been to the west! Now, either it was to the east or I was going insane! Or was I in a different, identical room, the victim of a fabulously expensive practical joke? Or had I died and gone to some irrational afterlife?

An unfair thought. A decent Atheist like me should not have to worry about that sort of thing!

The same lady brought breakfast, although this time she wore a pale blue dress, as richly embroidered and expensive looking as the last one, and of a similar cut. I guessed that if she had to work unnaturally long hours, she was at least well paid for it.

I slept for a few more hours, and when I awoke, my nurse was again sitting beside me. She began teaching me the language, starting with the parts of the body. The word for elbow, the word for finger. How you said that your finger was touching your elbow.

I was never much good at learning a foreign language. I'd gotten D's in Latin in high school, and had flunked out of Russian in college. But now, with a desperate need to get some questions answered and absolutely nothing else to do, I learned. Total immersion, I think it's called.

Her name was Roxanna. We were on the Western Isles, and the language was Westronese. She couldn't say exactly where the Western Isles were. Indeed, she seemed to think that it was a very complicated question to answer. I gave it up until I could speak the language better.

While the medical help was always there when I wanted it, the level of medical technology seemed to be as ancient as the style of my nurse's dress. Another, older, woman occasionally came by. She talked briefly with my nurse, changed my bandages, and checked my wounds. I never saw anything like the ordinary tools to be expected in a doctor's office. No one checked my blood pressure. I never saw a stethoscope. I never got a shot or took a pill. Slowly, my body healed.

My mind was already well. My physical pains were such that I was actually a few days noticing it, but somehow the deep, black depression that had plagued me for over a year was simply not there, gone as if it had never been. I could no longer even imagine what it had been like to suffer from it. Perhaps the brain cells that had caused it had died in the wreck. If so, they would not be missed.

As I slowly recovered, my nurse got sick. It looked as if she had a bad case of the flu, with a running nose and a fever, but she doggedly continued to serve me, to the point where I got to feeling very guilty about it. I tried to get her to take it easier, but my Westronese wasn't up to explaining what I meant, and my gestures were not understood.

My nurse gave me a thorough weekly sponge bath in a strictly professional manner, but never a shave. After much difficulty with my almost nonexistent Westronese and a lot of gesticulation, I found that Roxanna had never even heard of a razor. What she thought of my initially clean-shaven face remained a mystery for quite a while. As it was, the discomfort and itching of growing a full beard was added to my other physical problems, or perhaps it distracted from them.

It wouldn't have been a good idea to scratch the itching, healing cuts on my stitched up back, even if I could reach them, but I could and did take considerable satisfaction in scratching the stubble on my cheeks. Call it a counterirritant.

It was a week before they would let me get up and walk around for a short while, and over the weeks that followed I was allowed to explore a bit, but not to leave the mansion I was in.

I say "they" because I found that I was apparently at the head of a household with six servants. Besides Roxanna, my nurse-tutor, there was a maid, a cook, and three gardeners. Two of the gardeners were married to the maid and cook, respectively. How I rated such a royal entourage was beyond me.

Strangely, every one of them had the flu. By the time I commanded enough of their language to tell them about the Contact capsules in the ship's medical kit, I realized that there simply wouldn't have been enough for everybody, and I let it go.

The area in front of our windows was planted in

a carefully tended vegetable garden, but the two men and the woman who worked there were not the same people as the gardeners I had been introduced to. The garden and people apparently belonged to some other household, whom the people of our household didn't talk to, or look at, or even acknowledge the existence of. I tried to get Roxanna to explain about them, and for quite a while it almost seemed as though she couldn't even see who I was talking about. I put it down as just another mystery that would hopefully be answered someday.

After more than three weeks of convalescing, my nurse permitted me to go outside, at least up to our own roof. We went up a long spiral staircase, which, in my still weakened condition, was enough to force me to stop and sit down twice. I was a long way from being the healthy student who worked his way through college teaching Karate.

She led me finally through a small trapdoor in the ceiling and suddenly we were in the middle of a field of vegetables! Within a dozen yards of us, our household's gardeners were working diligently at their tasks, and seemingly oblivious to our entrance onto their domain.

When I had first met Roxanna's gardeners, I had assumed that their task was to tend the decorative gardens that I supposed our medieval castle was surrounded with. Now I learned that the roof of the incredibly spacious mansion was a carefully tended garden from which the household got all of its food, barring fish, dairy products, and the very occasional rabbit or chicken.

Looking about, I soon realized that these gardens were contiguous with those of our neighbors. Indeed, with increasing wonderment, I saw that every bit of horizontal land within sight was carefully used for growing crops. The terrain resembled pictures I had seen of the rice paddies of Bali, or of the sculpted mountain slopes in Peru. The difference was that the vertical surfaces here were covered with large windows and open doorways, which suggested that behind them there were hundreds or thousands of rooms like the one I slept in.

It soon became apparent to me that the mansion that I had been living in was not a building at all! I had been staying in a spacious cave, entirely below ground. My best guess was that originally, the mountainous countryside had been terraced to provide farmland, at what horrendous cost in labor I could barely imagine. Then the spaces below the fields had been laboriously hollowed out into huge apartments, work areas, and public spaces to free up even more land for farming.

Furthermore, as best I could see, all of this incredible amount of work must have been done by hand, for I saw not one single machine more complicated than a hammer, and even those more often than not were made of bone or wood or clay.

Farm animals were rare, and I can remember seeing only one ox-drawn plow during my first two months on the island. Even stranger, despite all these obvious indications of fabulous human industriousness, I don't recall ever seeing anyone working overly hard. Oh, people were generally busy at one thing or another, but you never saw anyone breaking his back, either.

After a half hour in the sun, we went back down for more language lessons. I *had* to get some questions answered!

# TEN

About the time that I was able to move about without undue pain, I was able to make simple sentences such that, with the aid of many gesticulations, I could begin to get some of my questions across. Again I asked about where in the heck were we. This time, Roxanna had an answer.

"The day before yesterday, I asked this question of a wizard for you," she said, and then rattled off some sort of a description where we were so many hours and minutes east and so many minutes north. It had to be longitude and latitude in some manner of coordinate system, but I could make neither heads nor tails of it.

I asked how the sun could rise and set in the same place, as it had persisted in doing, but I got no answer because Roxanna could not grasp what I was asking about. No amount of gesticulating or bad Westronese could get through to her. Giving up, I asked why this island was hidden, why my people didn't know it was here.

"Why are your people ignorant? What a strange question! How can I answer such a thing? You know them better than I. All I can say is that the islands have been in existence forever, I suppose, and people have been living here for more than four thousand years. They certainly haven't been hidden from me. How could one hide an island?" she asked.

How indeed? Fighting down my inclination to shout slowly when people don't understand me, I asked about Adam. I was given to understand that he was alive, but still too injured to move about. After I promised not to tire the guy out, Roxanna agreed to lead me to him the next afternoon.

"The forty days is over now, and thus it is permitted," she said, though I wasn't able to understand what she meant by that. Some sort of quarantine?

Despite the fact that he was sweating while running a middling fever, one of the gardeners was immediately sent with a note written by Roxanna requesting permission for a call on Adam's mansion. There was nothing like a telephone available.

Before we could do any visiting out in public, there was the matter of clothing. My shipboard wear on *The Brick Royal* normally consisted of a T-shirt and a pair of shorts, and while I had a single wash-and-wear suit with me, it had been damaged in the wreck.

Locally, except for the ladies' low necklines, dress was pretty puritanical. I had yet to see a Westronese ankle. I had been going around the house (or rather the cave) in the local equivalent of a bathrobe, sort of a belted pullover tunic that reached the ground, or maybe it was a caftan without the sleeves. Comfortable, I soon got to preferring it over the pants and shirt that I had worn all my life. But this, I was told, would be most improper to wear in public.

Roxanna and the maid, Felicia, soon had me up on a stool and were measuring me in more places than I had been aware of having places to measure. They went away for a few hours and came back with their arms full of stuff. There were three other people (from the store, I suppose) similarly laden behind them. All of it was brightly colored and richly encrusted with embroidery. They put some of it out

on the bed, and it soon was obvious that I was to
be dressed in the male equivalent of the ladies' outfits.
It was sort of Elizabethan, with tights, low boots, and
ridiculous, puffy shorts. There was a tight jacket, a
short cape, and a hat with a feather in it. All the
getup needed was a sword, but when I tried to ask
Roxanna about one, she hadn't the faintest idea what
I was talking about.

"A big kitchen knife? To wear?" she said.

The other thing about the heap of clothes they
brought was that, while it all looked fabulously
expensive, it was all used. There was not a new item
in the pile. I asked about this, and was told that,
of course, there hadn't been time to make anything
especially for me. I would have to make do for a
while, until the seamstress that Roxanna had hired
could start work on my private wardrobe. It seems
that off-the-shelf clothes were unheard of.

The next morning, decked out to play in a Shakespearian comedy, Roxanna and I set out for Adam's
place, in a section called Tintzin. To get there we
would have to walk the length of Lyonnesse, some
four miles or so. The maid was told to come along
with us, I suppose as a chaperone.

Leaving the apartment, we went through a hallway
with three right-angled turns. My guess was that it
was to control sound. It ended with a nicely embroidered curtain, past which we were in a public road-
way, or hallway. There was no door, and therefore
no lock on the door. In fact, there weren't any locks
anywhere on the island that I could see.

Maybe there wasn't enough wood or metal to put
a locked door wherever I was used to one, but then
I suppose that the total community here was so small
that everyone knew everyone else. If anybody was
ever caught stealing, I imagine that he'd never hear
the end of it from his maiden aunts and his great-
granduncles.

The way to Adam's place was entirely underground, through tunnels that were used as streets.
I was told that farmland was entirely too valuable
to waste on outdoor roads, and anyway, who would
want to travel in the rain? The only light was by
the occasional small glassless window, more often
set in the roof than in a wall. My eyes adjusted,
and it wasn't too dark.

There were many other people about, and every
single one of them seemed to have the flu. I asked
Roxanna about it.

"It is something that we must endure, my lord."

"To be sick, yes, must survive. But why, please,
everybody one time?" With my still limited Westronese, it was the closest I could come to expressing my question properly.

"Because you and your friend have just brought us
this plague, my lord. We can only hope that this is
the worst that you have gifted us with."

I expressed astonishment at the thought that I was
responsible for so much sickness.

"But it is quite true. We know that you did not
deliberately infect us, so we do not hold you morally responsible. Yet this illness was unknown to us
until four weeks ago. Your friend has assured us that
it will soon pass, and that it is not deadly, for which
we give thanks to God. In the past, other visitors
gifted us with things much worse. The last, more than
fifty years agone, gave us the curse of measles, and
many died."

Again I was astounded, first at the thought that they
had willingly risked so much to rescue us, and secondly that measles had proved so deadly to them. I
thanked her as humbly as I could for the rescue, and
said that if measles was deadly, then maybe the flu
was, too.

"We are all in the hands of God, my lord."

I realized that if I'd had something really deadly,

she would have been among the first to die. I said
as much to her.

"Better that than to be the last, my lord. I have
kept myself in a constant State of Grace since your
arrival. It is all that anyone can do."

Such stoicism was beyond me. I began to wonder
if I was a moral weakling, and to shut off such
dangerous thoughts I began noticing the people around
me again. Most of them were carrying loads of one
thing or another, since mechanized transport was nonexistent. There wasn't even any animal power in use
that I could see. Aside from the flu, people seemed
healthy, well fed, and reasonably well dressed, though
few wore quite as much embroidery as Roxanna and
I did.

Despite the fact that I had directly injured everyone here, people often tipped their hats to us, as
though I was the local squire. I asked Roxanna about
it.

"Of course, they all know me, and everyone has
heard of you," she said. "They are only being polite
to those they respect."

"I am most respected one here?" I said in my bad
Westronese.

"You are very respected. Great wealth is always
respected, as is great learning. But you are not the
*most* respected, of course. You are not the duke, or
the archbishop, or the warlock," she said, using
simple words and sentences, as one would do with
a child.

I had earlier gathered that the social structure hereabouts matched the clothing and technological level,
so the priest and nobility made some sense. At least
it made as much sense as anything else did in this
strange little fairyland.

The "warlock" business bothered me, though. We
had gone over it very carefully when I had learned
the word (which was one of the very few that was

pronounced the same in both Westronese and English). Warlock meant warlock, the same in both languages. They had magic here, or at least they believed they did. Even more curious was her insistence that *I* had magic, a great deal of it, apparently. When I assured her that I had no such thing, she became quiet for a while, and then said that the question was for wiser heads than hers.

I stepped aside to let a man with a huge bundle go by, and in the process scraped my knuckles on the wall of the tunnel. These walls, like those of the mansion, were plastered and painted, but the spot I had managed to hit had been chipped bare. The rock underneath was very sharp, like new, rough sandpaper. I lost a bit of skin, and it bled.

As Roxanna was bandaging my hand with my pocket handkerchief, I looked carefully at the living stone that was exposed. It was porous, bubbly, like brown plastic foam. Foamed glass? Was the whole place an artifact? But how could that jibe with the low level of technology that I saw everywhere around me?

We passed into a market section that had bigger skylights and was better lit than elsewhere. There was a great deal of buying and selling going on, but the goods on sale were all low tech. Farther on we walked through a food market that had a lot in common with things I'd seen in peasant markets in South America. Live animals, dead fish, and crude wooden scales. They were using corn husks for packaging. Utopia, this wasn't.

It was a two-hour walk getting to Adam's place in Tintzin. I asked Roxanna about why we were put so far apart, and she said that there were only two suitable positions available. This made no sense at all to me, but we suddenly had to walk in single file to get past a particularly busy stall, and the topic of conversation was forgotten for the time being.

# ELEVEN

Adam was living in a mansion that was much like the one I was using, except that it might have been bigger than mine. At least, he had seven servants to my six. He was propped up in bed, with his left leg and right arm in heavy plaster casts. Two attractive, well-dressed ladies attended him. They looked like they might be sisters, or possibly a mother and daughter.

Introductions were made. The ladies were Maria and Agnes Pelitier. I was about to ask about their relationship when Adam started talking to me in English.

"So you finally got your Errol Flynn outfit together. Only, it needs a sword, boss."

It was pleasant to hear someone speaking and to understand them without having to go through the mental struggle of translating it. Adam's Hamtramck accent was still there, but he had toned it way down. I had the feeling that he was no longer interested in playing the fool or the clown.

"I tried to get a rapier, but nobody here ever heard of one."

"At least you got the beard. 'Course here, everybody's got one. The guys, anyway. No razors."

"I noticed. Look, are they treating you okay?"

He put his good arm around the older of the two women, who smiled at the attention she received.

"Does it look like durance vile, boss?" Then he switched to Westronese and said, "Why don't you girls go someplace and talk nice to this other lady. Me and my friend got a lot of catching up to do."

His Westronese was far better than mine, but I swear that he was somehow able to speak it with that damned Hamtramck accent. The ladies left, leaving the maid behind in case we should want anything.

I sat down on a spindly, straight-backed chair and said, "Adam, just what in the hell happened?"

"What happened was that you are damn lucky to be alive. The real world is not like in the detective stories, you know. It takes a serious skull concussion to put a man out cold, and you was knocked out twice in one day. That's enough to kill most guys.

"You remember coming to help me bail? Well, you started down just after the ladder got carried away by all that junk that was floating around belowdecks. The water was sloshing back and forth a lot, and you managed to catch it right in the middle of a trough. You hit the lower deck when there was only about two feet of water down there to break your fall. You was out cold, but you was still breathing. I managed to get you propped up so your head stayed out of the water, but then I had to get back to the pumps, you know?

"Before I got there, we hit something big. The bow of the boat stayed up high, so I figured we was stuck on that island that couldn't be there. I got us both out the front hatch, since the back ones was both under water.

"There we was, propped way high up on some kind of a rocky beach. A lot of people was running towards us, and they looked friendly. I put you down and broke out that rope ladder to help them get aboard. About then, another big wave hit the boat in the rump, and I went straight off the end of the nose, like two stories down to the rocks and stuff down below. That's when I got busted up.

"Well, they took me and you into a cave, somebody's house by the look of it, and this old girl has six of them hold me down while they set my leg without any anesthetics! It hurt like hell, and to make it worse, they couldn't understand that in the boat, not a hundred feet away, there was a medical kit with morphine, Novocain, and all kinds of wonderful things in it! And when they got finished with my leg, they started it all up again, this time on my arm!

"When they was finally done, they left me alone for a bit, and I got a look out a window. They must of had three hundred people lined up, getting everything out of the boat and into some kind of warehouse. I felt better about that, since even if they was maybe robbing us, well, if it went to the bottom, it'd be gone forever, but as long as it was safe, we might get it back, some of it anyhow. I shouldn't have worried, though, since now that I can talk to them real good, they tell me that all of our stuff is safe and waiting for us. What's more, if we want to sell, they're real eager to buy."

I said, "I'm surprised that you were worrying about our property when our lives had just been saved."

"Hey, being broke in a strange country where you don't even speak the language is something to be scared about! You should of heard the stories my grandfather used to tell about how he got to America. Anyway, I had everything I owned on that boat. My coin collection, f'rinstance."

"I never knew that you collected coins."

"I never much told anybody about it, but, see, my grandfather went broke a second time during the Depression when his bank folded. Since then, us Kulczyinskis keep our savings in gold. That coin collection is mostly uncirculated Krugerrands. About forty-six pounds of them. That and I got a few hundred pounds of old-style silver quarters,"

"Shit on a shingle! I was paying you too much!"

"Nah, I could of got paid the same money anywhere. But, see, some of that gold was dad's, and a lot of it I got back when gold was thirty-five bucks an ounce. Shoulda sold it all when it hit eight hundred, but that's life, and anyway, I woulda had to pay taxes on it."

"I'm glad your fortune is safe, Adam. But what happened after they patched you up?"

"Well, your back was still bleeding a bit here and there, and the older women was fixing you up, still without anesthetics, but at least you was still out cold.

"Then these three guys in long capes come up riding on horses, waving their arms and yelling at each other. Everybody that wasn't working bows real low to them, but the three guys ignore the crowd and keep on arguing among themselves. This goes on for the longest time, and everybody sort of got tired, or maybe embarrassed about bowing to somebody who didn't seem to notice them, so one by one they stood back up and tried to look busy.

"Eventually, the biggest one seemed to win whatever it was they were yelling about. With the other two horsemen finally sitting quiet, he starts talking to the crowd on the beach. This guy can talk so loud they could all hear him above the noise of the storm. He points around and starts giving orders, and everybody starts moving a lot faster. I was picked up by eight hefty guys and taken off in one direction, and two of them took you in another. After that, you probably know as much as me. I been treated real good by the two fine ladies that live here, and everybody lives rich and dresses rich while in fact they're all absolutely dirt poor!"

"How do you figure that?" I asked. "I mean, their technology is pretty much nonexistent, but everybody lives well enough. People back home would drool over these mansions they've got. From what Roxanna tells me, even the poorest people here have at least twenty or thirty thousand square feet to live in."

"That's because they've been digging these holes for at least two thousand years, boss. What's more, they got to keep on digging them, since the rock here is all volcanic, good fertilizer. Rock, animal dung, and human shit are about the only fertilizers they got. Plus, of course, a certain amount of soil is always being washed away, and it has to be replaced."

"Call it inherited wealth, if you want to. It's still wealth."

"Boss, they got volcanic featherrock, they got a little clay, and that's all the minerals they got. Any wood they got was raised like in a nursery. They got no coal, no oil, and no ores of any kind. What's worse, they got no trade to anyplace else to make up for what they ain't got here. I call that *poor*."

"I guess I've been asking the wrong questions. So their lack of technology is due to their lack of materials to use it on."

"Yeah. Only don't sneeze at *all* of their technology, boss. In some ways, they're way ahead of us. Have you taken a good look at the clothes they wear?"

"Well, it's beautifully embroidered, but I'd hardly call that high tech."

"You would if you realized that half the clothes here are more than a hundred years old! These people got the growing, the processing, and weaving of plant fibers down pat. They do it way better that we do back in America. Their stuff lasts almost forever. That's why they can afford to spend so much time on the embroidery. Anything they make, they'll give to their grandkids someday!"

"Incredible."

"Believe it anyway. Maybe they know about

technology and maybe they don't. It wouldn't make any difference here, 'cause except for plants, there's nothing here to make a machine *with*."

"It could be you're right. Perhaps they really *are* poor. Adam, they made me promise to not tire you out, but there's one thing that has really been bugging me. Have you noticed the way the sun seems to rise and set anyplace it feels like?"

"Forty days and you ain't got that figured out yet, boss? You must have been hit harder on the head than I thought. You're asking seriously, aren't you?"

"Yes, I'm serious, damn it!"

"You'll be embarrassed you didn't figure it out yourself. This ain't an island, no matter what they call it. Islands stay in one spot. This place floats!"

"We're on a stone boat?"

"More like a stone raft. The other place you get featherrock is in Hawaii. It comes out of this volcano they got there. Sometimes it runs all the way to the ocean, and when it does, the rock just floats away. The specific gravity is way below one. It's so light it floats."

"Huh. That's going to take some thinking. But like I said, I promised not to tire you out."

"I'm not tired, and our ladies are the sort who'll throw you politely out on your ass when they think I've had enough. But before they do, there's something I got to ask you about."

"So ask. Since when did you need to ask permission to ask about anything, Adam?"

"Okay. You remember all those times you asked me to be your partner instead of an employee?"

"Sure, although we're both glad now that you never took me up on it. If you had, you would have gone bankrupt the same time that I did, and then where would your gold and silver coin collection be now? Or *The Brick Royal*, for that matter?"

"Yeah, well, I want to take you up on it now. We

go partners, Even Steven, sixty-sixty on everything but the ladies. The boat, the gold, the whole shot."

"Adam, that's crazy. The boat is a wreck, and its salvage value probably won't cover the costs of our medical bills, and whatever they'll charge us for pulling the stuff out and storing it. You'd be taking the short end of the stick."

"No, I wouldn't. There's a lot of metal on that boat, and any kind of metal is worth a fortune here. But that's not why I want the partnership. The real reason is, well, social."

"Social? I don't follow you."

"Look. In America, I could take your paycheck and still meet you after work for a beer. Things don't work like that here. On the Western Isles, the word for employee is the same as the word for servant. And being a servant here is like being a third-class person. Once I'm out of these casts, the fine ladies who have been taking care of me won't have nothing to do with me if I'm only a servant. It'll be like I'm tainted. If they knew, they'd even be embarrassed about having taken care of me."

"Oh. I can see your problem. But why worry? The fact is that you have not been my employee since the company went belly up."

"Boss, the way they look at it, if I'd *ever* been a servant, the best I could be afterwards would be something like a freed slave. Once I got the lay of the land, I told them that we was partners, and now I need you to back me up on that."

"I see. Well, don't worry. As of this moment, I hereby decree us to be the sole members of an undissolvable partnership, retroactive back to the beginning of time. Good enough?"

"Great, boss. I knew I could count on you."

"And I'll count on you to give me twenty-three pounds of gold for your enlargement to the ranks of free and noble men."

"The gold, you've got, and your share of the silver might be worth even more here, since they use silver for money, but gold only for jewelry. A tiny silver coin, smaller than a dime and as thin as paper is worth . . . well, it's worth a lot. Another thing. They take that 'noble' stuff pretty serious around here. You really think we should try and fake it that way?"

"Maybe we'd better not. It would be too easy to slip up somewhere, and that could mean big trouble. If we need the status later, we can always claim to be members of the Knights of Columbus, or something."

"Which I happen to be, but which you ain't qualified for. Oh, yeah. They take religion real serious around here, too. Keep that Atheism shit of yours under your hat, too."

"Now, do I rag *you* about *your* religion? Out loud, I mean, and in public. And is that any way to speak to your new partner?" I laughed as the ladies came back.

# TWELVE

"Felix, the Right Honorable Earl of Godelia, Lord of Privy Information," the guard beyond the door announced.

The earl entered, bowed, and then locked the door behind him out of sheer habit.

Duke Guilhem Alberigo XXI turned from his spacious desk. "Ah, Uncle Felix. I'm so glad that you could get here so quickly."

"My services are always instantly available to the crown, Your Grace, especially when your note said that all you wanted was my advice," he said, pausing to blow his stuffed-up nose. The earl's eyes were watering and his sinuses were throbbing as well. For a nobleman accustomed to long years of vigorous health, the head cold was particularly vexing.

"I see that you've got it, too. I'd be more sympathetic except that I was one of the first to be stricken with the damnable disease. We can only hope that the benefits we gain will be worth the price we're all paying. Naturally, what I wanted to discuss with you is the newcomers."

"I'm at your service, but I'm not sure what I can contribute, just yet. I haven't seen either of them, of course, but my men have carefully recorded every word they've said in either Westronese or English. What we've learned so far, which isn't very much, is that they are very probably exactly what they at first seemed to be, simply two men with a largish pleasure boat that had the bad luck to be caught in the worst storm we've seen in fifty years.

"The larger of the two might have been, at some time in the past, the servant of the smaller, but the relationship seems to have been more like a journeyman's service to a master, which isn't servitude in the ordinary sense of the word. They have since declared themselves to be partners, and I think that we should acknowledge them to be such. The larger also claims to be a 'Knight of Columbus,' and thus is perhaps a chevalier, but I'm not sure that we should consider him as such under our law."

"Their precise legal status can be deferred for the time being, Uncle. The real question is, are they our enemies?"

"It is most unlikely that they are the covert representatives of any outsider government. They seem to be genuinely surprised that we are here, so if our existence is known to their government, it is keeping us a secret."

"I see. Was there any difficulty in placing your listening devices in the homes of the ladies tending them?"

"None at all. There was easy access through the utility tunnels in both cases, so it was never necessary to inform the ladies of our actions."

The duke said, "I suppose that's for the best. I can't say that I like this business any more now than when we agreed on it in the beginning. I hope that you've been able to find a sufficient number of listeners with the requisite decency, discretion, and honor such that the ladies will never suffer by whatever is heard in their homes."

"Of that I can assure Your Grace. They know of the horrendous punishment that would fall on them should our snooping become common knowledge. But tell me, has anything been learned about the unusual instrumentation we found on their ship?"

"Little, except that it may not be so unusual in their eyes.

*The Warlock is working on it, but he hasn't had much to report yet. It is still very early. I'll keep you informed, Uncle Felix."*

On the way back from Adam's place, I asked Roxanna about the two Pelitier women. Were they a mother and daughter or two sisters?

"Sisters, my lord. They are separated by twelve years, so your confusion is understandable. The younger of the two, Agnes, was the wife of the Council Wizard Vintiere, before his untimely death. Before the marriage, Maria had been Vintiere's lover for many years."

"To live with two sisters, one for wife, one for girl friend. Very strange," I managed to say.

"Unusual, but within the law, my lord, and the three of them were happy enough. You see, Vintiere and Maria were of an age, and were lovers before their testing. He was a commoner while she was the child of a baron. This alone would not have stopped their marriage, had he been of but ordinary abilities. However, Vintiere scored at the top of his age group in the testing for the Wizard's Academy, and thus was required to attend a long and arduous course of instruction. As an undergraduate student, he was forbidden marriage."

"But didn't Maria wait for him?"

"No, my lord, it was not permitted. She married a fisherman, following her father's wishes. Maria had a son by this man. It was only after both father and son died in a boating accident that she was free to cohabit with her first lover."

"So many questions. Must be patient with me. Baron father felt fisherman good husband for daughter? And wizard not good husband?"

"A *student* wizard might pass or he might fail, and

if he failed he would be in a poor position to support a wife. A fisherman who owns his own boat is counted as wealthy, and an excellent provider."

"Why baron father not want daughter to marry son of another baron? Would be like that in my country." I couldn't figure out how to say "same social class."

She laughed a bit and said that such a thing would be impossible. When I looked confused, she gestured towards a bench in an alcove set into the wall of the tunnel-road and we sat down, leaving the maid standing and ignored. Adam was right. Servants here were treated like third-class humans.

"First, my lord, such a thing would be impossible because all of the barons are brothers or cousins, grandsons of the present duke's father or grandfather. You see, a duke is encouraged to have as many children as possible, to ensure the continuation of the line. On the death of a duke, one of his sons is elected by the earls, the duke's brothers and uncles, to be the next duke. After the election, the other sons, on reaching their majority, will become earls in turn. The son of an earl becomes a baron, one step lower on the ladder of the nobility. The son of a baron becomes a chevalier, although in fact only the duke, the archbishop and the warlock actually have horses. The sons of a chevalier are commoners."

"Hum. You talk of sons only. What happen to daughters?"

"Why, they mostly get married, I suppose, except for those who feel a calling for the church, and even then, marriage and casual lovers are not forbidden the clergy, as I have heard is done in some of the outsider religions. Oh, I see what you mean. Well, my lord, you must understand that there is only one noble family on the Western Isles, and obviously it would be against the laws of God, man, and good

breeding for a woman to marry back into her own
family. Therefore, they must marry commoners. Oh,
to be sure, they marry the wealthiest of these men
if they have a choice, for they are of the best stock
and come with good dowries. And of course, many
score high in the testing, and marry wizards or clergymen."

"Again you talk of testing. Explain, please."

"Very well, my lord, although it is taking a long
while to explain that two women are sisters!"

"Patience, please. We get back to sisters later. Talk
about testing."

"As you wish, my lord. At about the age of eighteen, every boy and girl in the isles is given a number of tests. The most important of these are written,
and the young are tested for their intelligence, learning
and piety. Other tests are physical, as in running,
jumping and acrobatics. Among the boys, the best
are selected for furthering their education either with
the wizards, or with the church. Once they have
satisfactorily completed their training, they enter into
the ranks of those organizations."

"And the girls?"

"Those maidens at the top of the lists who are not
themselves noble are wed to the nobility, and those
below them to the wizards and clergy. The great
majority of both sexes are rejected by the tests, and
may marry whoever they choose."

"Best girls are *forced* to marry nobles and wizards?"

"Yes, although it is equally true that the young
nobles and somewhat older wizards and clergymen
are forced to marry the maidens. Remember that none
of the tests were for beauty."

I didn't like the sounds of this system at all.

"In my country, people marry whoever they choose."

"In your country, you have a population of far
greater than our twelve thousand. Your gene pool is
large enough to permit such freedoms. Here we are

few in number, and the only way that we can assure
that genetic drift does not turn our children into
crippled imbeciles is with a program of deliberate
breeding, and ruthless culling."

Roxanna's expression was suddenly hard, but what
really shocked me was that this apparently medieval
lady was suddenly discussing modern genetics!

"Culling? You mean killed?"

"No, my lord, we are not quite that brutal, except
in the rare cases of serious birth defects." I could
she was getting upset with me, but I needed to get
at the truth of this business.

"What you mean, then?"

"I'd really rather not discuss it now. Come. We must
return home now if we wish to avoid an overcooked
supper or a cold one."

She got up and strode briskly down the tunnel. I
was forced to follow her, for fear of getting lost in
the maze of caverns under the surface of the island,
if for no other reason. After a half hour or so of
walking, she seemed to have calmed down, so I said,
"So Agnes scored high on test, and wizard Vintiere
marries sister of old sweetheart. Very lucky."

"That a thing is improbable does not make it
impossible, my lord. Also, well, sometimes things can
be juggled, just a bit. It is illegal, of course, but I'm
sure that it occasionally happens."

"But now poor Vintiere is dead, you say. What happens to two sisters?"

"You would know the answer better than I, my lord,
but it seemed to me that your friend Adam was much
taken by both of them."

"And if Adam does not marry one of them?"

"They have money for a year or two, I suppose,
during which time they might find husbands or lovers.
Barring that there is always the church."

From her expression, I could see that I was getting far too close to forbidden ground again. I

remained silent for the rest of the trip, and spoke
only of inanities through supper.

That evening, as I was getting ready for bed, the
maid, Felicia, came by to see if I needed anything.
I said yes, and told her to sit down. Since it happened that I was sitting on the only chair in the huge,
sparsely furnished room, I gestured for her to sit on
the bed. She did as asked, but she was suddenly very
nervous, sitting bolt upright with her hands clasped
tightly in her lap.

"What's wrong? I say something I should not?"

"No, my lord. You are well within your rights. But
still, I am a married woman."

"What does . . . ? Oh golly! Felicia, I'm not think
to have sex with you. It is just that on my country,
a man does not force a woman standing while he
is a friendly conversation with her. They would be
not a polite. Understanding?"

She relaxed, but not totally. "What do you wish,
my lord?"

"I want maybe answers to some few questions. I
try to ask Lady Roxanna about them, but she is averse
to give me straightaway answers. Would you help me,
please?"

"I'm not very learned, my lord. Even my parents
were servants. Perhaps my husband could give you
better help than I."

I could see that I wasn't going to get much out
of a woman who was worried about getting raped
on the spot, so I said, "Good. Go now and send back
husband."

I moved from the chair over to the bed, to fore-
stall any further misunderstanding. These people
lived by the sun and it was getting dark as the
man arrived, a spoon-shaped clay oil lamp in his
hand.

"I hope you'll forgive the light, my lord, but my
wife felt you thought the matter urgent."

"Not really a hurry, but I don't hate you the price
of oil. Put a lamp on the table and sit down. There
are some things I am about curious, and that Lady
Roxanna doesn't not want it to talk about."

"Uh, as you wish, my lord."

"First, what is you name?"

"Jacques, my lord."

"Good, Jacques. First time, about the lady herself.
I guessing that she was used to be married. Who was
man and what happened to him?"

"You mean the Baron Roland, my lord. He was a
fine young man, he was. He ruled the Barony of
Avalon as well as anyone had ever done before him,
he did."

"And he dead now?"

"Yes, poor man. Dead and in Heaven, if there's any
justice. There was a fight in a tavern between a gardener and a merchant. Drunk, the both of them, they
was. The baron went to break it up, as was his duty,
and the merchant hit him on the head with a full
pitcher of beer. Killed him dead on the spot. They
hung the merchant for it, of course, but that didn't
make the Lady Roxanna any less of a widow. It
happened almost a year ago, it did."

"I see. My friend Adam was put with young widow
like me. Just the coincidence, or was there some one
good reason behind them?"

"Well, it's not for such as me to second-guess my
betters, my lord, but don't you see that it just made
sense? I mean, somebody had to nurse the two of
you back to health, and teach you how to speak
properly and all, so why not put you with some
people who needed you as much as you needed
them?"

"Oh. I see. No one has asked me for money yet,
but I intend to pay for good services rendered. From
what Adam say, I can afford it."

"Afford it? My lord, you are one of the two

richest men in all of the Western Isles, and your partner is the other one. I mean, I wouldn't pry, you understand, but I was one of the men who was called up to help salvage your ship. There were *tons* of iron and steel and copper on that ship! And gold and silver, too, and other metals I don't even know the names of! There was stored food by the ton that the Warlock said would last forever, and you could see him looking just *greedy* at all the boxes of magic stuff we brought ashore. Yes, my lord, you can afford just about anything you can dream of!"

"Now, that's hard to me believe, but then maybe again I can probably dream a bit higher and broader than you can. So the Lady Roxanna is in need of money? Well, I'll be glad to oblige her."

"Yes, my lord, she needs cash, and don't we all know it. Not that I'm speaking on my own behalf, you understand. I mean, the wife and me will make out some way or another, no matter what happens. Even if the lady loses her lands and apartment, why, we'd probably go right with the land, so to speak, unless the new baron had some other servants that he wanted in our stead. Not that we'd want to stop serving the lady, of course, but if she really lost the land, what could we do for her? I mean, me being just a gardener and all."

"Relax. I don't think you lose a job, nor will the others either. Like I will say, I'll see that Roxanna is good paid."

"Thank you, my lord, and that's from all of us. And maybe we'd all be eating a little higher on the food chain if you could see fit to pay her something real soon," he said.

"Certainly. But if urgent things were now, why she say anything didn't?"

"Because she's a lady, and used to be a baroness. She's got her pride, she has. And mostly, I think, because what she really needs is more than money alone, if you get my meaning."

"No, I'm afraid I don't get meaning yours at all," I said.

"Well, confound it, I'm talking way out of line here, my lord, and if you want to have me whipped for it, so be it. But somebody has got to talk some common sense into you!"

"I'm not going to have you whipping, and I've punished never a man for speaking the truth. So if you have something to say, go out with you!"

"Yes, my lord, since you put it that way. The Lady Roxanna needs what every young widow needs. Namely, a new husband! And here she's been serving you and tending your wounds and even bathing you like a helpless baby, and you've not so much as patted her on the butt! You haven't kissed her, let alone pinched a tit, and what's a woman to think about that? I mean, what is it? Are you some kind of a pervert that likes to fondle little boys, or some such unholy thing?"

"Damn you, I'm not a *fucking queer!*" I had to say it in English, since if there was a word for those people in Westronese, Roxanna hadn't taught it to me. After a bit, I said, "Look. I am 'lost' my own wife not too long ago, and, well, I just haven't felt like it, that's everything."

"Sorry, my lord, I didn't know. How long ago did it happen?"

"A year ago. Just over a year from now."

"Again, sorry. But the time of mourning is long passed for you. Any priest would tell you that. You need a wife. Every man does, and you'll not find one better than the Lady Roxanna. A fine lady, she is."

"I'm . . . I'm not sure that I'm to be ready for that gross of a commitment."

"What commitment, my lord? You'll always need someone to manage your household, and there's none

better for that than Lady Roxanna. And if you tire
of her, or see another that you like better, why, with
your wealth you can always take on a concubine or
two. *God's Hooks*, my lord, you could afford dozens!"

"Dammit, I don't *want* dozens of concubines! One
woman was everyone I ever need. But the you talk
way about it, you'd tell me they for sale were. Or,
I mean, they aren't, are they? You don't own people
here, do they?"

"Slaves? No, my lord. Not for a thousand years and
more. But there are always more servants than people
to hire them, and many who would settle for a room
and the food they eat. And not the best food at that.
There's never been enough land to feed everybody,
even with the three crops a year a good gardener like
me can grow. But as to women, why they're mostly
just like men under the skin, if you get my meaning. They like a little extra loving now and then just
like most men do. And what with your wealth, why,
if you see one you like, just tell her so, and the odds
are fair she'll be in your bed that night."

Like most poor men, he was convinced that money
is the most powerful aphrodisiac. Having been well
off, once, I can testify that it just isn't so, but there
was no point in spoiling his dreams.

"You mean to tell me that around here is everybody into free love?"

"Well, of course, my lord, everybody isn't into anything. I mean, people are all different, you know. A
lot of us commoners, we married the women we
wanted and are happy with them. Me and the missus,
we're both well content with just one another. The
nobility and the wizards and the clergy, though, well,
the law says that they have to breed the best that
they can, so marriage to them is more like a business contract, if you get my meaning. So as long as
all the children born are from the married husband
and wife, well, the husbands have their friends on

the side and the wives do the same. They do it on the quiet or in the open, as it suits them."

"So you have method of baby control? What is it?" I asked.

The wick in the oil lamp started smoking, so the gardener adjusted it and put a bit of animal fat nearer the flame to be rendered into grease.

"In truth, my lord, I don't know. You'd have to ask a nobleman or a wizard. My wife and I are servants who were born of servants, and neither of us did really well on the tests, so we aren't troubled by that sort of thing."

"You mean that you don't care who the father of a child is?"

"No, my lord. I mean that we can't have children. We've both been sterilized. It's the law."

# THIRTEEN

In the grey dawn, Roxanna came to me and said that it was Sunday. My period of quarantine was over and I was well enough to get around, so therefore it was fitting that I should join the household and go to church with them. I wasn't happy with the idea, but wisdom and maturity had taught me when to keep my mouth shut.

You see, I was raised a Catholic, and I spent my teenage years vigorously fighting the system. It wasn't easy. The Christians had started indoctrinating me during the first year of my life, and they were so proud of this brainwashing of children that they publicly bragged about it.

"As the twig is bent, so the tree will grow."

They bent so me hard I damn nearly broke. They began programming their party line into me long before I was old enough to think rationally about what they were saying. They dumped a load of undeserved guilt into my young subconscious long before I learned enough discrimination to sort their turds from their shit. They gave me the same ugly guilt treatment that they shoveled into every other helpless child they got their hooks into, but because I was more honest, more sincere than most, I think that those hooks hurt me more than they hurt most of the others.

I was many years straightening out my mind and
my thoughts about religion, and in the process I
diligently studied all of the major religions. In the
end, my conclusions were very simple.

Western religions all feed on the most fundamental terror that a living being can ever face, the innate
fear of death. They all said that if you would just
live your life exactly according to the pattern that was
given to us on the high mountain, if you would give
up most of life's little pleasures, and if you would
shell out a major hunk of your after-tax income for
the greater glory of God, then by golly, they'd take
care of everything and you wouldn't really have to
die after all! They'd written vast piles of impossibly
obtuse and deliberately unintelligible theology to prove
that every word of it was true.

The real truth was that it was all a bag of nonsense designed for the sole purpose of keeping priests
well fed and comfortable without any of them ever
having to work for a living. It gave them a high-status
job, being the direct representatives of the absolute
boss, while letting them all live as lazily as any cheat
on welfare.

It was so simple. All you have to do is to invent
a God and then say that everything you wanted to
do was on his orders. Only to pull that off, you have
to explain just what this God thing is. Well, to be
a God, a being must have at least three main attributes. He must be all-powerful, all-knowing, and all-
loving.

What throws a wrench into the works of every
Western theology is the obvious existence of evil. There
is a lot of really bad shit happening in this world, and
God lets it go on happening. The innocent are wrongly
punished. The good die young. Babies are born with
incurable brain cancers. God lets it happen.

Obviously, if He and evil both exist, He either can't
get rid of evil, or He doesn't know about evil, or

He doesn't much care if evil exists or not. Yet if He has only two out of the three godly attributes, He just doesn't make it as somebody worth worshiping.

If He is all-knowing and all-loving, but not all-powerful, then He knows that evil is happening and really feels bad about it, but He can't do a thing about stopping it. Well, that's the same position that I'm in, and it would be pretty stupid to worship someone who's no better than me.

If He is all-powerful and all-loving, but not all-knowing, then He's sitting somewhere up there like a fat cat thinking that everything is just fine with us darkies down below. I could never worship so ignorant a being, and even if I did kowtow to Him, what difference would it make? If He doesn't know about something as obvious as evil, how could He notice something as insignificant as me? How would He know if I was worshiping Him or not?

And if He is all-powerful and all-knowing, but not all-loving, then the existence of evil proves Him to be one nasty son of a bitch. He must like it, that a baby is born with brain cancer! I'll be damned if I'll worship such a bastard! I may lack His power and knowledge, but I'm still a better, *more moral* being than He is, since if *I* could cure all the wretchedness and pain of this world, I would certainly do so!

All of which goes to prove that if there is a God, His character and abilities are such that He's not worth worshiping. Not that there is the slightest bit of evidence proving that such a critter exists in the first place.

It would take a very strange sort of mind to believe both in the painful world about us and in a full, three-attribute God. My mind isn't strange enough in that direction.

I'm a rationalist, and if that means that I will be dead when I die, and there's no pie in the sky by and by, well then, so be it. I'll just tough it out and

die dead. Better that than to live out the only life
I'll ever have as a fraud.

Curiously, there are people who are both rational
and religious. My best friend Adam is that way. How
he manages to do it is beyond me. All I can guess
is that he and the others like him must have minds
that are somehow compartmentalized. There are areas
where they are rational about everything, and areas
that are blocked off, like a computer memory in
"protect" mode. *These are things about which it is
not permissible to think.* Or something like that.

Growing up in a staunchly Catholic family made
breaking away from religion a very painful process
for me and everyone around me. I did it because I
felt that I had to, for my own self-respect, my own
integrity, and *for my own superior moral code.*

It was a battle that I fought long ago, but along
with wisdom and maturity comes a certain amount
of resigned cowardice. I wasn't going to change these
people. They were going to keep on believing in God
no matter what I did. Hell, they still believed in
*magic*!

There was also the fact that if these people sterilized their servants and let people starve to death
just because they couldn't afford the food, I wouldn't
put it past them to burn a foreign heretic!

Thus, I went to religious services with Roxanna and
the servants. Dressed in our best, we walked together
for a quarter hour to the church. It was in a section called Troicinet, where Roxanna had grown up.
There was a closer church, but she preferred her old
one.

Between the medieval schtick that pervaded this
floating island, and the fact that Roxanna never
mentioned any but the one religion, I had naturally
assumed that the church that we were going to would
be Roman Catholic. And maybe it was. Sort of.

Like everyplace else on the island, it was a huge cavern hollowed out underneath a field of growing plants. Also like the mansion I was living in, the walls and ceiling were heavily carved and decorated, but the decorations were not at all what I expected.

Every Catholic church has an altar in front, above which hangs that ancient instrument of torture and death, a cross. Nailed to the cross is a graphic representation of a dead, mutilated human body, with blood and gore dripping down. Here, though the centerpiece was still a persecuted Jew, it was now the Christ of three days later, after He had arisen. I thought that it was much less offensive than the way I was used to, even though they still displayed a dead man's body. There were other changes, too. There was a series of carvings on the walls of the room, where the bloody Stations of the Cross are usually displayed, only now they showed scenes from Christ's life, rather than his death. From where we sat, I couldn't see them all, but I recognized Christ with the little children, and the Sermon on the Mount.

In fact, glancing about, I saw not one single gory scene of slaughter and mayhem. Not one single martyr was being pincushioned with arrows or being burned to death at the stake. Oh, the decorations were done in a fairly heavy-handed, polychromed medieval style, but there was an attempt to suggest that maybe they weren't trying to make you worship a snuff movie.

In keeping with the general lack of metals, there weren't any of the usual heaps of gold encrusting the bastion of humility and austerity that you see in mainland churches, but there was instead an incredible amount of color and, of course, embroidery. I suppose it was pretty, in an abstract sort of way.

I leaned back, waiting for the boring thing to get over with. I noticed in the service a lot of small differences from the mass that I was used to, and I thought at first that I must be attending some sort

of Protestant ceremony, a thought that pleased me
not at all. The Catholics, at least, have a certain
amount of dignity about them.

Most of the service was in Latin, I think, and could
have been in Swahili, for all that I could understand
of it. There was a sermon in Westronese, but what
with my still-poor understanding of the language and
the lousy acoustics of the cave we sat in, I didn't
understand that, either. After what seemed like dozens
of hours, the long, dreary, and infinitely boring show
was finally over and we could leave.

# FOURTEEN

I asked Roxanna how far it was to the place where the wreck of *The Brick Royal* was kept, and it turned out to be pretty much on our way home. I insisted on visiting it.

There were three guards on duty at the only door into the warehouse. One each from the duke, the archbishop, and the warlock. It gave me the feeling that the local triad of powers-that-be weren't all that loving and trusting of one another. The guards wore various sorts of waxed leather armor, and carried carefully polished quarterstaves, but had nothing of metal on them except for small belt knives, with blades barely two inches long.

With Roxanna's help, I managed to convince them that it was all right for me to see my own stuff, but they weren't really happy about it. I had the feeling that they each wanted to immediately report our visit to their respective superior, but at the same time, they were each afraid to let the place be guarded only by the competition. But that was their problem, not mine.

The boat itself took up the center of the huge cave. It was pretty much lying on its side, since the massive, winged keel was still fastened on. I walked around it, inspecting.

There was an eighteen-inch hole in the bottom, near the keel, where the mast had punched through. This was much smaller than my memories of the wreck had made it seem. If Adam had a bag of concrete on board, and it hadn't gotten wet, doing a patch job wouldn't be that hard. The mast itself was surprisingly intact, as best I could tell, as was much of the rigging. Even the sails looked to be in reasonably good shape, and we had a spare set of sails around somewhere, the first ones I had purchased, made of Dacron. Crawling up on top, I saw that the cockpit had been gutted, but in a careful sort of way. The instruments had been removed, presumably for safer storage, but nothing was actually destroyed. The upper deck was cracked where the mast had come down across it, but the solar still and the solar cells seemed to be okay. The hole in the deck where the mast had gone through was a mess, of course, but I thought it was repairable. With a month or two of work, *The Brick Royal* could be made ready for sea again.

While I was looking over the ship, Roxanna and the servants were scrounging through the piles of stuff that had originally been on board. There was an awful lot of it, so much so that it was hard to see how we could have gotten it all packed into just the one boat. Roxanna had found the kitchenware, and was much taken by it.

"My lord! I had heard tales of your wealth, but the seeing of it confounds me! You ate with utensils of solid silver?"

"We used those for eating, but they're not silver. Silver tarnishes. That stuff is all stainless steel. It's harder and tougher than silver, and less expensive, too."

"But there is so much of it, and all for just you two men?"

"Well, first place off, while you people get along

just fine with one only single spoon each, a formal place setting in my country wants two forks, two spoons and a dinner knife, plus a steak knife if we're digesting big slabs of meat, which is many times. Then too, please, we started out with more that fifty people in boat, but most them got tired of sailing beside an ocean after a few months. I think Adam said that we had a table service for eighty with us," I said.

"How could that many people fit onto one boat?"

"It was pretty nicely crowded. Then, too, in my country, people don't have so much living space as you do here. Wealthy people live in houses that are ten times smaller than your apartment."

"Could . . . could we take some of this back with us, my lord?"

"Certainly. Take whatever it pleases you want. Just remember that half of it belongs to equal partner Adam," I said.

"Well, we wouldn't need half of it, but perhaps a service for ten?"

"Fine. Don't forget some plates, bowls, cups, and some sort of thing. All around here it's someplace. And let's make up a likely similar set to send for the Adam and Pelitier sisters."

It took me two hours to find what I was looking for. Adam's coin collection. It was half mine now, and I needed the money. There were two iron safes that each had a key lock with the keys still in them. Apparently, Adam had been less worried about someone robbing him than he was about losing the keys. The silver was all loose in one hefty strongbox that I couldn't begin to lift. The box was fireproof, and squeezed in on one side was a Manila envelope filled with passports, wallets, identification, and insurance papers. It was a good spot for all that currently useless stuff, and I left it in there. The gold was packed with each piece in a separate little plastic pouch to protect the finish of the beautiful coins, and then ten to fifty pouches, depending on the denomination, to the sturdy canvas bag. I took two bags of the gold, one for Adam and one for myself, and used four of the bags to hold a few fistfuls each of old silver quarters. Heavy stuff, it was all that I wanted to carry. I locked the chests and put the keys in my pouch, my present outfit not having any pockets.

Roxanna and the servants had the tableware sorted out by then, and had put some kitchen utensils in with them, which was fine by me. They were all ogling and talking about everything, even the plastic garbage bags that everything had been wrapped in. A minor case of culture shock, I suppose.

I did some scrounging myself, and in the course of things came upon the mirror-fronted medicine cabinet that had been on the wall of the boat's head. The face that looked back at me was ghastly. I'd never tried to grow a beard before, and now I knew why. It was scraggly and thin, and had twice as many hairs on the right side as on the left. The mustache was almost as bad, and I promptly resolved to get rid of the thing, local fashions or no local fashions. A few more minutes were required to find my shaving kit, and with the medicine chest under my arm, I rejoined the group.

As I put my reavings along with theirs, Felicia looked at the medicine chest and screamed. Soon, they were all crowding around the mirror, mumbling about what an incredible piece of magic it was. I was the longest time getting them calmed down, trying in my poor Westronese to explain that it was only a simple device, with nothing unholy about it. They eventually relaxed, but they never believed that it wasn't magic. In their eyes, I had become a mighty sorcerer.

"Well, you never look down on bowl of water? You never see face looked back?" I asked Roxanna.

"Yes, of course, but then water is magic, too."

I shook my head and went back to scrounging. The local beds were narrow, hard, and lumpy, so when I came across one of the big, queen-sized air mattresses that married couples had used early in the trip, and a sleeping bag to fit it, I put the bag and mattress into the "take it home" pile. I thought a bit, and put a second set of bedding in Adam's pile, since big people have even more trouble getting comfortable that us ordinary critters. Then I went back a third time and brought over enough air mattresses for our hosts and both sets of servants. They were people, too, no matter what the local mores said.

I found a sewing kit, and threw it in with Roxanna's booty, along with a few pounds of tea for myself.

"You'll especially want to throw away the thread, from what Adam tells me about your clothmaking abilities here, but you might find the scissors, needles, and thimbles useful," I said.

"Yes. Thank you, my lord, but why would you want scissors with a sewing kit?" She said, "But no matter, they will be very useful. But more to the point is that smaller boat."

The inflatable life raft was there, and still fully inflated, but I think perhaps that Roxanna didn't recognize it as being a boat. She was gesturing towards the yacht's twenty-foot-long tender.

"*The Concrete Canoe*. Yes, what about it?"

"I was going to suggest that it could be put to good use as a fishing boat, my lord. I saw no nets among your equipage, but there were many hooks, lines, and such," she said.

"I don't know as how I would like to be a full-time fisherman."

"No, of course not you, my lord. But a crew could be easily hired. It could be very profitable, as well as providing both your household and your friend's with the freshest of fish."

"Okay, if you wish. Would you see about hiring some suitable men?"

"Certainly, I would contact them, and select the best, my lord, but as to my actually paying their wages . . ."

"You can't, because you are just about out of money," I said, handing her one of the sacks of old silver quarters. "You should have said something about that sooner, but here. Take this and figure out how much more I owe you."

She spilled some of them into the palm of her hand and turned pale. "It . . . it is too much," she stammered. "This is a hundred times, more than that, more than I have earned for my hosting of you!"

"That much, eh? Well, keep it anyway." What I'd given her couldn't have been more than fifty dollars in quarters. I wasn't sure what the old silver ones were worth, but certainly I hadn't given her much more than the price of a good meal for two at a nice restaurant. Adam had definitely been right about metals being worth a lot here! I left Roxanna staring speechless at the money and went to scrounge up some food.

Everyone had gone to Communion except me, so we had skipped breakfast. The munchies were hitting pretty hard, so I broke out some food, the sort that didn't need cooking. Corned beef, Spam, Pringles and bean dip, some warm Cokes and some Snickers bars for dessert. Everybody loved everything, even the Spam.

On board, our usual "glassware" was plastic, but I'd found an unopened case of champagne glasses that had probably been saved for some celebration. These surprised them more than anything else. They'd heard of glass, but they'd never seen it before. I used the glasses to serve the Coke in.

We ate our fill, and I had Felicia take the leavings and an extra can of Spam to the guards. I was wondering where we should throw the trash when Roxanna carefully collected up all the tin cans and such and gave them to the cook for washing and preservation. Metal was that scarce here. I imagine that some craftsman will someday end up making something useful out of them.

It was well past noon before we were finally ready to leave. I gave two pouches of silver and one of gold to Felicia's husband Jacques, and told the three male servants to take them to Adam along with his share of the housewares, air mattresses, some instant coffee, sugar and a jar of Cremora. These people didn't drink anything with caffeine in it, and Adam used to need a few gallons of coffee a day to keep himself going. The men were to tell him that I would be dropping by tomorrow morning. The servants and Roxanna were astounded at my trust in the men, but I wasn't really worried. I mean, it was only a few hundred bucks worth, so what the heck.

Roxanna felt otherwise. She took the money back from Jacques, opened each of Adam's pouches and carefully counted out the contents, recording the amount, before returning the money to him.

"It is not polite to lead a good man into temptation, my lord," she said.

I tipped the guards a quarter each, thanking them for guarding my property so well, and telling them that I wanted them to keep up the good work. The truth was that mostly I just wanted to see the expressions on their faces. It was worth it, even with the one who couldn't believe that a coin so large could actually be made of solid silver!

Roxanna scolded me about it on the way home. I'd given each of them a half a year's pay!

I laughed at her, and gave each of our servant women four of the quarters, telling each them to give half of the money to her husband. It was fun. I hadn't exactly been poor in America, but here I was *rich!*

# FIFTEEN

"Sorry to be so long reporting back to you sir, but Lord Felix's people have managed to damage our listening equipment an average of three times a day since I installed it for them," Aldrich Skybolt said. "Since our illustrious nobility wouldn't admit to being able to tighten a loose wire, even if they did know how, they've been keeping me busy."

"Easy, my young friend. If they didn't think they needed us, they wouldn't support us, and we'd all have to go out and get honest jobs," the warlock chuckled.

"If you can call this business honest. Really, sir, we're snooping on three honest widows and a pair of shipwrecked yachtsmen. It's dishonorable, it's illegal, and it's a waste of time."

"It's also necessary. We have some very serious problems on this little island of ours, problems that we can't solve on our own. Maybe, just maybe, these Yanks will have what we need to survive. The duke needs to know how far he can trust our new guests, and we need to know what the duke's up to. I only wish we had a better way to keep an eye on the good archbishop's boys and girls."

"Yes, some of those monks think that it is more important to maintain our version of Christianity than it is to keep our people alive."

*"All too true, my boy. As to our eavesdropping, there can't
have been much to report yet. Our visitors can hardly be
out of their sick beds yet."*

*"True enough, sir. In the course of keeping the duke's
microphones working, I've managed to read everything his
snoops have written down, and what they've learned isn't
much more than that our guests aren't anything more than
what they seem."*

The next day, I shaved before breakfast. Roxanna
was shocked.

"I saw your face that way when first you came here,
my lord. I thought at the time that you must have
been badly burned. You did this to yourself deliberately?"

I said that I had, that it was the custom of most
men in my culture to shave regularly, and that I
couldn't grow a decent beard in any case. Roxanna
shook her her head but said nothing.

I took Felicia along so I wouldn't get lost and set
out for Adam's place. I found him with some wooden
poles lashed together to form a tripod, with a thin
string hanging down, supporting a series of heavy
weights. Apparently he was doing some tests on the
strength of materials.

"Hi, boss. You look better without the beard, but
I think I'll keep mine. Thanks for the money and the
coffee. Both have already come in handy. Besides
squaring up with the girls, I've bought me a sedan
chair, only it's more like a chaise longue. That and
I hired six guys to carry me around in it. Mostly, I
want to get down and check out the boat."

Six men was about right, Adam's size being what
it is.

"I've already been down there, of course. She's not
in bad shape, all things considered. The hole in the

bottom is about a foot and a half across, and the deck is cracked up a bit, but if you stored some cement on board, we should have her in shape in a month or two."

"No sweat. We had six bags, and each was wrapped up separately. We got everything else we'll need, too, if not too much is missing."

"Adam, I don't think that anything at all has been stolen. All the electronic stuff is gone, and so are all the books and maps and such, but I think that they did it just for safekeeping. I mean, if they were going to steal, they would have taken the gold, don't you think?"

"You're probably right, but then, different cultures do things different. Anyway, we don't really *need* any of the electronics. It's handy stuff, but we could sail out of here without it. And in a pinch, we could even do without the maps. I mean, if we just sail east, we'll come to the American coast, eventually."

"You're so eager to leave? I had the feeling that you were thinking about getting domestic on this weird little island," I said.

"You know, maybe I am. The girls here are so different from the ones back in America. I don't know quite how to put it, but it's like they're *real women*. The girls back home spend all their time playing games with your head, or trying to, anyway, since most of them don't have the brains to know that any man with a positive IQ can see right through it. They want to be respected, they say, and they want you to treat them like an equal. But if you try to do just that, to make like they're one of the guys, they get all pissed off 'cause they say you're talking vulgar in front of them. They say they want to be respected for their minds, but not one in a hundred has ever done anything to make her mind worth respecting. I mean, if they've read anything since they left school, it wasn't any more challenging than a teenage

romance. They say they want to talk with you, but
what they really mean is that they want to talk *at*
you. Then they don't have anything better to talk
about than what the other mindless broads had to
say at work. Give them a chance, and they will recite
to you, verbatim, every single word that every silly
twit muttered from her first coffee break to her rush
for the door at quitting time. And they'll get mad if
you don't act interested in every stupid word of it!"

"Most women are not that bad, Adam. There are
a lot of sensible, intelligent women in the States."

"Yeah, maybe a few. But by the time they get their
heads squared away, odds are that their bodies have
gone to shit. It's all the fault of the lousy training
they get at home and in school. They all grow up
believing every word of what those dykes who run
the National Organization of Women tell them."

"Well, I know that most of their leaders have
admitted to being lesbians, but that doesn't make all
of them sick that way," I said.

"Yeah? Well, I figure that if every libber in the
United States was laid end to end, they'd all be a
lot happier. Anyway, they've got the women of our
country believing that they have to be *both* men *and*
women. Trying a stunt like that, they just naturally
do a piss-poor job of it and end up being neither."

"I've sometimes felt a little that way. Personally,
I think that a lot of the fault rests with the news
media."

"By media, you mean television, since most of them
never read a newspaper beyond the comics and their
horoscope. And yeah, TV news has a lot to answer
for, when it comes to wrecking the whole damn
country. One person gets a bad headache tablet and
they hype it up until they have every twit in the
country afraid to take an aspirin. Some kid eats a
bad hamburger in Oregon, and they get a hundred
million housewives to pass up the ground beef in the

supermarkets. Do they ever think about what they're doing to the whole drug business? Or the thousands of people who depend on it for their livelihood? About how many cattlemen went belly-up because they couldn't get half of what they expected for their stock? But even so, it isn't all the media's fault. They're just out there trying to sell advertising time. It's the silly twits who believe every word of it who cause the real damage. These modern women lack perspective, they lack the discrimination to see the difference between a random incident and a real threat. Hell, they've even tried to make 'discrimination' a dirty word!"

"Come on, Adam. There are as many male twits as there are female ones."

"I don't believe that. For one thing, men have bigger brains than women, about twenty-five percent bigger. Women average nineteen billion brain cells up against our twenty-four billion. The male American is far more likely to take a rational view of things than the female. Women feel perfectly free to emote about things rather than considering them intellectually, whereas a man would be properly embarrassed if he let most of his emotions hang out in public. And this difference is not entirely caused by culture and environment. I tell you it's right in the wiring, and in the genes that programed that wiring. An intelligent man and an intelligent woman can take exactly the same input data, process it, and come to the same conclusion, yet I swear to God that their brains each took a separate path getting there."

"On that one, you're right, Adam. PET scans of brain energy consumption during problem solving show different patterns in men than in women. But that doesn't mean that one way is necessarily better than the other."

"I always knew it. And I'm not saying that the

women of the world are playing with half a deck. What I'm saying is that us men are using a poker deck and all the girls back there are using tarot cards."

I shook my head. "I take it that you find the fine ladies here to be an improvement over the ones you left behind."

"Yeah, they are, somehow. It's like they know they're women, and they know that's nothing to be ashamed of. They don't try to be what they're not, and they don't try to make you into something that you're not, either. They know that men are different from women, and that there's nothing wrong with that difference. That men and women can and should complement each other, in the mathematical sense of the term. Like nuts and bolts that work together, with neither being the most important, and with each being pretty much useless without the other."

"So which one are you going to marry, and can I be your best man?"

"Hey, there's no hurry, boss. Marriage here is more of a contract for having children. Until we're ready for that, there's no point to it. Anyway, maybe we ought to make it a double wedding. That was a real keeper you brought by here a few days ago."

"You too, huh? I've got a gardener who's trying to get me to marry his boss."

"Well, like I said, there's no big hurry. Maybe I'll really settle down here, but before I do there are a few hundred questions I got about this place. And if I don't like some of the answers that they give me, well, I'd feel a lot better if *The Brick Royal* was ready to sail at a minute's notice."

I said that I had questions of my own, and we spent an hour updating each other on what we'd learned. He just nodded when I explained the testing they put their kids through, and the forced marriages and all. He'd suspected something of the sort.

For his part, he had found at least six strange

vegetable products that had to be unique to this weird little island.

"There's this 'hemp' they grow which produces a fiber that I swear is stronger than Kevlar! Do you realize that they can't even cut the thread they use? They have to burn it through, and they do the same with the cloth they make! When the time comes to harvest their hemp, they have to pull it up by the roots. Then they just throw it into a tank, wet it down, and wait until it rots. What's left over is made into rope and cloth!

"They make their shoes out of leather that's generally made from the hide of a whale, but the soles are covered with this rubbery substance they get from another plant. It's as thin as paint, yet it lasts for over a year, usually. Then they just give the bottoms another coat and they're good till next Christmas!

"I think that they must have more and better medicinal plants than we do. We was both cut up pretty bad, but we healed up quick, with no infections and darn little scarring. And they tell me that these casts are coming off in a week. Can you beat that? A month and a half to heal five compound fractures, and me pushing forty-six from the wrong side?

"All of their dyes are vegetable, and they got as many bright colors as we do. What's more, those colors don't fade! They last hundreds of years, just like the cloth they're used on.

"The walls of all these rooms are plastered with something they get from a gourd plant, grind up and mix with water. There are some preservatives that I haven't checked out yet, but have you looked at the paper they use? It's not really paper! It's the leaf of a plant that grows without the usual veins in it. They just harvest it, press it flat while it's drying, and use it. It even turns white by itself as it dries."

I said, "So it's like you were saying the other day,

they do have a technology, but a very different technology than ours."

"Right. And there's a bloody huge fortune to be made from both sides by getting them together. We could do these people here a world of good by setting up a trading company."

"For which we need the boat. Incidentally, with your permission, partner, I've already taken the first small step toward our commercial empire here. Roxanna wanted to hire some fishermen and put *The Concrete Canoe* to work as a fishing boat. We never really used it much, and we've still got the inflatable life raft, so I told her to go ahead. That okay by you?"

"Sure, and I'm way ahead of you, boss. I had some fishnet makers in earlier today, and got them started on a two-mile-long drift net, something these people never heard of. Did I mention that this hemp of theirs doesn't rot, either? Whatever that stuff is, it sure ain't cellulose!"

"Drift nets? Isn't there some kind of international agreement restricting their use?"

"Who cares? The duke here never signed any international agreements, so where does some foreign country get off, telling him how to fish? And even if he had, do you think somebody's going to catch us using them? Hell, boss, they haven't even found this whole damn floating island yet!"

"Yeah, Adam, and why haven't they? I think that bothers me more than anything else."

"Me too. But for now, let's get the girls to pack a picnic lunch and go down to the boat."

# SIXTEEN

We made quite a procession, what with Adam and his six bearers, both of his lady friends, who were dying to see the ship, all of his servants except his three gardeners, plus Felicia and me. It was past noon when we got there, and within minutes Roxanna showed up with four fishermen in tow. We broke out the lunch we'd carried with us and augmented it from our ship's stores.

After some time spent on exclamations about the strange and wondrous things we'd brought (like paper plates and catsup in plastic bottles), the subject of conversation got around to the remuneration that Adam and I owed to the island's people for rescuing us and saving all of our property. It seems that local custom was for us to decide such things, rather than for them to present us with an exaggerated bill for us to argue over, as it would have been done in the outside world.

Our three ladies were of the opinion that each of the three-hundred-odd workers who had each spent two days lugging in our equipment, all the supplies, and the boat itself should each receive the equivalent of two cents worth of silver. This ridiculously low fee embarrassed us Americans. I mean, we're not the kind of people who hire scab labor. After some haggling with our womenfolk, we settled on a quarter to each man and woman. The guards at the door were each to get the same, with some of them already having been paid. The shire reeve was to get twice that, and various other officials, including the lady doctor who had patched us up, got up to a whole dollar.

Indoor real estate rented cheap in the Western Islands. Eight silver quarters rented us the warehouse for the next two years. We didn't argue about that, since landlords generally get more than they deserve.

When the ladies worked their way up to the duke, the tables were suddenly turned, and while we were trying to hold them back, they were trying to give away the store. The duke, they felt, should get one third of our gold, and the archbishop and the warlock one sixth each! Plus the same distribution in silver. This was something like a hundred thousand dollars, cash money American! And in a place where a quarter dollar fed a family for a year! The ladies simply felt that since we had it, the patriotic thing to do was to give it to the government.

I tell you, the IRS would have loved these women.

I couldn't see why we should volunteer to give them anything. Who ever heard of voluntarily giving money to the government? Governments always went in and stole whatever they wanted anyway. The only thing that ever slowed them down was the fact that they wanted you to be alive and productive so they could rob you again next year. If we started out being that generous, it would only whet their appetites. Look what happened when Montezuma sent whole baskets full of gold to Cortés, eh? And *I* should give real money to the bastards who run the local religion racket? No way, baby!

Adam, on the other hand, felt that a little cumshaw was a good idea, sort of like donating to the Policeman's Benevolent Fund. "Hey, it's good politics," he said.

We argued for more than an hour. In the end, we decided on two pounds of gold and four of silver for the duke, and half that for each of the other two high-muckety-mucks.

Even then, I insisted that Adam give all the money to the church, while I took care of the warlock. We went along with a suggestion from the ladies and threw in some other gifts in addition to the money. Some dinnerware and glasses, a few air mattresses, some food and drink, and a few dozen of the felt-tip pens that Roxanna was particularly taken with.

During all this time the servants just sat around, ignored, and astounded by the conversation. Nobody worked by the hour, so the general feeling was that their time wasn't worth very much.

"Okay," I said at last, throwing Roxanna the keys to the strongboxes. "You girls make up the lists as to who gets what, and count or weigh it all out. Adam and I have to get busy with the boat."

Before we could get into what should be repaired and how, there was the matter of the four fishermen and *The Concrete Canoe.*

It was a canoe to the extent of being pointed at both ends, but that was about it. In general proportions, it was more like a tubby whaleboat, or a fat lifeboat. Twenty feet long, it was seven feet wide and five high. It had an easily set up aluminum mast and was sloop-rigged with Dacron sails. It also had a small diesel inboard motor, and it was this motor that gave the fishermen trouble.

The sails were no problem, although they said that they would have preferred a gaff-rigged mainsail to the Bermuda rig we had. While the sail stays we used were new to them, they soon understood what they were for without any difficulty. They had never seen anything like a retractable centerboard, but once it was explained to them, they loved the idea. They adapted to what we had with surprising rapidity, especially considering that the local boats were more like kayaks than anything else I was familiar with, and we were told that the frames had more whale bone in them than wood. In fact, many of the things that I had taken for wood turned out to be bone with a sort of glued on cloth covering, to improve the tensile strength.

You see, locally, wood was incredibly expensive. Every single possible square foot on the island was in use for agriculture, and even so they were just barely able to keep people fed. To grow a single log, they had to take a fair-sized piece of farmland out of production for many years. Thus, a lightweight, cloth-covered frame made a lot of sense. When they needed more workspace for nets, equipment, and so on, they used two kayaks lashed together into a catamaran.

The fishing nets Adam had ordered wouldn't be ready for a few weeks, but our modern rods and reels would work for the time being. The fishermen were at first awestruck at being trusted with something as fabulously valuable as our fishing reels obviously were to them. Metals of any kind were extremely valuable on the Western Isles. I suppose that it was like giving a group of American carpenters a bunch of solid diamond hammers and telling them to go to work.

On finding out how weak (by their standards) our fishing lines were, they were soon talking about replacing them with the local product, for fear of losing a valuable hook or spinner. Nonetheless, they picked up on casting and reeling in pretty quickly. Actually, they were a very intelligent bunch of guys, a lot sharper than the sort of workers that you likely would have hired off the street in downtown Bay City.

Their reaction to the auxiliary diesel engine was less impressive. An hour's discussion on the theory and practice of internal combustion engines went right over their heads. We fired it up for a few seconds, the most we dared on dry land, without water in the cooling jacket, and they just got scared. Finally, Adam and I were reduced to teaching them by rote the names of the parts, had them chant through a litany on how you started a small diesel engine, and let it go at that.

Personally, I doubted if they would ever actually use the engine, no matter how far away from the island they were when they got becalmed. They'd been sailing all their lives without the safety of a backup engine, and anyway, there were always the oars.

It was late in the afternoon when we got all the men (including the guards) together and hauled *The Concrete Canoe* out to the water. It was quite a job, without machinery, or even rollers, and we barely had the manpower available to do it. Much later, it struck me as curious that none of the men, including Adam and me, ever even suggested that the women there should lend a hand, and that none of the six ladies present, even the servants, thought to volunteer.

The fishermen sailed around Avalon Bay for a while, until we could see that they were competent seamen who had the feel of *The Concrete Canoe*. We waved good-bye to them so they could get in a few hours of deepwater fishing before nightfall.

It was getting dark by the time Adam and I had settled on our work schedules for repairing the ship. We would use the bearers he'd hired as laborers, since otherwise they'd spend the time just standing around anyway.

We probably wouldn't need more men until we were ready to launch her, since more would be just that much harder to supervise. But come launch time, we'd need as many men to put her back as it took to haul her out, three hundred, at least. All of which meant that sneaking out "between two days" was out of the question, even if we wanted to.

At about the same time that we had things settled, the ladies had their task done and the fishermen were coming back as well. They had been lucky, and had brought back two dozen large Pacific salmon and a freshly killed bottle-nosed dolphin.

Roxanna was delighted with this first proof of her business acumen, but I was taken aback at the thought of deliberately killing a dolphin. In fact, I was about to raise a stink about it when Adam called me over to him in English.

"Dammit, we can't let them go on killing dolphins," I said in a stage whisper.

"And dammit, boss, you can't go blowing your top every time you run into a local custom that you don't approve of. We are strangers here in a strange land. These people have gone way out of their way to be nice to us, but they can change their minds about us any time they feel like it. If they want to eat large sea mammals like whales and dolphins, it's their business and not yours," Adam said, his nose inches from mine.

"But you're talking about some very intelligent animals! It isn't right to eat them!"

"What makes you think that those critters are so smart? They don't act smart. Whales would just bask around on the surface while those old-time whalers rowed up and speared them dead by the hundreds, and that's got to be acting about as stupid as you can get," he shouted.

"Those 'critters' have got huge brains," I yelled. We were both shouting in English, and the ladies, servants, and workers were staring at us, but what the heck. I had my dander up.

"Proves nothing. Maybe they need huge brains to control their huge bodies. Then again, monotremes all have abnormally large brains, and they're all dumber than your average empty beer can. They say that they don't have REM sleep, and the brains that

they have aren't organized very well. Well, maybe
cetaceans don't have REM sleep, either. Nobody's ever
tried to find out, you know. Maybe they don't sleep
at all, what with having to live under water and
breathe at the surface or something. The fact is that
we don't know. What we do know is that our dolphin was stupid enough to bite down on an unbaited
hook, and that it was dead before we ever saw it,"
he said.

"Making a mistake doesn't prove stupidity. There
is a definite correlation between brain size and
intelligence, and eating an intelligent animal is wrong."

"Bullshit. A pig is a very intelligent animal, probably smarter than a dog and *much* smarter than any
cat. Yet I've seen you order pork five nights a week
and bacon every morning. Anyway, where do you get
off telling another people what they should or should
not eat? Hell, some of your countrymen eat monkey
brains! And as for that fish juice you're so fond of,
hell, I got sick when they told me how they make
it!"

"Now that takes the cake! A *Polack* criticizing somebody else's eating habits! You people eat duck's blood
soup with *prunes* in it, for God's sake, and I've read
the ingredients on a package of *kishka*!"

I could see Roxanna wondering if she should inter-
vene, and then deciding that she was afraid to.

Adam said, "It is flat ignorant to read the ingredients label on *anybody's* kind of sausage, stupid, and
*tchanina* is the Food of the Gods! All of which goes
to prove that if the islanders want to eat dead cetaceans, it's their damn business!"

"Well, *I'm* not going to eat any!"

"Done!" Adam switched to Westronese, and was
suddenly speaking quietly and politely. "Lady Roxanna,
we've just decided. He would prefer not to eat any
of the dolphin, so don't fix him any of it."

I smiled and nodded to her in affirmation.

Astounded to see us agreeing, when she had been expecting us to get violent, Roxanna meekly nodded yes.

"Glad that's settled," I said.

"Good. Now you get to invite my whole crowd over for the night, 'cause it's getting too dark for us to take a two-hour walk home."

"Oh. All right. Roxanna, please make arrangements so that our guests here can spend the night with us."

She nodded yes again, and sent three servants scurrying off somewhere to do something.

# SEVENTEEN

I said, "Adam, I'm sorry I called you a Polack."

"Why should you be sorry about that? I mean, it's what us Polacks all call each other."

"I know that, but I'm not one of your people. You know. One Black Man can call another one a Nigger, but that doesn't mean that anybody else can get away with it."

"Well, *niger* is Latin for black, and it means nothing but the color, or rather the lack of one. To the ancient Romans, who spoke Latin, black didn't have the connotations of evil that it has for Northern Europeans. The Romans themselves were not the least bit racist. I mean, they'd enslave you no matter what color your skin was.

"Usually, when you want to say something that might offend somebody, it's safer to say it in a foreign language. If you're embarrassed about saying the Anglo-Saxon word 'shit,' it's generally okay to say 'defecate,' which is 'shit' from the Latin. Or to a baby, most mothers say 'kaka,' which was 'shit' in ancient Greek. Ditto with 'piss' and 'urinate.' So when 'Black' is a polite enough word, 'Niger' or 'Nigger' really shouldn't be considered derogatory when said by anybody."

"Well, *they* certainly seem to think it's derogatory,

124

and if you have any doubts, just go yell it for a while in some of the darker areas of Detroit," I said. "I wouldn't shout 'Nigger,' and I shouldn't have shouted 'Polack.'"

"But it's not like that. Polack means 'man' in Polish. Or maybe it means 'a gentleman of Polish persuasion.' Why should I get offended if you should take the trouble to speak my ancestral language? Now, I could see a Polish girl maybe getting ticked at being called a Polack, since properly, she's a Polka."

"Polka? Like in the dots?"

"Right. 'Polka dots' means like 'lady dots,' and 'dancing the Polka' means 'dancing the woman,'" Adam said. "You know, maybe the reason why the Blacks don't like the word 'Nigger' is because Latin isn't one of their languages. Maybe if we could find out how to say it in Swahili or Ibu or some such, we could find something to call them that they would be willing to use for more than three weeks."

"I doubt it. I think that they just do it for kicks. Every time the Blacks change their minds about what they want to be called, every liberal wimp in the country gets flustered and feels obligated to line up, kneel, and kiss every Black foot available, reciting the litany of the newly approved word. Some people *like* having their feet kissed," I said. "And anyway, I've seen a lot of Poles get fighting mad about being called 'Polacks.'"

"Yeah, well, then again, some people just like to fight."

We gave a hefty package to each of the three guards for them to take to their respective boss's boss's boss. Roxanna had included a duplicate inventory list with each package so as to keep the men out of temptation's way. I once read that such inventories were the reason why writing was invented in the first place. What with being in mourning for her last husband,

and after that being financially challenged (that's Political Correctese for "broke"), it had been a long time since Roxanna had thrown a party. Since this was to be the first time that she and I were to have guests over, Roxanna decided to splurge and do it up brown. A formal dinner on the Western Isles was a lot like those served in ancient Rome, except that the furniture was different. The Romans went in for big, bulky stuff, whereas on the Western Islands, the high strength of materials and the high price of them combined to make for some very spindly looking furniture. It was so skinny, in fact, that it was weeks before I felt comfortable using it. Supporting Adam's huge bulk, it always looked as though the furniture was about to collapse, not that it ever actually felt shaky.

"I must look like a watermelon propped up on three toothpicks," he said.

They used very little furniture, and kept their mansions very sparsely furnished. But whether it was out of storage or just rented, Roxanna arranged for enough for everybody. Besides Adam and his ladies, Roxanna's brother and his wife Melinda were there, and Roxanna's sister came in the company of the two men she lived with. I don't know why the idea of two men living with one woman should bother me, but somehow it did. I couldn't think of any reason why it should be any different, morally, than two women living with one man, as with Adam and the Pelitier sisters. So I just tried not to let my irrational feelings show. It's not for me to judge.

Another quirk of Westronese social customs was that when you invited someone over, you automatically invited their servants as well, so we actually had about thirty people at the party instead of just ourselves and the eight invited. These extra people helped our servants out with all the preparations and serving during the party, and with cleanup afterward. And in a strange way, they also joined the party.

When we got to the dining room, the servants had
a bunch of couches arranged in a circle, and you laid
down rather than sitting at a table. Each person had
a sort of TV table in front of him, and the maids
kept the food coming. There were dozens of bees-
wax candles burning, evidence of Roxanna's newfound
wealth.

"Silverware" was ordinarily restricted to a clay, bone,
or wooden spoon for soup and a sort of fondue spear
for anything solid and messy. They used their fingers for everything else. Tonight, though, Roxanna had
set out American-style place settings, to honor us, I
suppose, though it turned out to be not such a good
idea. A fork doesn't work very well when you're lying
on your side, because your mouth is now vertical
rather than horizontal. And you can't use a knife and
fork properly when you need your left hand to prop
your head up. By the third course, we all were eating
in the traditional Westronese way.

Since this was the first time we'd had guests over
since my arrival on the island, and since Roxanna
was wealthy now that I'd paid her, she had arranged
for entertainment. She said that the group she'd
engaged normally had a three-week waiting list, but
there had been a last-minute cancellation that made
them available for us with almost no notice at all.

They had a three-piece woodwind and percussion
band, a stand-up comedian and two dancing girls.
At first, the music was simple in structure, mostly
a sort of plainsong, or a bit like folk music, at least
while we were eating. Afterwards, while the tunes
stayed simple, some of the rhythms got incredibly
complicated.

I got to studying it and counting on my fingers,
and as best I could tell, the lead drummer was beating
out a nine count with his left foot and a thirteen
count with his right hand. His other extremities were
doing even stranger things, with the net result that

the music acted in a way analogous to the interference patterns you can get when you're playing with laser beams or moiré patterns on clear plastic films. They sort of automatically built up to a series of internally consistent crescendos. Hard to explain, but really interesting to listen to.

While the servants were generally ignored at all times when they weren't actually wanted for something, they in turn felt completely at ease at such times to ignore us. They would wander in, sit down on the carpet, and enjoy the show when they didn't have other duties elsewhere. Even the cook and the gardeners came in uninvited and watched what was going on, talking quietly among themselves as if we upperclassmen were pictures on a television.

I sometimes got the feeling that on the island, there were two separate realities, each populated by a separate group of people, who interacted only at certain prearranged points, and who were invisible to each other at all other times. Sometimes, I think I'll never get used to the Islanders' concept of personal service.

Most of the comedian's humor was topical, about local celebrities that I'd never heard of, and it went right over my head, but the ladies, our guests, and the servants thought it was a riot.

And the dancing girls, well, they were an eye-opener. First off, they were both outstanding dancers, they were remarkably attractive, and they were as lithe and energetic as Olympic gymnasts. Secondly, well, what with the almost complete coverage of most of the clothing worn on the island, and all the many and pious references to religion, I had gotten the impression that these were an overly strait-laced sort of people. I was wrong.

What these fine young dancers eventually built up to was wilder and sexier than anything I'd ever seen in New Orleans, Las Vegas, or even the western suburbs of Detroit! Long before their act was through, they were completely naked, and taking remarkable liberties with our aging male bodies. Oh, I've seen things raunchier before, but only at a stag party and never in front of a mixed audience. Yet Roxanna and the Pelitier sisters seemed to be enjoying the show as much as anyone else!

Talking with Adam about it later that evening, he said that dance was the "Glorification of Woman," and since our ladies had no doubts about their own femininity, they didn't feel threatened by any one else's. They took our applause as compliments to themselves. If American women took offense to such things, he claimed, it just supported his thesis that they were trying to be both sexes while in fact being neither.

"And did you notice that neither of the dancing girls had a hair growing anywhere below their necks?" Adam said. "If nobody here ever heard of a razor, they must have some sort of vegetable product that's one hell of a depilatory. You might want to look into it, if you decide to keep your face cleanshaven, since your supply of blades won't last forever."

For a finale, the comedian set out a number of sharp stakes with wide bottoms, sort of like daggers that stood with the point straight up. When the dancers started to move among them, I got a bad feeling, and signaled it to Adam. Then one of the girls did a back flip and came down between two of the deadly things, missing each by millimeters. I was on my feet, but Adam, casts and all, was quicker.

"Stop! No more of this! In our country, we do not enjoy watching beautiful women risk their lives. Waste not, want not, after all. So get rid of those knives and do something else."

Which was the right thing to say, with just the right touch of levity. I only wish that it had been entirely true.

We had brought a selection of wines, carbonated beers, and various liquors from the ship, including one of the barrels of rum that we had picked up in Puerto Rico. All of these were new to the locals, who had never tasted carbonated beverages, fortified wines, or distilled liquors before. The servants and performers joined in, of course, both because Adam and I, being Americans, are natural born egalitarians, and because our ladies stayed with the local habit of pretending that servants were not there when they weren't needed. Perhaps because of their inexperience with hard liquors, the party got pretty loud and rowdy, but even then the two social classes didn't acknowledge each other's existence. It was as if two parties were taking place in the same space.

When I went to talk to some of Adam's litter bearers, they did a bit of a double take, as though I had just somehow materialized right in front of them. Then they talked to me formally, as one would to a superior in a work situation, rather than as a fellow party goer.

The performers were an exception to this strange dichotomy, apparently being members of both planes of existence. But then, I suppose that show business people are on a different plane everywhere. Anyway, I was introducing this supple and still-naked young thing to the mysteries of a rum and Coke, with a twist of lemon peel, a local product, when Roxanna came up. In the States, this might have caused an embarrassing moment, but here there was none of that sort of thing. And Roxanna fell in love with *Cuba Libre*s, too.

Anyway, after months of stress, strain, anxiety, injury, shipwreck, depression and confusion, a good party was definitely in order, and indeed was had by all.

I woke up on the floor with the morning sun in

my eyes, with my head propped up on the small of a sleeping dancer's bare back and Roxanna curled up at my side, her head on my shoulder.

It's actually not such a bad life after all.

# EIGHTEEN

The Reverend Cardinal Deacon James of Ys approached the Most Reverend Phillias XIV of Caduz, D.D., Archbishop of the Western Isles. He knelt, kissed The Ring, and looked up, awaiting instructions.

"Ah, James. You may stand. I have need of your thoughts. Tell me, what do you think of of the new strangers?"

"Well, Your Excellency, in the short term, they are a public nuisance. Almost everyone on the islands has been infected by their influenza. Thus far no one has been killed, but I call your attention to the many thousands who died during plagues brought to us by just such outsiders cast up on our shores in the past."

"Yes, yes, but in the long run?"

"In the long run, they are far more dangerous. In the past, it was a simple matter to keep rescued outsiders from bringing the entire outside world down upon us. We needed only to keep them away from the boats. If one still escaped despite our precautions, and somehow managed to make it home alive, he would never be believed because any ship sent in search of us would find nothing but open sea. But now, it is my understanding that the new ship contains communication devices far in advance of what the Warlock possesses, devices that could call the outsiders directly to us, no matter *where we moved. Droves of outsiders with their diseases, their weapons, and their ungodly ways."*

*"Yes, James, and I think that last point is what bothers me the most. They tell me that not one outsider in fifty considers himself to be a Christian, and even among those few, well, have you ever listened on the Warlock's devices to what passes for a sermon out there?"*

*"Yes, Your Excellency. I learned the English language just so that I could understand them. For my pains, all I heard was a so-called 'preacher' who was screeching about God in the most atrocious manner possible. Yet this person repeatedly claimed to be a Christian! I fear for the souls of our people if such foreign influences were let abroad on our islands."*

*"Indeed. And those so-called 'spiritual' infamies are but a part of their bad influences. Many of our people have fallen to the sins of drunkenness when overindulging in the beer and wines made on our islands. Now, rumor has it that the two outsiders have brought in no less than eighteen new forms of drink to tempt our people. What other abominations can yet be in store for us?"*

*"What, indeed, Your Excellency? In truth, I fear for our little island!"*

*"As do I, my son. Come, let us pray . . ."*

Shortly thereafter, the dancer got up, bid us a polite and somewhat formal good-bye, and left, still completely naked. Roxanna kissed me lightly on the cheek, went to her bedroom, and wasn't seen until evening.

I started to sober up.

This condition was soon combined with the grand-mother of all hangovers. It was past noon before Adam and I got back to the warehouse where *The Brick Royal* was stored. The main reason why we went there at all that day was because we hadn't thought to bring the medical kit with us the day before.

After a long search through our scattered property, I found it at last, and the Alka-Seltzers. Felicia already had two plastic glasses of water ready and, bleary-eyed, Adam and I toasted our survival of the previous night.

Then I sent the maid home with blue packages for Roxanna, Maria, Agnes, and, almost an afterthought, for Felicia herself, since her eyeballs looked as bad as Adam's. Or my own, I suppose, though the technology hereabouts didn't run to mirrors, and I hadn't been up to shaving that morning.

"Vitamins!" I said, enunciating carefully. "The only way that I could possibly feel this bad is that I must be suffering from a severe vitamin depletion. They must not put enough vitamins in the food here. You stored lots of vitamins, didn't you?"

"Megadoses. I bought cases of the stuff when I was thinking that maybe we might actually have to spend a few years wrecked on some desert isle doing in the tons of dried beans I'd just bought. But are you so sure that you're suffering from a deficiency disease? Couldn't it have something to do with those thirty-six rums and Cokes, on top of all that wine and beer and scotch and gin and stuff? I mean, you were drinking and keeping up with four ladies, each one individually."

"Maybe," I said slowly and quietly, carefully enunciating each word so as not to be accused of inebriation. "But a hangover has definite physiological causes, like dehydration, and salt depletion, because you pissed it all away, and a depletion of the soluble vitamins, like B, C, and the rest, for the same inalienable reason. Had my vitamin and mineral levels been up there where they belong, I wouldn't be feeling nearly this bad."

I found what I had been scrounging for, and

mouthed down some One-A-Days, a couple of B-50s, a gram of number C, and then some vitamin E, because it was there.

"You want some, Adam?"

"They couldn't make me feel any worse," he said, chewing up a random handful.

"We ought to give some Alka-Seltzer to your bearers," I said.

"What for? I didn't invite them to the party. Did you invite them to the party? So why should we be beholden to a bunch of party crashers?"

"Don't be that way. They're in pain, and the thing about pain is that it hurts a lot. Anyway, if they all quit you, you'll be stranded here, because I'm not going to carry you anywhere today. Furthermore, they *were* invited. When I invited you, the invite covered them. Local custom. Roxanna said so. So be nice to the boys."

"If I gotta."

He waved them over, handed out some of our dwindling supply of tablets, and told them how to take them.

"Maybe there is something to these people having some vitamin deficiencies. Let's get the girls on vitamin supplements and ask them in a few weeks if they really feel better."

I said, "Good idea."

About then, two gaudily dressed individuals came up to us, bowed, and presented us each with an oversized envelope. Adam had the presence of mind to open his first.

"Well. It seems that I have been formally invited to lunch tomorrow with 'His Excellency, the Most Reverend Phillias XIV of Caduz, Archbishop of the Western Isles.'"

"Wonderful," I said. "Me, too. Only I get to meet the warlock, just after lunch. I wonder what you wear to a formal meeting with a warlock?"

"I don't think it much matters as long as you bring

the proper gifts with you. Some bat wings would be nice, or maybe a roc's egg, and don't forget a negative pound or two of phlogiston."

"I've already sent him a positive pound of gold, and after that, he's just going to have to suffer or live with it," I said.

Not much got accomplished that afternoon, and, since it was still a two-hour walk back to his place, I invited Adam back to Roxanna's place again.

"Yeah, thanks, but you know, we can't keep doing this forever. I mean, if it was just you and me, there wouldn't be any problem, but women got these nesting instincts. Roxanna and my girls act real friendly and all, but if we force them together too much, they'll start infringing on each other's territoriality. I think I got to buy or rent someplace near this warehouse to live in."

"Seems silly to me. I mean, I got a good fifty thousand square feet at Roxanna's place. Why should we bother with getting more?"

"I'm not saying it makes sense, I'm saying we got to do it or we'll eventually have a female explosion on our hands. I don't want to lose mine, and after last night, you don't want to lose yours, either. So be reasonable and do it my way."

"If you say so. Anyway, we're rich. You can afford it."

Supper that night was quiet and subdued.

The next morning, Roxanna invited me to the local bathhouse, a weekly bath being the local norm. I'd gotten to looking forward to the sponge baths she'd been giving me, but I was out of quarantine now and I wasn't an invalid any more. Also, I thought that I'd better look my best, if I was to meet a warlock in the afternoon.

The public baths turned out to be as big an eye-opener as the party had been. There was something almost schizophrenic about the way these people were super strait-laced at some times and totally uninhibited at others.

Roxanna and I went through a curtained doorway into a small changing room. Without any preamble, Roxanna promptly stripped herself completely naked. Just not what I had expected, at all.

Her actions, that is, not her appearance. She looked just like what I'd been dreaming of for weeks. Fine, firm breasts with tiny pink nipples, a very small waist, nicely flaring hips and wonderfully long legs that went all the way down to the floor. Like the dancers of a few nights before, she was completely depilated, a custom that I found myself liking.

But this was not the right place for an erection, not when I could hear a crowd of people on the other side of the curtain. There was nothing for it but for me to strip down as well, hang my clothes up beside hers, and hope that my body wouldn't do anything embarrassing.

We went into a huge room full of naked people, and I soon started to feel less awkward. I mean, if everybody was doing it, well, why not? After a bit, I realized that I would probably have felt more awkward if I had been the only one who had clothes on.

In some ways, the bath was sort of Japanesey. I mean, you washed up first, and *then* you took a bath. Roxanna led the way to where a fountain squirted warm, fresh water into the air almost like a shower. We wet ourselves down, and went to the side to suds down with a soft, brown soap. She scrubbed down my newly healed back, so I returned the favor by doing the same to her back.

And to both sides, and to her front. She took it as nothing out of the ordinary, as did the people all around us. She was even talking to a lady friend of

hers as I finished up. I don't know why I was so
forward. I mean, I'm usually rather shy. But it seemed
like a good idea at the time so I did it. After rins-
ing off at the fountain, we went to something that
was halfway between a small swimming pool and a
monster Jacuzzi.

Once we were sitting in the almost too warm water,
I said, "Roxanna, why were you walking different?"

"Walking different? What do you mean?"

"Well, when you women are wearing a long dress,
you sort of glide along, as if you were on skids, or
skates, or wheels. Now that you're naked, you walk
like everybody else I've ever known. Why is that?"

"You don't like the way I walk?"

"I absolutely love the way you walk. I only want
to know why you walk one way some times, and
another way at other times."

"Oh. Well, it looks nicer that way."

"I don't understand."

"All right. Look." She got out of the pool and
walked away. "When your legs aren't covered, you
want them to look as nice as possible, yes?"

She walked towards me in a normal fashion, her
feet pointed straight forward.

"Yes, Roxanna, you have very lovely legs."

She accepted the compliment as only being her due.
She walked away again, and came back walking like
some comedian from a silent movie, with her toes
spread out almost sideways and her knees slightly
bent. It looked absolutely ridiculous, but after a bit
I realized that this strange method of locomotion made
her body above the waist absolutely motionless.

"You're right," I said. "I can see now why you'd
want a thing like that covered by a long dress."

She had really been walking like that all the time?
Well, some cultures think that a bone through the
nose is the high point of beauty, and by comparison, I suppose that I lucked out.

After a long soak, Roxanna asked me if I felt like a massage, and I said yes, hoping that she meant to do it herself. Unfortunately, such things were done here by professionals, and I soon found myself stretched out on the table next to hers. The masseurs were both men, I suppose because it takes strong arms to do the job properly. I am nonetheless convinced that sometimes there is much to be said for inefficiency. After that, we took a swim in a larger, cooler pool.

Perhaps I had a misspent childhood, and was entirely too serious and formal myself, but this was my first actual experience with public nudity, at least when I was one of the nudes.

It's a very odd thing. At a stag party, where the ladies aren't wearing clothes and you are, you just naturally feel lecherous towards them. But when you're naked too, and in public, you just don't feel that way anymore. Oh, you can certainly appreciate a beautiful body, in an intellectual sort of way, but the sexy feeling isn't there anymore. Maybe that's why less than one American in a thousand is a nudist. It's not that nudists are being overly sexual with each other, but the precise opposite. And most people, given the choice, would really rather be lecherous.

Which launches another thought. In most countries in the civilized world, church and state agree vigorously in condemning public nakedness. They instill this taboo into their people with great vigor and effectiveness, to the point that people have been known to choose death by fire rather than leave a burning building naked. Many men (and some women, although they seem to be less effected than we are) would prefer torture, mutilation, and bankruptcy to walking down the street without their pants on. The prohibition of nakedness seems to be stronger than that condemning theft, or even violence. Being naked in public is probably the most common childhood nightmare, far more prevalent than bad dreams about, say, stealing from the neighbors.

I suspect that the reason for this is that the leaders of both church and state desperately want to increase the size of the populations subordinate to them. More people means more taxpayers, more cannon fodder, and more contributors to the holy cause. They say that whenever the old Indian chiefs got together, the main topic of conversation was always the relative lack of Indians.

The best way to make more people is by keeping your men sexually frustrated most of the time, and then permitting them to release those frustrations when they are locked away in private with their wives. Forcing people to cover their bodies increases the level of frustration, and thus, from a ruler's point of view, it must be a good thing.

Consider the way the populations of the Arab countries, where women are often forced to wear mobile tents, are exploding. On the other hand, in the Scandinavian countries, Sweden, Denmark, and Norway, where public nudity is common, populations are actually declining.

The next time you see a particularly attractive young person undulating along across the street, and you wish that she was wearing a whole lot less, just remember that you are but the victim of yet another wretched government plot.

# NINETEEN

*His Royal Grace Duke Guilhem Alberigo XXI sat with one hip on the corner of the desk of Tom Strong, E.E., Warlock of the Western Islands.*

*"So, Tom. What have you and your people learned about the various equipments our visitors have brought to my island?"*

*"Less than I'd hoped, Your Grace. Over the shortwave, they have been talking for fifty years about the rapid progress that has been made outside in electronics, but it wasn't until I actually saw some of it that I realized, on a gut level, just how much has really been accomplished. Everything is a thousand times smaller than what we used in the war. It does a thousand times more, and seems to use less than one hundredth of the power to do it with. With most of the devices I've opened up, the truth is that I don't have any idea of how they work. I often don't even see how they could be built in the first place. Wires almost too tiny to be seen are somehow glued to thin sheets of hard plastic, and then soldered somehow to the legs of other devices as small as insects. I daren't try to unsolder anything, for my own equipment is so crude by comparison that I would surely do damage. And my understanding is far cruder than my equipment!"*

"But surely there's something that you've learned."

"I think that I know what some of this stuff is supposed to accomplish, Your Grace. Five of these things are radios of various sorts, that operate on various frequencies. This suggests that the shortwave sets that I have managed to keep operating can receive only a small portion of the broadcasting that is actually going on out there.

"There are several televisions, which receive a full-color moving picture, along with the sound that an ordinary radio would reproduce. There are two devices that also reproduce a picture, but do it on paper. This is in addition to a printing device that connects only to a thing called a 'computer,' but which seems to do other things besides computation. This disc, clearly labeled 'The Encyclopaedia Britannica,' fits into a slot in the computer, which suggests all sorts of things."

"And what might this Britannica thing be?"

"When I was out there, it was a set of large volumes printed on very thin paper that took up seven feet of shelf space. It was a summation of all human knowledge."

"And now all of that is apparently on this small, shiny disc, along with all the new things that they've learned in the last fifty years. Yes, I see your problem. I take it then that you will recommend that our visitors explain it all to you."

"Yes, Your Grace, and that they get it all working again. This equipment can teach us a great deal about the outside world, things that we will need to know, if we are ever to deal with them on any but disastrous terms."

"And you think these men can be trusted? When helping us might mean hurting their own world?"

"Sire, you are used to thinking of the outside as being a single entity, as the Western Islands are a single social, political, and economic entity. This is a mistake. The outside world consists of many separate, disorganized governments, with many conflicting interests. This fact is one of the few in our favor."

*"We have other strengths, Tom. Don't forget that we of the Islands are each the result of seventy-five generations of very careful selective breeding. We are a superior people, and that will tell more than any other factor when we go out to face the world."*

*"I hope so, Your Grace, for face them we must, and soon."*

Spiffed up and dressed in my best, it was with considerable trepidation that I followed the warlock's page past two clerks who doubled as armed guards, up a bodaciously long spiral staircase, over a stone bridge that spanned a cleft in the central mountain that had to be over three hundred feet deep, and finally into the great man's inner sanctum high above the Bay of Avalon.

It wasn't at all what I had been expecting. The room was huge, as were almost all rooms on the Western Isles, but whereas every other area I'd seen was extremely underfurnished, to the point of looking naked, this place was crowded with tables that were piled high with arcane equipment.

The equipment wasn't what Hollywood told you a warlock's workshop should have, either. There was not one eye of newt or ear of toad in the place. No bubbling retorts, no imps and devils staring out from sealed bottles.

On the wall, where one would have expected stuffed owls and mummified bats, there was instead a hand-drawn chart of the Periodic Table of Elements, with the last ten or so at the bottom missing. There was some ceramic chemistry equipment standing long unused in one corner, but mostly the place was filled with books and old electrical junk. In truth, the room looked more like a World War II electronics lab than anything else that came to mind, with lots of ancient tube-type equipment lying around in various states of disrepair.

In addition to all the old stuff, three big tables were covered with all of the new electronic stuff that had been taken from *The Brick Royal*, while a fourth held much of our library.

"Ah! G'day, mate," said a voice in English with a strong Australian accent. "Tom Strong here. Welcome aboard and all that."

I turned to find the warlock sitting at a rolltop desk on a swivel chair. The fellow looked to be in his sixties, with white hair and clear blue eyes. He was wearing a long black robe, and there was a tall pointed black hat on the credenza behind his desk, but his outfit wasn't embroidered with the astrological symbols that you'd just naturally expect. It was embroidered with tube-type circuit schematics.

"Thanks for the gifts you sent me, though you really sent too much. The gold in particular, well, you might as well take it back. I just wouldn't have any use for it. Later on, if you still feel generous, maybe I can talk you out of some of your incredible electronic gear."

"As you wish, sir. You're Australian?" I said.

"Right. I was on a bomber during the last big war, one of your B-17s, actually, when our navigator and our pilot got each other lost on a dark and stormy night. The twits had us a thousand miles in the wrong direction, the fuel ran out, and the pilot had to make a dead-stick landing on the island. Made a complete hash of it. Been here ever since. Have a chair, won't you?"

"What happened to the rest of you?" I said, sitting down.

"Well, only three us survived the crash, and one of the gunners was killed a few months later doing something really stupid. That was over fifty years ago, and Johnny died last year. Cancer, I think it was, although they're not much for autopsies around here. I'm the last one left. It's one of the reasons that I'm so happy that you bastards have arrived. Someone from the outside world to talk to, you see."

I reminded myself that "bastard" was a polite term, if you were an Australian.

"Then why have you waited two months before you asked me to visit you?"

"In part because of the quarantine rules, in part to give you time to heal from your wounds, and to give you a bit of time to start learning the language. Also, it took me a few weeks to recover from that mild form of influenza that you chaps gifted us with. Then, too, there's a bit of politics going on between me and the good archbishop, but you don't want to hear about that. Anyway, after fifty years, what's a few more months?"

"So you've been here the whole while? You never thought of going home?"

"Oh, at first I did, but there was really no way to do it. I didn't bring a boat the way you folks did, and the old bird I came in on was total loss and no mistake. Then, after a while, well, this place sort of grows on you. I married, settled in, and prospered. But look here. I'm the one who is supposed to be questioning you, and not the other way around." He pulled out a sheaf of papers. "Nguyen Hien Treet. That's Indochinese, isn't it."

"Vietnamese, actually."

"But it says here that you're a U.S. citizen."

"I am. I was born and raised in the United States. In fact, this 'vacation' is my first extended trip away from there."

"And how does a Vietnamese fellow like you get born in the U.S.?"

"It didn't take much talent, I assure you. After the same war that you fought in, my parents found work

as a nanny and a gardener, employed by a British
general. He promised them long-term employment and
British citizenship if they would go back to England
with him. Naturally, they jumped at the chance, and
sailed there with him. But after the war, England was
forced to go on an extreme austerity program. The
general found that he could no longer afford many
servants, and was forced to let my parents go. He
was an honorable man, however, and even after they
were no longer his employees, he used his influence
to see to it that they received the promised citizenship papers. Despite this, my parent's financial pros-
pects in England were not good. Those few jobs that
were available always seemed to go to Anglo-Saxons.
In time, though, they discovered that as British subjects, it was fairly easy to get a visa to the United
States, and their friend the general was able to arrange
free military transportation for them to Michigan. They
got there in 1948, and eventually, as you say, they
prospered. I was born in 1953."

"I see. I was wondering why you had a Yank accent
and not an Indochinese one."

"I'm sorry to say that growing up, I learned very
little Vietnamese. My parents felt that I would be
better off learning only English. The problem with
that was that they barely spoke the language themselves, so my first language was actually *broken*
English. To make matters worse, they used Vietnamese
between themselves when they wanted to discuss
something that we children shouldn't know about.
I think that I must have internalized the strange
attitude that somehow, other languages were something that I shouldn't know. Anyway, in school, I
really blew it, trying to learn Latin and later Russian."

"But I understand that your Westronese is coming
along quite well, Treet," he said in Westronese.

"I think they call it total immersion. But look. Could
you answer just a few questions for me?"

"Certainly, mate, in a few minutes. First though, what was your profession? I mean, you seem to be an educated man, but what did you do with yourself?"

"I was an engineer, working in the special machine tool trade in Michigan. My partner and I owned our own company, and we mostly designed and built special machines for the auto companies."

"Special machines? That's like lathes and drill presses?"

"Hardly. Most of the machines we built were completely automated, without any workers at all. They did things like assembling automatic transmissions or rebuilding used crankshafts."

"Humph. Not much call for that sort of thing around here, I'm afraid. Your friend Adam Kulczynski was also an engineer?"

"Yes, we were partners. Mostly, he took care of the shop and I took care of sales, although we each filled in wherever needed."

"Pity. Well now, I'll answer your questions then. Within reason, of course."

"Thank you. First, could you please tell me just where in the hell we are, and just how someplace as obviously impossible as this island can seem to exist?"

"Now that takes quite a long answer. I don't imagine that there's any chance that you brought any tobacco with you, is there?"

"Sorry. I used to smoke, but everybody back home is quitting it now, since the habit was proved to cause long-term damage to one's health. We've got some Foster's beer stored somewhere, though, if you could see fit to answer my questions."

"Bribery, I see. Very well, then. I'll expect a few cases tomorrow. To answer your question, I suppose that the story starts some fifty thousand years ago, during the last ice age. So much water was tied up

in the ice caps that covered half of Europe, Asia and
North America that the sea level was down several
hundred yards, and most of the world's continental
shelves were exposed.

"A series of volcanoes erupted in an area that was
then dry land, but is now a hundred miles off the
west coast of France.

"Now, most volcanoes come in one of three varieties. They spit out either lava, or dust, or mud, or
sometimes all three. But there is a very rare sort where
the lava is glassy and has just the right amount of
gasses absorbed in it. When this sort of lava oozes
out slowly, the absorbed gasses come out of solu-
tion and form bubbles in the lava. There's one like
that in Hawaii, they tell me, and when the molten
rock flows out on the ocean, the fluffy stuff just floats
away. Well, the lava from our ice-age volcanoes didn't
float away just then because it was a hundred miles
from the ocean. It just kept on oozing and solidify-
ing, and piling higher, wider, and deeper.

"When the ice age ended, the sea level rose and
our volcanoes became a collection of islands. Now
they didn't float away because they were stuck quite
firmly to the continental shelf, and there they sat for
the next forty-nine thousand years or so.

"In time they were discovered by people. It happened quite early, we think. While we have no records
of the first landings, there are written records on this
island that go back to 2754 B.C., and since they used
to have five times our current land area, there were
about as many people then as now. The old histo-
ries make fascinating reading. You might have that
lady friend of yours check out some of our early
books from the library, when your reading skills pick
up, that is.

"For the most part, due to their remote location, the
Western Isles were spared the invasions and empires
that have wracked Europe from the earliest times. We

have tended to be a fairly peaceful people, at least compared to the other European nations. Oh, we've had our wars, rebellions, and assassinations, but they were fewer in number and lower in ferocity than the average.

"Also, we were the first nation in the world to become Christians. You've heard of the apostle, Doubting Thomas? Well, about in the middle of the first century he came to our islands, and converted us from paganism without much fuss and bother at all. St. Thomas became our first bishop, and the church he founded has been the only one here ever since.

"I gather from your expression that you're not very religious, but you have to realize that Christianity is a powerful force hereabouts, and has been for almost two thousand years. Aside from our unique geology, it's been the dominant molding force both for the culture and technology of the islands."

"Christianity is responsible for your low level of technology?" I said.

"No, mate. It has been responsible for the *high* level of our technology. We both know that on the mainland, there has always been a tension between science and religion. It's not that way here, the current political differences between me and the archbishop notwithstanding.

"Think about the stories that you've heard concerning Doubting Thomas. He wouldn't believe that Christ had arisen, even after he had personally seen Him himself. He insisted on positive proof, putting his fingers into Christ's nail holes, and his arm into the spear wound in Christ's side.

"Can you understand that such an attitude was just what was needed to foster the scientific method? St. Thomas always insisted that one should always examine everything for one's self, and never trust to dogma or unsubstantiated folk tales. As a result, there has been a formal scientific organization here for over eighteen hundred years. The whole scientific revolution started here fifteen hundred years before it caught hold in Europe."

"And you are the current head of this scientific organization?" I asked.

"Right. The Wizards. Oh, the titles and all are a bit archaic, but that's to be expected with so old an organization. We've been carrying on our scientific researches for almost two millennia."

"Then why are you so far behind the rest of the world?" I said.

"First off, we're not as backward as we might appear to be. True, our clothing styles haven't changed much in the last five hundred years, but that's because of some of our high technology, not because of any lack of imagination on our part. When any article of apparel can be expected to last several hundred years, there is very little incentive to make much new clothing. We have no group of garment manufacturers here eager to increase their sales by making last year's fashions obsolete. What little new clothing we need to make is done as a hobby by the women here. They like to compete with each other on their embroidery, but if they changed the basic styles, everything they inherited from their grandmothers would be obsolete. A change in style would make them poorer, not richer.

"Then too, as you well know, in certain fields, horticulture, for example, and the study of ocean currents and weather patterns, we're considerably ahead of the rest of you.

"But for the rest, there are several obvious reasons why we're presently behind. You know that we have always been in a really dismal state when it comes to raw materials. We have no ores, no fossil fuels, and almost no minerals at all. Furthermore, there are damn few of us. There are only about twelve thousand people on all of the islands together, compared to upwards of six billion of you in the outside world.

"You can't expect us to stay ahead of the rest when we're outnumbered by a half million to one!"

# TWENTY

"But we're getting sidetracked, and you asked for a history lesson," the Australian warlock said.

"So, for a thousand years after the coming of St. Thomas, the Western Isles prospered. While we avoided most of the invasions that plagued Europe, and managed to beat off three major Viking attacks, we did stay in touch to a certain extent. The Romans never got around to invading us, but we did enjoy a lively trade with them until the Germans took over the western half of Roman Empire. Luckily for us, the Germans never were much good with boats, so we stayed free. Still, there was a certain commerce going on in goods, and pilgrims, and ideas."

"Then why didn't your islands show up on the maps that the ancient Romans made?" I asked.

"I suppose that they did. The curious thing is that not one single authentic ancient Roman map managed to survive into the modern world. We have Ptolemy's text on how to draw a map properly, but none of his maps themselves. The only thing approaching them, outside of our libraries here, of course, are some highly distorted medieval copies. The Western Isles show up on them, of course. On the famous tenth-century Beatus map, they are clearly shown right where they are supposed to be, south of England and west of France. Your modern scholars have decided that they must represent Scotland, of all things, though what Scotland is doing as a separate island and south of England is left unexplained."

I resettled myself in the hard, straight-backed, armless chair and said, "So they were taken for granted at the time, and later passed off as a myth when they weren't there any more."

"Precisely. There were even a few tourists back then, going both ways. King Arthur's father, Uther Pendragon, was born not two miles from here, and despite what *your* history books will tell you, St. Patrick was born here a mile in the other direction. It was *our* church that baptized Ireland and parts of Scotland, not the Church of Rome. In fact, the Irish did not join the Romans until the time of Henry the Eighth. When he made the Church of England split from Rome, the Irish joined the Roman Catholic Church, mostly as a political protest. But I'm digressing again.

"So a vast mass of bubbly glass was stuck to the French continental shelf, and I'll leave it to you to think about the stresses involved. Glass, of course, is slightly soluble in water, and glass under stress is degraded faster than unstressed glass. In the winter of 1099, when everyone else in Europe was looking eastward at the First Crusade, a storm of monumental proportions swept in off the Atlantic Ocean, and broke the Western Islands free of the ocean bottom. The earthquakes were devastating, and there was hardly a building left standing. The entire city of Ys was completely lost. Some four thousand of our people died in a single night, most of our winter's stores of food were destroyed, and our standing crops were ruined. If the duke's library hadn't been kept in a mountain cave, our records would have been lost as well, but we thank God for small favors.

"As soon as the storm had blown itself out, our

duke ordered every ship to be launched, to go to the mainland and beg for aid. This in itself turned out to be no easy feat, for to the wonderment of all, the very level of the sea had gone down six yards, and this was no mere freak tide. Indeed, as far as anyone could tell, there were no longer any tides at all! Our land area had increased considerably. But despite all the strangeness, some eighty ships were launched. Of these, only two returned, after great hardship and long voyaging, for when our ships got back to where the islands should have been, our islands were gone entirely! The Western Islands had floated off with the Gulf Stream, and we stayed on that great merry-go-round for seven hundred and fifty years."

I said, "I'm amazed that in all that time you didn't snag yourself on some seashore or seamount."

"Well, we did, and fairly often at first, until we had the ocean currents thoroughly mapped. Once, we were hung up on the west coast of Ireland for three years. But the action of sea and tide eventually broke us free, which made us glad. You see, there were some very nice advantages to being adrift in the Gulf Stream, and the biggest of these was the weather. With a bit of coaxing, it was possible to spend the winters in the warm, southern latitudes, and the summers in the cool north. We found that we could easily get two and three crops a year from our fields.

"Excuse me," I said, "But how do you go about 'coaxing' something as massive as these islands are, without any machines to speak of?"

"There are ways. You can drop an anchor at one end of them and cause the rest to spin around. You can put down cloth sea anchors—rather like parachutes— into a lower ocean current, and pull yourself a bit in that direction. The currents below are not always the same as those above, you see. We've even used huge kites, on occasion. But no more of these digressions, or the tale will never come to an end.

"Another advantage to floating free was that our travels took us as far south as South America, along what would one day be known as the Spanish Main, and past Central America as well. There were still forests on our islands then, and we could still build fair-sized ships. With them, we could bring back still more timber. We still had a fair stock of metal tools to work with then, as well. We traded with the natives as much as we could, and picked up from them many interesting plants and animals, but no tobacco, more's the pity. Most of our dyes and medicines were acquired during this period, and of course, we've been improving on them ever since. We'd developed the rules of simple genetics in the third century, you see. Oh, nothing like the recombinant DNA work that has been going on in the last few years outside, but a few thousand years of careful selection and breeding can work wonders.

"Also, we found that by restricting our contacts with the outside world, being at sea was healthier for our people. You see, by 1250, we had worked out the germ theory of disease, and it was obvious to us that if deadly germs couldn't get to us, they couldn't kill us. Bacteria and such must have hosts to live on, and our population was small enough that, eventually, most diseases died out. It wasn't until much later that we discovered what a horrible trap this was that we had fallen into! But more about that later."

I said, "But how did you keep yourselves hidden?"

"Why, we didn't even try to! Lots of people saw us. The legends of Ireland are full of sightings of our islands, and many a mariner and fisherman has gone home with tales to tell about us. The simple truth was that nobody believed them. There was no way for any of those people to substantiate what they saw. We were moving around, you see, and anytime anyone went out to find us again, we simply weren't there any more! People even went so far as to invent an optical illusion to explain what people who saw us thought they saw, the *Fata Morgana.*"

"But the Atlantic Ocean is one of the most heavily traveled bodies of water in the world! Eventually, enough consistent sightings would convince people that you really existed," I said.

"So what? It is not as though we were actually trying to hide, after all. As long as no one sent an invasion fleet out after us, we really didn't care what the world thought about us. We merely wanted the world to leave us alone. Until around 1850, that is. Then it was that we realized the biological trap that we'd fallen into. You see, we'd picked up some shipwrecked sailors, and one of them had smallpox. It cost us a third of our population, even though we learned the accepted methods of treating it from one of the other castaways, who had been a ship's doctor. We simply had no immunity against the disease, nor, as it turned out, for any of the thousand other ills that mankind is heir to.

"Do you realize that from the time I first came here, in 1943, until a month ago, I was not sick a single day? Oh, it's been very nice, I suppose, though one generally doesn't notice being healthy. Also, look at me carefully. How old do I seem to be?"

"Well, sir, when I first came in, I pegged you at about sixty, but I guess you must be a bit older than that, from what you say," I said.

"I'm much older than that. I was thirty-six when I crash-landed here. I wasn't regular aircrew at all, you see. I was in charge of aircraft electronics at my base, and when a radio operator got sick, and I got a chance to see something of the actual war, I jumped at it. Treet, you are looking at a ninety-two-year-old man. Clean, healthy living and the lack of disease can do wonders for you. The immune system takes a lot of one's vital energy to run, but mine hasn't had much work to do at all. But if I were to go back to Australia now, I likely wouldn't last the month out. Every disease that I hadn't gotten before would jump on me all at once, and that would be the end of me.

"So, as I was saying, in 1852, the wise men of the islands realized that we could no longer risk being discovered by the outside world. They held a major public debate about what to do about the situation, and the grand council decided to leave for a less populated part of the world's oceans. Together, we managed to steer the islands from the Gulf Stream south to the similar current in the South Atlantic. From there, it was south of the Cape of Good Hope, through the Roaring Forties, which by all accounts deserve their name, south of Australia and then north into the fairer climes of the South Pacific. It was a rough trip, but we made it, and it served us well for almost a hundred and fifty years.

"But no more. Now you blighters have satellites flying up there at all hours of the day and night. If one of your military spy satellites was to gam in on us, the show would be over, though we've managed to stay out of what they would call 'sensitive' areas. Worse yet, we're big enough for your geosynchronous weather satellites to see, if anybody would believe what they were looking at. As it is, our best guess is that when they do see us, they put it down as some sort of an electronic glitch, and ignore it. Nonetheless, it is obvious that the situation can't go on forever. Some power or other is going to spot us, and with peaceful intentions or otherwise, they will likely invade us. And for the medical reasons I've mentioned, not many of us will survive it."

"So now you need a way to keep your island hidden from satellite surveillance," I said.

"That would solve one of our problems, but not the other one."

We were interrupted as a young woman came in wearing an abbreviated version of the warlock's robes.

All of the other women's costumes I'd seen on the island had floor-length skirts, even when the bodice was cut as low as possible. This outfit exposed nothing below the neck, but the loose black smock ended just below the serving girl's crotch.

"Always been a leg man, myself, and my mother always said that a woman should never expose both ends at the same time," the warlock said.

When I agreed that it would be a shame to cover up such attractive legs, the warlock nodded in agreement, and the young woman winked at me. I'd been impressed with the warlock's status before, but a man's having so much power that he could actually get the ladies to dress in a fashion that pleased him, well, it was a thing that was beyond all experience!

It was a moment before I noticed what those lovely legs had carried in for our afternoon snack. Besides the weak, flat beer that the islanders made, I was surprised to find a large plate of *sushi*!

"We weren't the only plane to crash here during the war," he explained. "A Jap patrol plane pulled the same stunt, and one of their gunners turned out to be a pretty good cook."

"You were saying that you had yet another problem," I said.

"Right. You see, we're sinking. Over the centuries, water has been slowly working its way into the tiny gas bubbles that keep the place afloat. We've been able to compensate for this reduction in buoyancy by hollowing out all of the mountains above the water level, and by sinking shafts below it, again to reduce our weight, but as one of your songs has it, we've 'gone about as far as we can go.' And the coral buildup on the underside hasn't helped things a bit!"

"Just how fast is it going down?"

"We've sunk a foot in the last six years. In twelve more years, a major storm might be able to flood out some of our lower galleries, and that would bring on a total disaster. Do you see the spot we're in? We can't leave and we dare not stay!"

"It can't be that bad. I don't know much about medical things, but I'm a hell of an engineer. Why don't you simply go down below the islands and scrape off the coral and the waterlogged featherrock?"

"The islands draw more than half a mile, that's why, and there's a little problem with breathing down there!"

"Going all the way down to the bottom might be a problem, but there has to be a lot of excess weight within a few hundred feet of the surface. Ever heard of a SCUBA rig?"

"There have been a few scattered references to such a thing on the radio, but they weren't very clear," he admitted.

"SCUBA. Self contained underwater breathing apparatus. We have two of them with us, along with a compressor to pump up the tanks. You are welcome to them, and we'd be happy to teach some of your people how to use the things."

"Marvelous! Can we start tomorrow?"

"No reason why not. Also, while I'm not sure of all of your needs, there might be a lot of other things that we can help out with."

"That's the spirit, mate! Now then, before you go, could you explain to me some of this equipment you had on your boat?"

Which got us into a three-hour-long conversation, and this time with me doing all the talking. On parting, we agreed to meet the next morning down at the boat.

# TWENTY-ONE

I got home to find that everyone else had started supper without me. As I caught up with the rest of them, I filled them in on my remarkable conversation with the warlock.

"So what they have is a very old, do-it-yourself scientific organization, with a little World War II technology thrown in. There isn't any magic at all," I said.

"But, you say that you are able to see hundreds of miles in the dark, that you can look down to the bottom of the ocean, and that you can hear people speak when they are on the other side of the world. If that isn't magic, I would very much like you to tell me just what is!" Agnes said.

"With Americans, I guess that you could say that technology is something that we understand, and magic is something that we don't," I said.

"Then for me, it's still magic," Agnes said. "I don't understand any of it!"

"Call it magic, if you want," Adam said. "One word's as good as another, but 'magic' has two syllables and 'technology' has four."

"I suppose that the symbols themselves aren't important, but I'd still rather be called an engineer than a magician," I said. "But tell me, Adam, how went your meeting with the archbishop?"

"It was beautiful," he said, with a calm and glowing smile. "I don't think that I've ever met so holy a man before in my entire life. They're Christians here, but it's a purer sort of Christianity than anything I've ever heard tell of. It's like they are all living by Christ's actual teaching rather than what a bunch of abstracted theologians have done with those few parts of it that they understood. There's . . . Aw, you wouldn't understand it, Treet, but there's sort of a joyful acceptance here of the beauty of God's world, with love being far more important than sin, and heaven being emphasized more than damnation. I don't think that these people even believe in Hell, or if they do, they aren't worried about it. It's like Christ is too nice a guy to do that to somebody."

"You almost sound as though you're ready to convert," I said. In fact, he sounded more like he had gone through the kind of brainwashing that the Chinese Communists always wanted to be able to do, but never could quite get down pat. But I couldn't tell him that. Trying to argue with a fanatic just hardens his resolve. All I could do was wait and see if he recovered.

"I might convert. I just might, once I've learned more. Anyway, I will be taking religious instruction from one of their priests, starting the day after tomorrow."

"I never thought that I'd see you giving up on being a Catholic."

"Maybe I'm not. Right now, I don't see why I have to stop being one thing in order to start being another. I don't know enough about this whole setup yet, but I intend to find out, and soon."

If I was still a teenager, I would have gotten into a frothing hot argument with him, but much of wisdom and maturity has to do with being just too tired to bother with the ones that you know you can't win.

"Okay," I said. "There seems to be some sort of friction between the warlock and the archbishop, but the warlock didn't want to talk about it. Did the archbishop say anything enlightening?"

"Some. There's a big faction in the church hierarchy that doesn't want to have anything to do with the outside world. They cite the problems that the warlock mentioned, you know, the problem with diseases and the fact that the island is slowly sinking, but those aren't the biggies with them. They're more worried about cultural inundation, only they don't call it that. They say the big problem with outside contact is that it would make the people here materialistic and sinful. That the people would leave the ways of their forefathers and pick up on an evil American lifestyle."

"You mean that the churchmen are worried about losing some of their influence, not to mention their cushy lifestyle," I said, and then noticed the shocked expressions on the faces of the servants and our ladies.

"A heathen like you might put it that way," Adam said in English. "I think that they are worried about more spiritual matters."

"Whatever. So the church as a whole takes no great joy at our arrival here."

"I didn't say that," Adam said, switching the conversation back to Westronese. "I said that there was a faction that was worried about us. There's another faction that looks forward to going out and converting the godless, so-called Christians in the rest of the world back to what Christ had in mind in the first place."

I said, "Doesn't sound like there's much we can or should do about it."

"True. Getting messed up in somebody else's politics is dumb. Our best shot is to try to prove to them that we're really very nice guys."

"So I trust that you don't object to my giving our SCUBA stuff to the warlock?"

"Not when they need it as bad as they do. What's more, we got to start thinking about some kind of submarine, to really give the bottom a good scrape, and maybe rig some kind of additional flotation devices down there as well, some kind of big air bags or something."

"Makes sense. We also ought to think about donating some of our duplicate electronics stuff to them. All they know about the outside world, they're getting from some old AM and shortwave radios, and they can only keep them working about a quarter of the time," I said.

"I've been thinking about that, too. We don't really need the satellite stuff, or the solar cells, or the genset, for that matter. The televisions can go, as well as the VCR, the tapes, and the CD library. See, eventually, the Western Isles will have to be integrated in with the rest of the world. The archbishop doesn't like the idea, but I don't see how anybody can stop it from happening. And when it does happen, the Westronese had better know a lot more about the outside world than they do now. Some serious preparations are going to have to be made, and all the legal angles figured out. And it wouldn't hurt a bit if the people here all learned to speak English. I mean, it's the closest thing to a world language there is."

"You're figuring on making a pretty big commitment to these people?" I said.

"Hey, Treet. We fell into something really big here, you know? I mean, most people spend most of their lives doing their jobs and trying to be decent and all, but never getting a chance to do anything really significant. Here, we've got a shot at doing something absolutely earthshaking. Something that can really make a difference in the world. I say we go for it! Anyway, you got anything better to do?"

I thought about it for a while, and you know, I really *didn't* have anything better to do. I leaned over to his couch so that I could shake his hand. "Adam, you're right! Let's do the job, full bore and balls out!"

I leaned back, feeling good. I had a job to do, and a company to run again! The old Treet was back!

The ladies weren't exactly sure of what had just happened, but they picked up on the way Adam and I were happy and confident, so they were happy, too.

Roxanna and I didn't say much to each other through supper, and later, as we all had a few drinks, we just sort of held hands for a bit. Then, when it was time for bed, we went to her room as though it was the most natural thing in the world, as if we were an old, married couple who had done this a thousand times before. The night was calm, wondrous, and lovely, and when I awoke the next morning, I found that I was thinking of myself as a married man again. For the first time in years, I felt a lovely, warm, confident glow. The dark, empty depression that had plagued me for over a year was totally, absolutely gone and buried.

"Roxanna, let's get married."

"My lord. You pick the strangest times to say things!"

"What? I mean, you don't want to?"

"I didn't say that. It's just that you must learn to do things properly, and proposing matrimony while lying naked in a lady's bed is *not* the way it is done!"

"All right, all right. Forgive my ignorance, but it's all your fault. You are supposed to be my instructor, after all, and if I wasn't told something that I should have known, it's not my doing. In my country, the typical lady would have at least kissed me for the biggest compliment that a man can give to a woman, even if she was going to turn him down."

She kissed me, and lingered at it.

"There. I trust that your customs are now satisfied. Now then, to satisfy mine, you must first approach me when we both are fully dressed, and before witnesses. You must go down on one knee, you must accurately describe both your affections and your financial situation, and you must ask my permission to speak to my father. *If* I give it, and *if* you then talk to him, and *if* he gives you his formal permission, *then* you may put your proposal to me, but not before. End of lesson."

"I didn't even know you had a father. You've never mentioned him. Is there anything I should know or do before I look up this man I've never met and ask him for a daughter?"

"Yes. You should spend a lot more time thinking the whole matter out. Talk it over with your good friend, Adam. I think that he might be wiser than you."

I should have been smart enough to keep my mouth shut at this point, but I wasn't.

"You think that Adam is smarter than I am?" I asked. "That his IQ is higher than mine?"

That put Roxanna off on another one of her long lectures.

"Again, that's not what I said. From what you've told me, your people seem to measure mental abilities along a single dimension. Here, we use three dimensions, and after testing, we place an individual's mental abilities within a three dimensional solid, rather than along a straight line, as is your people's custom.

"The horizontal X-axis is graduated to display education, with ignorance at the left and learnedness at the right. Education is what can be taught in school. One's position on that axis indicates how much one has actually learned.

"The vertical Y-axis is for innate problem solving ability, with stupidity at the bottom and intelligence at the top. This faculty is controlled by one's genetics, although severe environmental factors can sometimes degrade it. It cannot be taught.

"The Z-axis is used to display the ability to make appropriate actions at the appropriate time, with foolishness at the far side of the cube, and wisdom towards the viewer. The nature of wisdom is much debated among our educators, since it above all else is what we humans strive for in the mundane world.

"Suffice it to say that each of these three is independent of the others. People exist with every possible combination of these attributes. There are no blank places in the cube. It is quite possible, for example, to be wise while also being stupid and ignorant. The traditional old peasant was often like that. The teachers of higher education are sometimes intelligent and learned while still being foolish."

"Remarkable," I said.

The whole situation had gotten about as unromantic as it could get, and I found myself thinking that maybe she was right, maybe I was rushing things. And maybe I was getting myself involved with a rather cold fish. Only there had been nothing frigid about her the night before!

I think that I must have dozed off for a bit, because when I woke up again, I was alone. When I got to the balcony that we used for breakfast, the maid told me that Adam and his ladies had already eaten. He and his bearers were at the boat, and Maria and Agnes were out looking for an apartment closer to the warehouse than their home was.

Roxanna didn't show up, and I ate alone.

# TWENTY-TWO

Arriving at the warehouse where our ship was stored, I found Adam directing his workers in further disassembling the ship. They were laboriously chipping out the plastic that had been poured around the ship's batteries, down next to the keel. Adam felt that if we were going to give the warlock the solar cells, we'd better give him most of the batteries as well.

"What with these casts still on, I can't get in there to see what they're doing. I've told them the difference between what a battery looks like and the stuff we encapsulated them in, but they've never seen a battery before. Maybe you'd better get in there and give it a look."

"Right," I said. "We don't need battery acid all over the place, or wrecked batteries, either."

I climbed up into the hull, which was still on its side, and checked out what the men were doing. It was slow going, but they had gotten down to the batteries in two places, and were carefully working around them. I got back out.

"Looks fine to me. You figure on giving the warlock all of them?"

"All but two, and we'll need the starter battery for the engine. That's all we really need to run her, and the electronics. Without the solar cells and the genset, we'll have to fire up the engine every other day, but what the heck. I figure that we'll only be shuttling between here and South America, and that's less than a few thousand miles."

"Makes sense. What about the prop-shaft generator? Won't that help?"

"I was thinking that by hooking that generator up to some wooden blades that could be made locally, we could rig up a windmill and put it on top of the mountain here. With enough wind, it could probably make more juice than the solar cell array."

"Why not? We can replace it all in Lima, anyway," I said.

"Right. Now then, there's one little job that you're going to have to handle alone, since I'm wracked up and I'd rather that nobody else knew about it."

"What's that?"

"The arsenal. It's encapsulated just forward of the batteries."

I stopped and stared at him for a bit. "You never told me we had an arsenal on board. Why do you have it, and why didn't you tell me about it? Just what do you have in there that had to be kept so secret?"

"It's not all that much, and there's nothing illegal in there, but you got to be careful with guns. On the one hand, if you need them, you *really* need them, and then they're worth a lot more than gold to you. I mean, what if some drug runners had decided that *The Brick Royal* was just the thing they needed to make a little midnight run into Miami Beach? On the other hand, more Americans are shot each year by their friends than by their enemies, so until needed, it's better if your friends don't know they're there. Also, some of the girls we started out with would have freaked out at the thought of having guns around. Then there was you. In case you've forgotten,

for about a year there you were slopping around in
the worst case of depression that I ever saw a man
live through and survive. You're better now, so I don't
mind telling you about the weapons, but back then
you were awfully suicidal. Enough said?"

"If I'd wanted to kill myself, I could have jumped
overboard any night."

"I know, and if I coulda hid the ocean, I woulda
done it. The guns I could just not talk about."

"All right, and I suppose I owe you my thanks. But
for now, just what exactly do you have buried over
the keel up by the stem?"

"Two of everything I thought we might need. There
are some Remington autoloading 30-06s with Leopold
scopes, for hitting something hard when you don't
want to get near it. Some Remington 12-gauge autoloading shotguns, for blowing it away if it's up close.
Some Remington Nylon 66 .22 caliber plinking guns,
with scopes, for target practice and small game. Some
Browning 9mm Hi Power automatic pistols, purely for
self-defense. Some Ruger .22 caliber plinking pistols,
for just screwing around with, and some Street Sweep-
ers, for when we're not screwing around. All the guns
are made out of stainless steel and plastic, so corro-
sion won't ever be a problem. There's two thousand
rounds of each kind of ammo, except for the .22 long
rifle. We got twenty thousand rounds of that, plus
cleaning equipment, spare clips, belts, holsters, some
knives, and other accessories. It's a good little arsenal."

"Wow. What's a Street Sweeper?"

"It's a 12-gauge autoloading shotgun with a twenty-
five-round drum magazine. It has a collapsible stock
and a shoulder sling like what you use with a
submachine gun. It has a minimal legal length barrel, and a flashlight that mounts on top where you'd
think a scope would go. Where the spot shows is
where your shot pattern hits. I thought they would
be nice to have if we ever had to stand guard duty."

"What? No Uzis, assault rifles, or grenade launchers?" I said facetiously.

"The Uzi is a very overrated weapon. It's as big as a real gun but it only fires puny pistol ammo. As to assault rifles, I think that the army went over to those .223 caliber M-16s because militarily, you're better off wounding an enemy than killing him. After all, you wound a man and they have to dedicate three medics to haul him away and take care of him. It's that or getting a hell of a morale problem when they start abandoning their own injured. Wounding an enemy takes four of them out of the fight, but if you kill him, he's just one more dead martyr. But I don't ever plan on fighting an army, and if I ever have to shoot somebody, I want him dead! Grenades? They're illegal and way too dangerous. If we had explosives aboard, somebody would likely drop one, and blow a hole in the bottom of the boat and us, too."

"Thank God for small favors."

"You shouldn't say things like that unless you mean it. Anyway, we are among a bunch of very peaceable people here, and I think the guns would make a bad impression. I'd hate to have to throw them away, so I figure to just hide them somewhere."

"Why not just leave them where they are?"

"Because it's three hundred more pounds that could be cargo, each way, every trip."

"Whatever you say. I think that it was stupid to have them in the first place. Anybody we'd have to defend ourselves against would know so much more about that kind of fighting than we do, that shooting back at them would just get us killed quicker. I mean, I used to be pretty good at Karate, and I've always had the feeling that you were something of a street fighter when you were a kid. If it came to trouble, we could probably make a good showing for ourselves with our fists and our feet. But with firearms, we'd be flat outclassed."

"Nah. People who rely on violence are mostly pretty dumb. We could out-shoot them if we had to. But we're not faced with that situation, so I think we'd best hide the arsenal."

"So how do I get the arsenal out of the boat without taking five hours to chip it out of the plastic? I mean, I know you, so I know you wouldn't put something like guns someplace where we couldn't get at them if they were needed in a hurry."

"Well, chipping would work, and it would only take a half hour or so, even if you had to be quiet about it. Or there are the explosive squibs."

"I figured as much."

A squib is sort of a hydraulic cylinder that uses a powder charge to move the piston. They work fine. Once. There's an engineering joke about a new military quality-control specification for squibs. They required one hundred percent testing. That's funny when you say it in Engineerese.

"Yeah, well, if you want to blow the squibs, there's a screwdriver in a clip right near the stem. Next to it, there's a screw that's just barely covered with clear plastic. Clean out the slot in the screw and then twist it ninety degrees *clockwise*, like you were driving it farther in. Ten seconds later, the guns should pop up nice and easy."

"Okay, I'll do it while everybody else is at lunch. What happens if I turn it the other way?"

"You expected a booby trap, maybe? Nope. Not when I could be the one to get boobied. But the screw will come off and you won't be able to get it back on again."

# TWENTY-THREE

Such was the feeling of urgency on all sides that it took Tom Strong, E.E., Warlock of the Western Islands, only half a day to set up a meeting with the archbishop.

The meeting of the two rivals took place on the nearest thing they had to neutral territory that was secure from public notice, the rectory of the Monastery of St. Thomas the Doubter. Although the monks here constituted a religious order, as part of the Regular Clergy, they were completely independent and not subordinate to the archbishop's Secular Clergy. Furthermore, the Order of St. Thomas the Doubter spends most of its efforts on scientific research, much of it in coordination with the wizards.

"Ah, Thomas! It is so delightful to see you again!" the archbishop said, with not a trace of insincerity in his well-trained voice. He sat down at the stone table, opposite the warlock, in the otherwise empty room.

"The feeling is completely mutual, I assure you, Phillias," the warlock said, smiling. "I feel that we need to talk with regard to our recently rescued castaways. They will soon be helping us with the sinking problem, and it would be good if we could coordinate our programs, so as to cause as little confusion as possible among our respective subordinates and the people at large."

"I agree, Thomas, and as much as we both would enjoy an extended chat, I suppose that it's best to get on to the business at hand immediately. The church of course would welcome your help in alerting the people, and more importantly the duke, to the dangers that these outsiders represent."

"Well, your priests have their pulpits, Phillias. When it comes to influencing the masses, you are far stronger than I. As to the duke, well, he seeks the counsel of many, of course, but makes his mind up for himself. And while I don't want to be a spreader of false hope, you know as well as I that our guests have access to the new technology that has recently been developed out there. They seem willing and able to assist us in solving many of our problems, major as well as minor."

"The major problems that I am concerned with are the bringing of the diseases of the outside world to the bodies of the people of our islands, and the bringing of its many unholy ideas to their minds. We do not need the outsiders' help to alleviate these problems. They themselves are the problems."

"That seems unduly harsh, Phillias. They seem to be decent enough sorts. Isn't one of them taking religious instruction from your people already?"

"Well, we could hardly decline such a request. Yet still it remains that the best help they could possibly give us would be for them to cease to exist. Then I could get on with my proper work of saving people's souls."

"We have survived diseases a hundred times before, Phillias, and since our faith is strong, you need not fear that any other belief will supplant it. But you cannot save souls unless the bodies they inhabit are alive! I have told you again and again that the featherrock the island is made out of is slowly getting waterlogged! In the past, we were able to compensate for our loss in buoyancy by enlarging and extending the tunnels we have inside, especially those below the water-line, but it is getting to the point that further digging will begin to destroy the island's structural integrity, weaken it until a major storm could crack us in half."

" 'We are in the hands of God, as we always have been and always will be. Have faith, my son, and fear no ocean's storm.' " The archbishop was quoting from a favorite ser-mon he had written sixty years before.

Changing tactics, the warlock said, "Has it occurred to you that this is the only place on earth where our particular variety of Christianity is practiced, Archbishop? That if the Western Islands are lost, your religion will be lost along with everything else that we have here?"

"You are such an alarmist, Warlock. If the tunneling that your men are doing is weakening the island, then by all means bid them to stop doing it! Surely that's simple enough for even you to understand! The islands have been afloat for a thousand years, and all previous warlocks were com-petent enough to keep them thus. The end of our world will not happen this afternoon."

"Perhaps not this afternoon, Your Excellency, but it could well happen this decade, or even this year. As to stopping the digging, the waves now lap to within three yards of the main entrances of the island. If sea water ever started to flow in with any large volume, it would flood the lower galleries, and the island would promptly sink. Call me an alarmist if you wish, Your Excellency, but I definitely pre-fer being a living alarmist to being a dead nitwit!"

"Warlock, you are as single-minded as always. And as close-minded as well!"

"And you are as bone-headed, as self-seeking, and as stupid as you've always been, Archbishop! You'd be a laugh-able clown, if you didn't have the power to get us all killed!" The warlock was standing, glowering at his adversary.

"All conversation with you is a waste of God's good time,"

*the archbishop pontificated, standing and leaving by the
nearest exit.*

The warlock arrived with his entourage, some two
dozen people.

Our workers stopped what they were doing and
bowed to him, so I thought it would be a good idea
to do the same. Adam did the best he could from
his sedan chair.

"Thanks, mates," the warlock said in English. "That
sort of thing isn't necessary when we're alone, but
it helps keep up appearances when in public. My,
this is a fine-looking craft you have here. I understand that you built it yourselves."

"Not exactly, my lord," Adam said. "I directed our
workers in the construction of *The Brick Royal*."

"That's about what I meant," the warlock said,
switching back to Westronese for the benefit of his
entourage. "I've brought six apprentices with me who
are particularly good swimmers. I'd like to have them
start cleaning off the coral and waterlogged featherrock
as soon as possible, so if you would be so kind as
to show us these SCUBA rigs you mentioned, we can
get on with it."

"Of course, my lord," I said. "But you must
understand that they can be dangerous if they're not
used properly. Adam here has taken a formal course
in their use. He's taught me how to do it, but I think
it would be best if he gave the course to them before
work actually starts."

"That would be excellent."

In a few minutes, the tanks, weights, masks, flippers, depth gauges, and other paraphernalia were
gathered up and put in front of the sedan chair, and
Adam was talking to a rapt audience. After a half
an hour or so, the warlock was starting to look a
bit bored, so I took him aside to talk with him about

the master plan Adam and I had started working on
the night before.

"My lord, we've started to develop a plan that
would let us help you and your people out of your
current difficulties. Talking with you yesterday, you
mentioned the problem of the Island's sinking, and
the problem of the way your people don't have
immune systems ready to fight off modern diseases.

"Well, we're starting work on the first problem this
very minute, with the SCUBA rigs. Also, we have
aboard a dozen or so snorkle outfits, which are sim-
pler. They consist of nothing but a pair of flippers,
a face mask, and a short breathing tube, and they're
normally used for fishing and sightseeing near the
surface. We've got the compressor and a few hundred feet of hose around, and between them, we think
we can cobble up some system that will let another
dozen men work under water, but not very deep. Still,
any weight removed from the island is to the good,
so it won't hurt at all to get to the easiest stuff first.
We plan on making a number of trips back to the
outside world, and one of the first things we plan
to bring back will be a larger compressor, one that
could support perhaps a hundred workers, down to
about one hundred feet. Some time later, perhaps we
can come up with some sort of machine to give the
bottom of the island a proper scraping, since our preliminary estimates make it look as though putting in
some sort of additional flotation would not be cost
effective. Nonetheless, the work we do now will gain
us time."

"Excellent. Go on."

"As to the medical problem, well, as I said, neither of us is a doctor. But we can get one. When
we get to the mainland, we can find a good immu-
nologist, or whatever what we need is called, and
hire him, or her. These islands are such a wonder
that I don't think we'll have any problems keeping

him once he's here. Also, thinking about it, we don't think that the problem here is either as bad or as unique as you have made it out to be. After all, isolated jungle tribes turn up every now and then in the Amazon or New Guinea, and they don't all die the first time a missionary shows up. To be sure, in the long run, the population of these tribes does go down, but for the most part those natives don't get proper medical attention, and we will see to it that your people do."

"I see. Well, you realize that I don't have the final say about all of this, but so far, I'm impressed. Go on, please," he said.

"Adam and I both feel that the eventual joining of your culture with that of the outside world is inevitable. It's going to happen, whether anybody wants it to happen or not. It would be better if it was put off as long as possible, but at the same time, you'd better start preparing for that eventuality right now. The first step is cultural. We have to teach your people about the outside world. For a start, we've got a VCR and a tape library here. That's sort of like a movie projector and a lot of movies. I'll set it up sometime in the next few days, and show it to you. I think you'll love it, and since our tapes are all in English, it should encourage your people to learn what is becoming the world language. We would like to see you start some formal classroom courses in English as well."

"Yes, I don't see why that can't be done," the warlock said.

"Some legal preparations ought to be made. I don't know what this will entail, exactly, but when the world discovers you, we'd better have all the legal angles covered. I mean, twelve thousand is a very small population for an independent nation in this world. Possibly you might be best off being under the protection of some larger power. A number of small nations are currently doing this, and without exception, they are better off for it. Nauru, for example, is under the protection of Australia. Monaco has an arrangement with France, and San Marino is somehow connected with Italy. I don't know what Liechtenstein and Andorra do, but I can find out. All of these countries have populations of about your size."

"Well, that's something for the duke to decide, of course. In fact, none of this can be done without his permission," he said. "But please continue."

"Then there is the welfare of your people. Your country is currently doing a number of things that I'm sure that most of you wish it didn't have to do, simply because you have more people than you have land. I'm talking about such draconian measurers as sterilizing people who have been servants for two generations, for example. With trade, we can easily solve these problems. Consider. The current price for grain on the Chicago market runs between three and seven cents a pound, depending on which grain we're talking about. I think that we could sell that high-strength fiber of yours for at least fifty dollars a pound. In terms of vegetable mass, that's a ratio of something like a thousand to one. One pound of fiber for a thousand pounds of grain. You've got the room to house a far larger population than you have, and with trade, you can feed them better than you ever have before. Besides food, there are a thousand other products that you could use. I'll bet that some chemical fertilizers would do wonders for your crop yields. Electric lights would give you three or four more hours a day to enjoy yourselves in, and they are a lot healthier than breathing the fumes of smoky oil lamps, too. Not to mention obvious things like good steel tools, as well as some sort of transportation devices. Heck, a *wheelbarrow* would triple the productivity of your porters, and some very simple farm machinery could vastly multiply the work your gardeners get done. Do you realize that in the United States, which is the world's largest food exporter, less than three percent of the population works on the land?"

"Interesting, mate, but I'm not sure that we should become just another one of your 'modern countries,'" he said.

"Nor should you be. What you have and what you are is unique. I'm not suggesting that you should buy the whole bag of toys. Look over each item one at a time, pick and choose what's best for your people. I'm just saying that there are some options that you and the duke should have, and I'm offering to get them for you."

"I'm delighted to see that the two of you are taking our welfare so much to heart. While I'm sure that you are very generous men, still I expect that you will want more than just a handshake for all of this. What is it you want in return?"

"We want two things. The first is a monopoly on the trade between your islands and the outside world, with this monopoly to last until at least ten years after the Western Isles have been discovered by the outside world. The advantages to you are that we will be doing our darnedest to keep you a secret for as long as possible, and that through us, you will be able to control exactly what comes in and what goes out. The second thing we want is money. We propose that we will bring in anything that you want on an item cost plus transportation cost basis. We will sell any of your products for all that we can get, and keep twenty-five percent of the selling price for ourselves. We suggest that the duke should take fifty percent of that selling price and use the money for improvements on the islands, and that the producer of the product get the remaining twenty-five percent. Thus, if, say, two pounds of fiber were to sell for one hundred dollars, then we would get twenty-five dollars, the duke fifty, and the producer twenty-five. Since the producer could then buy five hundred pounds of grain with his money, he won't be hurt by the transaction."

"And you won't make any profit on what you sell to us?" he asked.

"We would charge you only for our actual costs in purchasing it and getting it here. Our books will be open to you. We will provide you with the manufacturer's catalogs and price lists on any product that you might want to buy, so you'll know that you're not being cheated. Since we will be making our profit only on what we sell, you can be sure that we will try to get the best prices possible for your products, and since we want you to produce as much as possible for us to sell, we will want your people to need money, and thus we will be trying to get them to buy as much as possible from the world outside. It's as fair a deal as we could come up with. Also, Adam and I plan to live here as much as we can, and so much of our profits will be spent right here, with the money going right back into your economy."

"It all sounds reasonable to me, except perhaps for your proposal to put a quarter of the entire nation's production into your own pouch. But those are details to be discussed later. What specifically do you propose for the near future?"

"Well, we must get the boat repaired. That will take a few weeks, but then it would be best if we let the patch cure for at least two months, to harden properly. During that time, there will be plenty of mechanical and electrical things to keep us busy. After that, it will be another week before she is ready for sea. While all that is happening, I think that I should spend much of my time doing an inventory of the local products available here on the Western Isles. We've talked about your amazing high-strength fibers, but I'm sure that you have many other things that would be of interest to the outside world."

"Good. That will give me perhaps three months to work on the duke and, more importantly, the archbishop. As to familiarizing you with the state of our technology, I will arrange for you to have a technically competent guide to show you the island, and to take you through our various horticultural and animal husbandry research facilities. Perhaps we can schedule it in a few days. But for now, it looks as though your good ladies have a lunch prepared for us, so I think that we should oblige them."

"Agreed, my lord. One last thing. You might want to mention to your friends that it would be a profitable idea to plant as much of your high-strength hemp as possible. Adam and I will be putting our entire fields in hemp, and buying such food as we need."

# TWENTY-FOUR

Indeed, while I had been talking with the warlock, Roxanna and the Pelitier sisters had arrived. They had set up an American-style banquet table, and were loading it with food. The fine ladies here took pride in taking good care of their men.

The table was filled with the usual Western Islands fare, but as a treat for our guests, I broke out some of our supply of foreign "delicacies," such as canned sardines, Hershey bars, and Spam. Again, Spam was a major hit, so I passed out cans of the stuff for people to take home with them. Adam must have gotten that canned pork fat cheap, since we had cases of the greasy stuff. I never could stand it, myself. I found the case of Foster's I'd mentioned to the warlock, and gave him one of the oversized cans.

"It's warm, I'm afraid, but then you Brits like your beer warm, don't you?"

"First off, mate, I'm not a Brit. I'm an Aussie. Second, while there are some British ales that are better served at room temperature, Foster's is a lager, and is best served chilled." Switching back to Westronese, he said, "Page! Run these off to one of the nearest cold shafts, won't you? And the rest of you, take some of these other beers and wines there as well."

As the men went to the door with cases of beer and wine, I said, "A cold shaft, my lord? What's that all about?"

"It's a place where it's cold. You haven't done much exploring around here, have you? I'll have to see that they're covered on the tour we'll arrange for you. In the meantime, haven't you wondered why it's always cool and pleasant here, even though we're at sea level and near the equator? It's because of a system that was built in the first century after the islands started floating. You see, while the water at the surface of the ocean is often quite warm, if you go a few hundred feet down, it's as cold as it can get without freezing. Our ancestors dug tunnels down to below that level, and arranged a series of check valves to keep the cold water flowing no matter which way the relative currents around the islands were going. There are a number of large, shallow ponds of cold water within the bowels of the islands. Air currents are forced over these ponds, and then circulate through all of our living spaces, keeping the temperature pleasant. The shafts that bring these air currents up are naturally much cooler than the rest of the structure, and are useful for chilling things that are better cold."

"That's quite a system," Adam said. "But you're cooling down the air and then moving it up. That requires external power. How are you doing it?"

"The water is raised by the ramming force of the winds and water currents around us. In general, we are moving with the ocean currents, of course, but wind and chance make for some slight differentials. The water taken in isn't warmed very much, so its density isn't very different going up or going down. Only friction has to be paid for, and that's kept small by the large size of the tunnels.

"As to the air currents, well, on the ocean there's generally a wind about, and there are tunnels all about the islands with shutters on them that let air in, but not out. To get back out, the air must flow over the cool ponds before it can come out through someone's house. This cools only the leeward half of the islands, of course, but we see to it that the islands turn fairly often. The stone they're made of has a lot of thermal mass, so being without cooling for a day or two isn't noticed. We have to be in a dead calm for a week before it gets uncomfortable around here, and that's a very rare event. Come visit my office and I'll show you a diagram of the system."

"I'd like that," Adam said. "We're going to need those diagrams when we give the bottom of the island a good scrape job."

"There's another thing that's bothering me," I said. "I can see how they could dig tunnels down to below sea level, so long as there wasn't any water in them. But how did they mine their way through to the ocean without drowning the workers?"

"They used gunpowder to blast their way out. We've had gunpowder here since the fourth century. How else do you think that a bunch of peaceful farmers and scholars could have beaten off three major Viking raids?" the Australian warlock said.

"I'm surprised that I never heard of any legends of such a battle."

"That's simple enough. We don't write songs about killing people, and the Vikings didn't live long enough to sing about it!"

After the meal, it was decided that the smaller cans of Budweiser were cool enough to drink, and the party settled back for a while. I figured that this would be a good time to do something about the stupid arsenal that Adam had hidden aboard.

Excusing myself, I climbed up into the boat, and used a ten-foot ladder to get from the hull wall up to the keel. I found the screwdriver and the screw that Adam had talked about. I had only used a squib once before, but I knew that despite the fact that they were powered by an explosive charge, one going off really isn't much of an explosion. It's more like a fast, strong push, and they are not all that noisy when they are used properly. This was one of Adam's engineering jobs, so I wasn't worried about bothering anyone in the least. I cleared the encapsulating plastic from the screw, inserted the driver and gave it the clockwise twist that would energize the squibs.

The resulting explosion blew two large footlockers sideways out from the keel, taking the ladder and me with it out into the hold. I bounced off the now-vertical upper deck, slid down the ladder, and sat down hard. Both lockers broke open on the way down, spewing weapons, ammunition, and various instruments of death and destruction all over everything in sight, including me.

I spent a few moments wondering if both my legs were broken before everyone started crowding into the hull of the ship. So much for secrecy. The warlock was the first one to get to me.

"Are you all right? Try wiggling your toes," he said as he removed rifles and boxes of ammo from my battered body.

"I seem to be all right, my lord. More damage to my pride than anything else."

"Good. I'd hate to lose you. What are all these guns for?"

"They were Adam's idea. I didn't know about them until today. He was worried that we might run into some rough characters on the high seas, and, well, better safe than sorry, you know? But now, since we are in civilized company, we thought that it might be best if we just hid them somewhere, so as not to give you the wrong impression of us."

"I see," he said, pulling the case from a shotgun. "This is quite a beauty! Chrome plated?"

"Stainless steel. They all are. Please understand that all of these weapons are legal back where we come from. There are no machine guns or heavy explosives."

"Right. Well, if you were just going to store them somewhere, how about if I took care of that for you? We could put them in the duke's arsenal with the rest of the weapons."

"The duke's arsenal?"

"Yes. It's mostly just a bunch of interesting antiques, but all of the machine guns and ammunition from my old B-17 and the Jap plane are there as well. We haven't had any need for such things here, of course, but waste not, want not, you know."

"My lord, we would be delighted if you would take these embarrassing things away and store them properly."

As the warlock's men were hauling the arsenal away, I went over to talk to Adam.

"The one time you really screw up an engineering job, and it has to be with a truckload of guns in front of the number two man on the whole island! Damn you, Adam!"

"Yeah, well, your timing could have been a bit better, you know. Why did you have to do it when everybody was here?"

"We agreed that I should do it during lunch."

"That was before we knew who else would be here eating with us. You should have thought it out better. Anyway, it's all worked out just fine. The guns are gone, and maybe we can make the duke a gift of them. I mean, if he keeps an arsenal, he must like guns. Most guys do, you know," Adam said.

"All right. So why did your squibs overreact?"

"I'd sized them to lift the cases straight up, boss. I forgot that with the boat sideways, no lifting was necessary, and the resultant extra energy had to go someplace. In your lap, as it turned out."

"Grumble."

Some time later, the warlock was getting ready to leave.

"My lord," I said. "One thing you might want to do is to start writing up a wish list, things that you would like us to buy for you once we get to the mainland. And you might suggest to the archbishop that he write up such a list as well."

"A clever thought, that. If he gets his mind going on what he wants you to bring back, he might forget that he was against your going in the first place! Oh, yes. What did you want done with all of your electronic equipment that is up in my chambers? Shall I have my people bring it down here to you?"

"Adam and I have talked that over, my lord, and we've decided to give you everything that is not essential to running the ship. Perhaps I could come up there tomorrow, and we could sort through it together."

"Uh, Treet? Tomorrow is not a good day. They're taking my casts off tomorrow, and somebody is going to have to take the boys swimming," Adam said.

"Nor is tomorrow a good day for me," the warlock said. "I expect that I'll spend the day closeted with the duke, discussing your proposal. But there's no hurry. It'll be months before you sail."

Despite my new bruises, I got home feeling that it had been a profitable day. We were well launched on what I felt sure was to be the most profitable and worthwhile business venture of my life, and it was certain to be the most interesting. At dinner, Adam and the ladies were equally enthused. Roxanna was intent on learning English, with the hope that the duke would give her permission to join us on the voyage to South America. Maria and Agnes soon joined in with her plans, and the meal turned itself into an impromptu language lesson. It was late when we turned in. After Roxanna's rejection of my methods of proposal that morning, I was afraid that I would have to go back to sleeping alone.

Luck was still with me, though, and Roxanna had returned to being her loving self.

# TWENTY-FIVE

After breakfast, I went down to the warehouse and found four of the warlock's apprentices waiting for their first swim with a SCUBA rig. Some of them might have been waiting there for an hour, but ten minutes went by before the last two straggled in.

It wasn't as though these were slovenly or recalcitrant students. They were all enthusiastic and eager to learn. They were being as prompt as they had ever been, for anybody or anything. It was simply that there was no such thing as a clock or watch on the entire island. They couldn't get there on time because they didn't have the slightest idea of what time it was!

I had never realized just how important timepieces were, but these people regularly wasted about two hours of working time a day just waiting around for everybody else to get there. That's a tremendous amount of waste. Consider. Two hours *per capita*, twelve thousand people, and two hundred fifty working days a year. If one assumes an average hourly rate of only ten dollars an hour, that comes to sixty million dollars a year, flushed down the toilet for no good reason at all.

Wrist watches. Our first cargo back had to contain at least a thousand wrist watches.

Because of the sharpness of both the coral and the underlying featherrock, it was customary for these people to swim fully clothed, even to wearing thin socks and gloves. Their swimsuits looked like long winter underwear, but they were made of the same incredible fiber that all their other clothes were made of. That is to say, they were not only coral proof, and featherrock proof, but they were probably bulletproof as well.

We gathered up the SCUBA equipment, as well as the snorkeling stuff, and headed for Avalon Bay. On arrival, I discovered that the air tanks were empty. As a safety measure, Adam must have drained them after the last time we used them, back in the Caribbean Sea.

I decided that some snorkeling practice should be held first. I was starting them out with the snorkeling rigs to get them used to flippers and face masks, and to being under water, I said. They loved it.

They'd been swimming all their lives, but without goggles or a face mask, you can't see anything down there but a fuzzy blur. Water has about the same index of refraction as the cornea of your eye, and with no air gap in front of it, your eye's optics simply don't work properly.

Now the boys were in a beautiful new world, filled with strange things that they had always been near, but had never seen before.

There was much to see. The structure of the island went entirely under the bay, such that the average depth was about thirty feet. While I'm no marine biologist, I'm sure that I saw both Atlantic and Pacific varieties of fishes there. The Bay of Avalon was as rich with sea life as any coral reef I'd ever seen on television, and it was totally unpolluted. Magnificent!

Unfortunately, this marvelous coral structure was just what was sinking the islands, and threatening to kill everything, including the coral itself. After all, if the island did sink, the coral and most of its attendant sea life would be at the bottom of the Pacific Ocean, where it couldn't live any more than I could. Yet clearing the lagoon out down to the featherrock seemed like a crime.

In the end, I resolved to start chipping at the edge of the island, where the rock cliffs dropped sheer down into the nothingness that was below. And in truth, it would be much easier, per pound, to simply break loose the coral and waterlogged rock, and let them fall to the ocean bottom, than to have to put what we'd loosened on some sort of raft and haul that raft off to the edge of the lagoon for dumping.

It made me feel much better to have a sound, engineering reason for doing what I wanted to do in the first place. There was plenty of other weight elsewhere to get rid of, and maybe someday I could get the warlock down here and convince him that the bay should be set aside as a nature preserve. Maybe.

At lunch time, as we had arranged, Roxanna had a meal set up for us on the small beach by the bay. As we ate, she talked to the boys about the advantages of learning English, and it turned out that half of them already had at least a smattering of the language. By the end of the meal, it was decreed that all instruction would henceforth be given in my native language rather than theirs.

The old saw about not going swimming for an hour after eating, because of the danger of stomach cramps, is nothing but a stupid old wives' tale. In the first place, unless you've eaten something that has given you ptomaine poisoning, there's no particular reason for newly eaten food to cause cramping. Nor is there anything about being in the water that can cause them. Severe stomach cramps are a rare malady. And even if you do get the cramps while you are in the water, there is no reason for them to be any more dangerous there than on dry land. Stomach cramps don't interfere with your breathing, after all, or with the use of your arms. You can keep on swimming with your face above the water even if your knees are up around your chin.

We went back into the water right after eating, went to the mouth of the bay, and started work on the edge of the ocean proper. Adam had arranged for some four-foot lengths of reinforcing rod to be ground to a point at one end for use as picks and pry bars. Still using only snorkel rigs, we each had one of these tied with a two yard cord to our waists, and as a safety measure, I had each of us wearing a safety line that went back up to the rocks on shore.

It was pretty easy to tell what needed removing and what should remain. If it was coral, break it off and let it sink. If it was rock and it didn't put out a spray of bubbles when you poked it, get rid of it. If it floated to the surface after you broke it loose, you did it wrong, stupid, and don't do it again!

We didn't accomplish much that first afternoon, but we did work out the basic techniques needed for the job. Picking and chipping didn't work well under water, but prying did. We resolved to get some longer and stronger bars made up soon. Also, a lot of time was wasted going up and down, so we rigged some weighted lines down to the work area. It was easier to pull yourself up and down than to swim the whole way.

By midafternoon, the light down there was getting bad, and we knocked off. We were exhausted, anyway. When you haven't been swimming in months, seven hours in the water takes a lot out of you, especially if you are working your way, very gently, into middle age.

I invited the group over to Roxanna's place for tomorrow's breakfast, mostly to insure that we wouldn't have to wait for the stragglers before starting the next morning. I also asked them to bring along another eight of their friends. Since we had a dozen snorkel rigs, plus the masks and fins from the SCUBA rigs, there was no reason for not putting them all to work.

I had been thinking of them as boys since I was over forty and they averaged about twenty. "Young men" would have been a better term.

Watching them leave, I felt a lot of admiration for them. I've worked with many groups of men in my life, most of the time as their leader. For the last ten years, most of my subordinates have been very competent people, degreed engineers and skilled tradesmen, mostly. But I swear that I have never worked with an entire group of people before who were *all* as exceptionally intelligent, outstandingly eager, unflaggingly hardworking, and uniformly lighthearted as these young men all were. I tell you, it was like working with a totally different kind of humanity, a better kind.

I've heard that the Japanese average about ten points higher on IQ tests than white Americans. It is difficult to write an accurate interracial or cross-cultural test, but if the data are true, I suspect that it might be because, for a thousand years, a Japanese Samurai was morally required to immediately decapitate any commoner who didn't "act in the manner expected." Since the Japanese had an extremely complicated code of behavior, it must have taken a fairly intelligent person to always know just what "the manner expected" was, in any given situation. I think perhaps that the Japanese were not only selecting for people who were well mannered, but also for those who were intelligent, or at least smart enough so as to have been able to learn all the rules.

The policy of reducing the population by selectively sterilizing the less successful members of their society must have done the same thing for the people of the Western Isles, only much more so, since it was systematic. I can't say that I approve of the method, but I can certainly admire the results.

Adam was walking the next day, albeit a bit unsteadily. We figured that swimming was just the exercise he needed, so he took the eight new kids into Avalon Bay in the morning while I had the old-timers chipping and prying coral. His crew joined mine in the afternoon, and I let him run the show from then on.

I had to get the genset up and running as well as the diesel engine that powered the SCUBA tank compressor. It took me the better part of two hours to partially disassemble both rigs, and to repair the damage caused by the dunking they got when the boat was sinking. Then I was over an hour figuring out a way to get diesel fuel from the big tanks built into the boat, which was on its side, to the small tanks on the small engines.

Once I had the diesel engines producing both pneumatic and electrical power, I started filling the SCUBA tanks. Then I put the batteries Adam's men had extracted from *The Brick Royal* to charging, since we had exhausted them in trying to bail her out during the storm. Scrounging around, I found some of our electric lights and set them up, ready to switch on, come dark.

About that time, some of the warlock's men came by with all of the electronic gear that had been taken from us by him for safekeeping. They brought a letter from him saying that we might as well keep everything together, and could I please see what could be done about generating some power for them. I answered his question by switching on the lights for his men. It would have been more dramatic had it been dark, but they acted impressed, anyway.

I set up the satellite dish just outside of the cave, and soon got its automatic tracker going. The guards stared bug-eyed and nervous at the dish, never having seen an inanimate object move before. Culture shock all over the floor.

After that, I got antenna wire, data lines, and power cables to the computer, the television, and the VCR before deciding that the system needed a more thorough test and that I wanted a break, anyway. I was just getting into a tape of *Star Wars* when Adam and his dripping-wet crew came in. The boys were enthralled.

I stopped the tape and set it to rewinding.

"Gentlemen, this entertainment is best seen from the beginning. Before we start, I want to mention that one of the highest art forms practiced in the outside world is called science fiction. It exists mostly in the form of written stories and in theatrical presentations like the one you are about to enjoy. In this art form, the writer creates not only the characters and all of the things that happen to them, but also the very universe that all of the action takes place in. Thus, he is absolutely free of all constraints, and may exercise his art to the limits of his creativity. Done properly, this fictional world is as internally consistent as the real world around us, so that it becomes easy for the reader or viewer to suspend his disbelief and become thoroughly immersed in the story.

"I tell you this because to you, the real world outside of your island might seem to you to have some of the aspects of science fiction. Out there, they have many devices and forms of communication and transportation that you are not yet familiar with. Please remember that they do not have ships that can travel between the stars, or robots that can talk and think like human beings, or weapons that can destroy entire planets, although they are working on it. Anyway, the following is fiction, it has no purpose but to stretch your mind while you are enjoying yourself, and I wish you a pleasant few hours."

Then I turned the set back on and let them watch those marvelous opening scenes. Judging from their comments, they seemed to be able to follow the plot reasonably well, despite their lack of proficiency in English. It was dark when I sent them home. They had missed supper, except for some junk food I'd broken out of stores, but they didn't seem to mind. They'd just seen their second totally new world in two days.

# TWENTY-SIX

"Your Grace has heard of the entertainments now being proffered by the outsiders? Brutal tales, where men are shot down in the hundreds, where entire planets are blown up and destroyed, and where even the hero and heroine perform the entire play without ever going to church, or even once dedicating themselves to God?" The archbishop was shaking in his rage.

"I heard that the boys who are spending their days working underwater to keep the rest of us afloat saw one of those 'movies' we've been hearing about for the last fifty years. By all counts, they completely enjoyed themselves. And as to the lack of religious content in the thing, well, Phillias, would you really have been happier if the hero had been worshiping the God of the Jews, or perhaps one of the many Hindu Gods?"

"No, I suppose not, Your Grace. Still, there is great danger in these entertainments. They will have to be controlled."

"I suppose that you are right. Did you know that almost every political body in the outside world makes some efforts to control the sort of entertainments available to its citizens? Some of those nations are so haphazard that it boggles the mind to try to think of what it is that they could possibly find offensive. Indeed, I'm not sure that I want to know."

*"You would doubtless be much happier in your ignorance, Your Grace. I take it that you agree that any new outside influences will have to be carefully controlled?"*

*"I'll agree with that in principle, although the details of how it is done and what precisely will be forbidden will have to be worked out. It is too early yet to do anything definite."*

*"But not too early to at least think about it. Thank you, Your Grace,"* the archbishop said as he left the royal chamber.

The next morning, I was getting ready to go back to the warehouse, eager to get to work, when Roxanna reminded me, rather coldly, that this was Sunday. Working on anything but absolutely necessary tasks was improper, and anyway, we had to go to mass.

Adam was right again. There wasn't any point in getting married, since I could get plenty of nagging without having to go through the bother of the ceremony. I gritted my teeth and wasted half the morning sitting with a room full of other equally bored people, listening to some fool in a fancy outfit spout off about something or another that I neither cared about at the time nor ever remembered afterward.

In the afternoon, we joined Adam and the Pelitier sisters and went to the beach. The girls had heard about snorkeling, and had to try it. It was a busman's holiday for two men who had just spent two days under water, but what can you do? Furthermore, the scenery at an American beach is much better than the beach scenery on the island, what with their use of long johns instead of bikinis or less. The girls fell in love with the face masks, the flippers, and the snorkeling rigs, but I'd been spending enough time underwater lately.

Afterward, I found out that, in honor of the guy

who came up with the wine at a wedding feast, the bars were all closed on Sundays. Grumble.

I spent the next morning getting the rest of our electronic equipment going. I started without very high hopes. Our equipment had all been through a ship-wreck, with all the mechanical shock, saltwater immersion, and other trauma that implies. It had been dismantled by clumsy if well-meaning hands, hauled all the way up to the warlock's chambers and there inspected by who knows how many less than competent people. It had then been hauled back down to the warehouse, and left on the floor, where I was trying to get it all back together again. Some of it, like the navigation gear, had been built to withstand the rigors of a nautical environment, but much of the rest, like the stereo equipment, was only built to the usual, shoddy commercial standards.

Most of the nautical gear had originally been mounted in the aft cockpit, but that was on its side now along with the rest of the ship, so I set all the gear out on top of garbage bag covered cases of who-knew-what and started wiring it up with cables I'd scrounged from the boat. I gave myself even odds that I could get maybe seventy percent of it going again in three days, but I surprised myself.

By noon, I had every single piece of equipment up and running. Every single one of the radios, trans-mitters, telephones, fax machines, stereos, navigation gadgets, and computers worked. Not to mention the refrigerator and the microwave from the galley. Amazing! Even the radar and sonar equipment checked out, though of course they weren't actually working, the radar dome and sonar transponders still being affixed to *The Brick Royal*, which was on dry land and in a stone warehouse.

When they had gotten back to their barracks last Saturday night, the boys had naturally told all of their friends about the wonders of television and *Star Wars*.

By noon, Sunday or not, word of these wonders had filtered all the way up to the warlock and the duke himself.

Modern people in the outside world keep in touch mostly through the television and radio news programs. Without these conveniences (or curses, depending on your point of view), people keep in touch mostly by talking to one another.

On the islands, they do what people must have been doing throughout the history of mankind, until recently. Everybody knew everything because of constant gossiping. It is a remarkably efficient system, and I have had things that I told to people as I was leaving the warehouse repeated back to me within minutes of my arrival home.

And while television or radio news will let you know, in general, what is happening to the nation at large, gossip can be, and often is, personalized. Each bit of information actually tends to direct itself to those people most concerned. The case in point was that one of our workers told Adam that the duke was coming over. He'd heard about it through a string of nine people starting with his grace's chamberlain.

Think about that. Since people tend to talk about what their listeners want to hear about, the information steered itself through increasingly more interested people until it got to us!

The modern world lost a lot when we traded gossip for the news, although we just might be getting some of it back with the internet. Time will tell.

Not that knowing about the duke's visit made me any happier. I wasn't looking forward to meeting the duke, or the archbishop either, for that matter, for the very same reason that I have never looked forward to meeting any other governmental figure.

Governments are essentially negative organizations. Their whole function in life seems to be to tell you to not do the things that you want to do. Since you naturally don't want to not do the things that you want to do, they then take great pleasure in causing you as much pain as possible when you do them anyway. (Think of it as a cryptogram.)

They'll kill you or throw you in jail unless they think that you can make more money for them to steal if you are on the outside. If you've ever wondered why the rich hardly ever go to jail, well, that's the reason. It's not that they have undue influence with the courts. They don't. Judges and juries don't like rich people either. It's that when a rich man is free, he can make more money than a poor man can for the government to plunder. Now you know.

Oh, governments also tell you not to do the things that you don't want to do, too, but that doesn't count, since you can generally ignore such rules and not get into too much trouble. The fact is that they have so many laws that it is impossible for anyone, including the numberless and nameless people who work for the government, to know exactly what all those rules are.

To get on in this world, your best bet is to do what you want, to do it in as quiet a way as possible, and to avoid governments whenever you can. It's the only way to get anything done. One of the quickest ways to spot a nonachiever is to see if he starts out on a project by asking somebody's permission. The shakers and the movers of this world just go ahead and do things, and the best ones try hard not to be noticed by anyone. The people who show up in the news and on talk shows are mostly phonies.

The ladies had again provided an excellent seafood dinner, I had some Mozart going on the stereo, and Adam and the boys were eating with us when a gaudily dressed herald stepped in and announced that His Royal Grace Duke Guilhem Alberigo XXI was here, along with Thomas Strong,

E.E., Warlock of the Western Islands. The dozen or so people who were with them were not announced, and therefore must have been flunkies.

I felt a moment of panic, not knowing what to do. Then everyone else stood and bowed deeply, which made me feel better. Now I knew what one did when the duke interrupted your lunch. You stood up and then bent over.

Thinking about it, bowing is just like what baboons do when approached by a superior male. The subordinate male bends over and the boss mounts him, just as if he were a willing female. Which shows that "the powers that be" have been fucking us since before we were people.

The duke was a tall, athletic-looking man, and looked to be in his mid-fifties, though his white hair and white full beard suggested a greater age. His clothing was vaguely Elizabethan, like that worn by everyone else on the islands, except that his was richer in texture, and the embroidery was much finer. When he came close, you could see that the needlework was so tiny that it gave the impression of being photographic lithography, rather than being done by hand. He wore a simple, unpretentious crown made of gold wire that was not much thicker than a man's wedding ring, but it was his bearing that hit you first and hardest. Here was a man who was born and bred for leadership, and no one who saw him could possibly doubt it. All told, he was pretty impressive, having nothing in common with the typical American politician.

"Welcome, Your Grace," I said in my best Westronese. I *hoped* "your grace" was right.

"Yes, welcome, Your Grace and Your Excellency. Could we offer to share our poor dinner fare with you?" Adam seconded.

"Why, thank you, yes," the duke said in English that had the slight Oxford accent favored by announcers on the BBC. "I've heard a great deal about the excellent preserved food that you brought with you, and I'd rather enjoy trying some."

"With pleasure, Your Grace," I said as I went to the cases of canned food we had there.

I picked up at least one of everything, plus four cans of the absurdly popular Spam. Back in Bay City, I would have been embarrassed serving Spam to my lowest minimum-wage employee, but here, well, if the duke wanted Spam, he would get Spam. I was but a stranger in a strange land.

The table was full, with as many people as chairs, but with the speed and precision of a crack drill team, the apprentices picked up their plates, glasses, and silverware, left the table, and went back by the wall, to picnic there on the floor, out of the way. The ladies and their servants quickly cleaned up where the boys had been eating, spread a new tablecloth that appeared as if by real magic, and put out new table settings fresh from the packing cases. By the time the duke, the warlock, and both of their entourages had walked the length of the warehouse, their places at the table were ready, almost as if we had planned it that way.

The duke sat down opposite me, and the rest of the entourage took their places without further ceremony. Our ladies then started to sit, so Adam and I took the hint and joined them.

Why a pair of staunchly egalitarian Americans like us should feel so awkward around an insignificant country's nobility was hard to explain, but there it was. It probably had something to do with the way the duke had trained long and hard in the art of being impressive, and we poor slobs had never been exposed to the tricks of his trade before.

The duke puzzled for a moment with a fork and then put it down. I opened a can of Vienna sausages, showing how the key worked, and the duke promptly opened a can of Spam in the same fashion.

"What method is used to keep the meat from spoiling?" he asked, switching back to Westronese so everyone else could understand. Seeing me use a fork, he promptly used his in the same manner.

"First sealing the food away from any further contamination, and then cooking, to kill any decay organisms present. In practice, the meat is soldered into the cans when raw, and the cans are cooked under pressure for several hours to insure sterility," I said.

"Interesting. Still, it seems an expensive way to do things." The duke was sampling each offering directly from the can. Naturally, nobody tried to stop him long enough to put the things on a plate.

"Not really, Your Grace. Not with mass production. If you are making millions of the same product, it becomes practical to build specialized machinery that operates quickly and almost by itself. This makes each product very inexpensive. In my country, a skilled workingman's daily wage will purchase a ton of steel, which is what the cans are mostly made of. They have a thin coating of tin, or sometimes plastic, since iron would react with the food in the can. With mass production, the price of that can of Spam would be at most a quarter hour's wages after taxes for a minimum-wage worker."

"Hmm. And what would be the wage differential between your least and most skilled workers?"

Having tried everything I could offer, and passing the cans down to his subordinates, the duke settled in on a can of Spam, as I had somehow known he would. He was really chowing down.

"Oh, perhaps five dollars an hour for the least capable beginner up to perhaps fifty for a master machinist or model maker. Certain professions, medical doctors and lawyers, make much more, although they pay for their own offices, equipment and staffs."

"I see. On the Western Isles, the range is not so large." The man was actually opening *another* can of Spam.

"True, Your Grace, but here, people spend much of their income on food, whereas in the United States, a person can buy enough to survive on for ten or twenty dollars a week. Oh, they spend more than that on food, normally, but most of the difference goes to buying more-convenient, already-prepared, or better-tasting food. What I'm trying to say is, among us, most of what most people earn goes towards the purchase of things that they don't absolutely need, but merely want."

"So with their most basic needs easily supplied, they spend their time earning money to buy toys. Yes, I suppose that makes sense."

"It's also true that most of our people worry so much about their toys that they have made them into absolute necessities, psychologically, at least," Adam said without a trace of his usual Hamtramck accent. "Because of this, from an objective standpoint, all wealth beyond a certain point is largely an illusion. Still and all, I think that we lead richer lives than your people do. We are better informed, physically more comfortable, and intellectually more stimulated, on the average, than I think the people of the Western Islands are."

"Perhaps this is true, although you still know very little about us. Time will easily cure the problem, I'm sure. For now, well, the good warlock has discussed your proposal with me, and I must say that I find it interesting. Some of the things you propose, reducing the dead weight to increase the flotation of our islands, for example, are so obviously beneficial to my people that they need no discussion. Increasing our food supply would be equally wonderful, could I be convinced that it can be done without subjecting my people to a series of deadly plagues, or the invasion of some foreign power. The other things, the 'toys' as you have several times called them, I am not sure about. Consider, for example, that your excellent machines are currently serenading us with Mozart's *Haffner* Symphony. An excellent piece of work, one of my favorites, and your equipment reproduces it better than I could have possibly imagined. But we are ignoring it as we talk together here. Not only are we spoiling our own enjoyment of it, but I think that Mozart would not be altogether pleased. Wouldn't it be better to listen to it in a concert hall, with live performers?"

"Yes, Your Grace, it certainly would be far more moving as a live performance. And Mozart, were he still alive, would be annoyed at our treating his music so casually. In fact he *was* annoyed with the noblemen of his time who had hired him, when they proceeded to talk while he was performing. You see, they chose to ignore him just as we are currently choosing to ignore the servants who are waiting on us. This gets us to another advantage of an industrialized culture. In America and the Western world, there are very few servants, except for the case of a working mother who sometimes needs help with her children. Here, the wealthy enjoy a leisurely life largely at the expense of the poor. Among our people, the poorest are at least theoretically equal with the richest. I, for example, have often met with my own employees after work and enjoyed a beer or two with them."

"Indeed. For my own part, I think that when a person tries to be what he is not, he becomes an unhappy person. He may even become a dangerous one. In all cultures, there are leaders and there are those who are led. That is the way it should be simply because nothing else works. I suppose that some of my attitude comes from my being the product of seventy-eight generations of very careful breeding, but so be it. I am exactly what I am, and I'm not the least bit ashamed of it. Rest assured that if I ever permit my people's culture to change, it will change very slowly."

There had been no change in the duke's pleasant demeanor, but his words said that he was not entirely pleased with my ideas of democracy. Sometimes I think that I have a permanent case of foot-in-mouth disease.

Adam came to the rescue. "Your Grace, I wonder if I might interest you and your vassals in seeing some of the sights of your own islands that you have never seen before. Would you like to go swimming in Avalon Bay with a snorkeling rig? The coral and fishes down there are unbelievably beautiful."

"Yes, I definitely would. It was one of the reasons that I came down here today. I also want to see your television and such, but I expect that the bay would be better seen while the sun is yet high."

Everyone on the islands could swim, and the duke's party had brought their swimsuits because of the rumors they'd heard.

As Adam led them off with fins and masks borrowed back from the boys, the warlock stayed behind for a moment to talk to me in English.

"Look, you ninny!" he said in a whisper. "You can hardly expect a hereditary absolute ruler to be enthralled with the glories of democracy! He is a good lord who takes the welfare of his people very seriously, but he also has an obligation to almost a hundred generations of ancestors, to hand his country intact down to his successor. He takes that duty very seriously as well. Any more nonsense out of you and you could spend the rest of your life under house arrest! Understood?"

"Yes, Your Excellency."

"Good. Don't forget it."

The warlock followed the rest of the group to the beach, and I sat back down and put my head in my hands, wondering just how badly I had screwed the whole thing up this time.

# TWENTY-SEVEN

Roxanna came up behind me and started rubbing my neck and shoulders. "My lord, it is not that bad. The duke is a very wise and understanding man. He knows all about the social customs of your country, and you have not seriously offended him by telling him again about them. Come. You have yet to show me the wonders of your television and your VCR. Show me something light and amusing."

A truly marvelous woman. I resolved to propose marriage to her again, and this time with all the formalities.

Roxanna's English wasn't up to understanding the verbal byplay of most comedies, so I found a pair of old silent films, Harold Lloyd's *His Royal Slyness* and then his *Haunted Spooks*. And by the end, I was laughing as much as the ladies, apprentices, and servants, or perhaps a bit harder.

The duke returned with his crowd as I was rewinding the tape. Adam kept the whole thing in hand, starting with giving the boys back their equipment. He put one of them in charge, and told them to get to work without us.

Adam started at the far end of the warehouse with some of the navigation equipment, displaying a laser ROM disk that contained charts of every sea, coastline, and harbor in the world. Then there was the Global Positioning System, that could locate us to within ten meters of our actual position. Combining these two, it was possible to navigate in complete darkness, without radar or sonar, through most of the channels, coral reefs, and harbors of the world. Providing, of course, that you didn't hit something that wasn't on the electronic charts. Another ship, for example.

He talked about how the radar and sonar worked, but couldn't actually demonstrate them with the ship being where it was. Then there were the radios. An all-band receiver and two marine-band transceivers. The duke was familiar with shortwave. Indeed, it had been his main source of information about the outside world. The satellite phone system really surprised him, however.

"Do you mean to tell me that it is possible to contact any single person anywhere in the world? Instantly?"

"Anyone who has a telephone, Your Grace, which is most people in the civilized world. And almost instantly. There's a half-second delay. Watch. I'll demonstrate. It's been too long since I called my mother, anyway. She worries about me, you know," Adam said.

And with that, he picked up the handset, dialed up her number, and put the phone on speaker mode, so everyone could listen in.

"Hello?"

"Good morning, Ma. It's Adam."

"Adam! Where are you? You haven't called in months! I was getting worried that you got shipwrecked or injured or something horrible like that."

"I'm just fine, Ma. I'm in the middle of the Pacific Ocean. We had a little trouble with our satellite phone and I couldn't call, but we got it fixed now. The good news is that I met this girl, or rather these two girls. They're sisters, and each of them is as good a woman as *your* mother was. I just might get serious about them, as soon as I can figure out which one I want."

"Then Adam, if either one of them will take you, you should marry her right now before the poor girl comes to her senses! If you are ever going to get me any grandchildren, you'd better start soon, because you're already almost too old."

"Forty-six is not too old to get married, and I'll keep you posted on the ladies. Got to run now."

"Good. About the nice girls you've met, I mean. You call me every two weeks from now on, you hear?"

"Yes, Ma. Good-bye."

"Good-bye, Adam."

The line went dead.

"You see, Your Grace. It's that easy."

"Remarkable. Those buttons you pushed before you contacted her, they were some sort of instructions for the machine?"

"Yes, Your Grace. It's called a phone number. They have books listing them, or if you know where a person lives, and that person has not given instructions that they wish their number to be kept a secret, an operator, a person who works for the phone company, will give you their number."

"I see. So if a person wishes privacy, he is granted it."

"Yes. Privacy is very important in our culture. If there had been an emergency, however, the police would be able to contact anyone who needed contacting," Adam explained.

"So your people don't have privacy from their government."

"Well, yes and no, Your Grace. Sometimes it's difficult to know exactly where to draw the line, if you get my meaning."

"Indeed, I do. Another thing. I just observed you telling your mother a lie. Two lies. You were both shipwrecked and seriously injured. Do you often tell her lies?"

"Your Grace, had I told her that I had been in a shipwreck, that I had broken five bones, and that I nearly drowned, she would have been upset for months. There's nothing that she can do about it, and all the danger's over, so why should I make her worry? So to answer your question, yes, of course I lie to my mother. In fact, I do it fairly often."

The duke thought about it a moment, then shook his head, declining comment.

The next item was a personal computer, and explaining everything it could do took a half hour. The only surprise for me was when Adam produced a CD-ROM that had the *Encyclopaedia Britannica* on it. I hadn't known that we had such a thing, but then most people never use an encyclopedia anyway. It's just important to *have* one.

That left the entertainment equipment. After the stereo, there was only the TV and the VCR. Some of the duke's party wanted something religious and others wanted an adventure story, so Adam put on *Ben Hur*.

All four hours of it.

It was well past dark when the last tape finally started to rewind, and I was eager to get home and in bed with Roxanna.

People were actually getting up to leave when Adam said, "Your Grace, were you aware of the various news channels available to us?"

And so we watched CNN until midnight, which left not nearly enough time for properly loving Roxanna. Sometimes Adam blows it, too.

Entirely too early in the morning, five more of the warlock's subordinates were waiting for us. Three were scholars who wanted to do research with our computerized encyclopedia, one was to watch the news channel and take notes for the bulletin boards, the local equivalent of a newspaper, and the fifth, who was to take us on the warlock's promised tour of the islands, was Journeyman Judah ben Salomen ha-Cohen.

"A remarkable name for a Christian," I said.

"I chose it myself," he said. "You see, my father was a chevalier, a great-grandson of the old duke. As a great-great-grandson, I of course am a commoner. But if every descendent of the ducal line kept the family name of Alberigo, well, there wouldn't be much left but Alberigos in the entire country. Because of this, the custom is for those in my position to chose our own names. I wanted something different."

"You certainly got it," Adam said.

It took only a few minutes to get the reporter and the researchers set up and familiar with the controls of their equipment. As I've often said, these people were all remarkably intelligent. Roxanna used the time to give instructions to her cook about making sure that the apprentices were fed lunch, since she wanted to take the tour as well.

Judah ben *et cetera* had brought a map with him, the first I had ever seen of the Western Islands. It was now obvious why they were sometimes referred to in the singular and sometimes in the plural. It was one single land mass, one rock, really, which naturally made it singular. This rock was irregular in shape, about seven miles long and four miles across at the widest. Most of the rock was not above the waterline. There were five separate peaks that went above the waves, so that from the surface there appeared to be five islands plus a number of smaller, mostly barren outcroppings. Hence the frequent use of the plural.

These peaks enclosed a fair sized lagoon, the Llyr,

toward the center of the complex, and a number of channels going out to the ocean. Much of the islands' local transportation went on in these protected waters, along with some fishing, aquaculture, and water sports.

With Roxanna and the Pelitier sisters along, we had a pleasant day. I won't bore you with the whole tour, but some things we saw are worth relating.

There was a lot more depth to the culture of the islands than I had been led to expect. Besides libraries and churches, there were concert halls, dance halls, bars, inns, and restaurants. They had public beaches, small but carefully tended parks, and picnic grounds. Many people were active in sports, and they were served by gymnasiums, playing fields and arenas, most of which were underground. In fact, everything that could possibly be underground, was, including most of the beaches. At least, they usually had a massive overhang cantilevered above them, with carefully cultivated plants growing on top. There was even a five team semipro league, playing a sort of water polo.

All of these facilities were open to the nobility, the wealthy, and the servant class, although the same two-world mentality that I had noticed at the party was maintained, with the nobility and the wealthy on one team, and everybody else on the other. A weird attitude, but it had the benefit of effectively doubling the facilities available to everyone. People acted as though members of the other caste simply didn't exist. You actually got the feeling that they *couldn't* see each other, and maybe they didn't. What would have looked crowded to a normal person simply had half as many people there so far as they were concerned.

I've heard that the reason why native speakers of Japanese have difficulty pronouncing the "L" and "R" sounds in English is that they never learned, as small children, to differentiate between the two. To them, both sounds are alike, and they can't hear any difference. Well, if acculturation can account for such an obvious (to me) auditory illusion, why can't the same process result in a visual one? Maybe the islanders actually could not see members of the other class when they were in certain social situations!

Not having been raised in their culture, I could see everybody who was there, and I never could get used to the Westronese way of ignoring some people. It was never obvious to me how they told a member of one class from a member of the other. There was no class difference in the swimming suits worn, for example, but everyone still seemed to know who was who. It couldn't have been that they all knew each other as individuals, not with twelve thousand people around.

Roxanna was of no help in solving the problem for me. To her, the difference was so obvious that it was difficult to talk about. It was as though I had asked her how to tell a fish from a milk cow. The best I could get from her was that it depended on how the other person looked at you, but that just begged the question, since I then had to ask how the other person knew who was who. I still could get no satisfactory answer.

The school system was run by the church, for the first twelve grades, and was both free and mandatory for all children. Yet here too, the double world thing went on, with the nobles and the wealthy sitting to the right while the servants sat to the left. Instruction was absolutely equal, but also absolutely separate.

Instruction was absolutely unequal and separate when it came to sex. From grade one, the girls went to some classes and the boys went to others. Girls had women teaching them and boys had men. Women's Lib wouldn't get very far around this place.

After graduation, the kids were tested, as I mentioned earlier, and some of the boys were sent off to get a higher education. The rest found jobs. Some of the girls were sent off to mandatory marriages, and the low scorers got to find the husbands that they wanted. I wondered how many of the girls tried very hard on the tests, and how many boys deliberately passed up a higher education in order to marry the girls they wanted.

I suppose that any child anywhere has a hard time expressing his individuality, but the amount of personal freedom allowed them on the islands was less than anyplace else I've ever heard of. When I was a child, I'm not sure that I could have stood it here. Or maybe I could. Kids are pretty malleable. But if I had gone through this educational system, I would have been a much different person than I am today. It makes me wonder if I would have been a better one.

We ended the day at a pleasant bar with a three-piece dance band. A curious island custom was that the woman normally paid the tab, anywhere she went with her husband or protector. This was in line with the way they handled all the other household expenses, but it struck me as being rather strange. In the real world where I came from, the man always prefers to pick up the tab, in part to affirm his dominance over the situation. Here, the wife always acted subordinately, yet she had complete charge of all the money. I don't think that it could have worked in America. In Japan, maybe.

We enjoyed ourselves. Roxanna actually got me out on the dance floor, showed me the local steps, and I never once fell down. This was rare accomplishment for me, since something in me always used to confuse social dancing with the katas used in Karate training. Before long I always used to end up treating dancing as training rather than as social intercourse. Most of my dance partners were not amused, although a few thought I was hilarious.

Our guide said that the next day's portion of the tour would be more technical, and thus probably wouldn't interest the ladies. They promptly agreed with him, saying that they had found suitable lodgings near the warehouse for Adam and the Pelitier sisters, and would rather spend the day getting the new household set up. That night in bed, I asked Roxanna if she had really wanted to go on the next tour.

"A woman should never go where it is suggested that she might not be amused."

"An American woman wouldn't say a thing like that," I said.

"Would you rather that I was an American woman?"

"No."

"Then you should consider yourself answered."

# TWENTY-EIGHT

After the heralds finished their long-winded introductions for three men who had known each other for more than half a century, the duke waved them and the rest of the lackeys out except for the privy secretary, who sat quietly taking notes.

"Gentlemen, I have called you together for a short meeting of the privy counsel to discuss what we each have learned about our guests, Mr. Kulczynski and Mr. Nguyen. This is to be a preliminary discussion only, but sometime in the next several months a series of decisions must be made concerning them. I will ask our good Warlock to start us out."

"Thank you, Your Grace. The short of it is that my own impressions have been entirely positive. Both men are well educated, remarkably intelligent, and quite competent in both engineering and business. They are basically honest and hardworking. They are becoming increasingly dedicated to the best interests of the Western Islands, in part because Your Grace's choice of women for them was particularly good. Both men are bonding well with the ladies who have been hosting them.

"As I have often said to both of you before, it is becoming increasingly necessary for us to prepare to come to terms with the outside world. Aside from the fact that we are sinking, we are becoming increasingly visible to their satellite cameras. Our discovery is inevitable, and our political and economic positions will be far better if we go to them than if we wait and then have them come to us. Especially since they just might come to us with an army behind them! Do you realize that a single one of their aircraft carriers can have more adult men aboard than we have on our entire island? There are hundreds of unruly nations out there with armies big enough to conquer us without difficulty.

"I have discussed our friends' proposals concerning a trading company with both of you. I think that we should act favorably on it as soon as possible. I think that we are extremely fortunate to have two such outsiders come to us at this time. So much so that I can't help but think that their arrival on our shores was divinely inspired."

The archbishop was getting increasingly fidgety, so as the warlock sat down, the duke gestured for the clergyman to take the floor.

"Divinely inspired? Damn you! I'll tell you what's divinely inspired!"

"I'm sure that God is delighted to hear that," the warlock drawled.

The archbishop was red faced, and sputtering so badly that the duke said, "Phillias, relax a moment and get yourself under control, so that you can *calmly* explain your views to us concerning our guests."

Long minutes passed before the archbishop again stood up.

"Your Grace, my own views are diametrically opposed to those of the Warlock, who himself started as an outsider. I consider the many serious dangers that the outsiders pose to be far more worrisome than whatever heavenly spying they are doing to us, whatever possible future invasion we are told may be in the offing, or any tragic structural failure or sinking of our islands that may occur if the Warlock's men continue doing or not doing, as the case may be, whatever it is that they are actually doing.

"I am worried about the health of the bodies and souls of every one of your subjects. The danger of diseases is well documented. Small numbers of outsiders have repeatedly started plagues that have killed off one third to one half of our entire population. That is four to six thousand of your people dead! Now, think about what could happen if hundreds, even thousands of outsiders come all within a short period of time. Hundreds or thousands of plagues could be started simultaneously, and every single one of us could die! Even those who are sick but not deathly ill, and who might have recovered, will not, for lack of anyone to tend them!

"The outsiders themselves, who, over the painful centuries, have developed immunities to most of their diseases, worry daily about their own safety. The U.S. Centers for Disease Control would seem to be an organization as large as our whole nation, yet it can not control the diseases it tries to eliminate.

"With our handicaps in size and immunity, we would be helpless, and soon dead. Our religion, so carefully preserved over the ages, would be gone. Our culture, so carefully nurtured by over seventy generations of your ancestors, would be no more, and your heir would be nonexistent. Our people, bred to be brighter, more fit, and more civilized over so many difficult years, would be gone, and all their promise a wasted effort.

"Yet one thing that we have learned from the machines of the outsiders gives me some insight into God's plan for our tiny band of islanders. We hear repeatedly on their news that the outsiders themselves are destroying the world, or at least making it uninhabitable, if not by war, then by pollution. If they do this horrible thing, and if we are still hidden at sea while this tragedy happens, it may be God's will that we are destined to inherit the earth!

"We may be the future of all mankind! Think long and hard on *that* before you debase us into becoming just one insignificant nation among hundreds of others!"

The duke was silent for several minutes before he said, "Now *that* is a remarkably heady thought, and one that the Warlock and I will have to ponder long on before we dare make comment. Certainly, I will have nothing more to say today, so I think that we might as well consider this council closed."

In the morning, we spent a half hour at the warehouse getting a few details ironed out. Adam's six "bearers" were laboriously chipping the concrete away from the edges of the hole that the mast had made, to insure that the patch would be grounded on sound ferrocrete. Another day should do it, we figured, and that included the damage to the upper deck as well.

There were two SCUBA divers working separately from the snorkel crew now. Their program was to go down to a hundred feet or so and clean up a six-foot-wide swath, working upwards, to the fifteen foot level where the other divers had to leave off. That took them three hours, and exhausted their tanks. They took a two-hour lunch break while their tanks were being refilled, and then repeated the operation in the afternoon.

We calculated that at their current rate, it would be thirty years before they cleaned off the edges of the entire floating rock, but every little bit helped.

Journeyman Judah arrived to take us on his tour, and Adam and I left with him. Again, I'm only going to give you a summation of the high points of the day's activities.

Because of the space required, orchards, forests and vineyards were in the hands of private growers, but the wizards themselves maintained extensive experimental fields of annual, biennial, and nonwoody perennial plants, and we toured these first.

The total number and variety of plants there was surprising, until we found that the majority of them had no known practical use. Some of their lovingly-cared-for plants were known weeds, and I actually spotted a patch of carefully cultivated crabgrass. It was simply their policy, if possible, to never let a species of plant get lost, on the theory that you never knew what would turn up as useful someday.

The chief gardener, Master Maimonides ibn Tibbon, took us through those veggies whose usefulness had been proven. There were a lot of these.

They had more than fifty spices that I had never heard of. We made a note to buy a large variety of dried spices on the open market to take with us to the mainland. We'd have to see if any of them attracted any commercial interest.

There were sixteen plants from which insecticides were prepared. Each of these was quite specific, repelling or killing only a distinct type or class of pest. One of them was a repellent for black flies, and I knew we had a sure winner there. Northern Maine and much of Canada are almost uninhabitable for months during the summer because of these pests, and here we had a defense against the little bastards!

And, of course, we'd be taking samples of all the rest back with us as well.

More than two hundred varieties of plants were used for making dyes and pigments. Since all the possible colors were already available to the outside world from chemical dyes, I said we had little hope of commercial success with these vegetable ones. This hurt Maimonides' feelings a bit, since dyes had always been a special interest of his.

"You're wrong, Treet," Adam said. "Their dyes don't fade with washing, age, or sunlight. Furthermore, they work on the local Super-Hemp, and we don't know how that stuff will react with our chemical dyes."

We promised to take back samples and to try to find a market for them. Even if Adam was wrong, it was good PR.

The extracts of seven plants were known for their preservative qualities. Since we had no way of comparing these with commercial, chemical preservatives, all we could do was to figure on taking samples and instructions to a testing lab, and see what they said.

There were several plant extracts that I suppose you could call cosmetic, but they weren't paints or oils. One was the depilatory we'd noticed the effect of. It was claimed to stay effective for over a year. Another reduced wrinkles, and a third turned all your hair blond, permanently!

Thinking about what women in the United States paid for treatments that only claimed to do such things, temporarily, all I could see were dollar signs floating in front of my eyes!

Almost five hundred varieties of plants supposedly had various medicinal qualities. Most medicines on the island were mixed up as a sort of tea or soup and simply drunk by the patient. None of them was claimed to cure cancer, and nobody here had ever heard of AIDS, but there was one that made a male contraceptive. They said that one dose lasted six months. There was a female contraceptive available as well, and it was good for a year. There were also two drugs that induced permanent sterility, one for men and one for women.

Most of the rest of the medicines were for diseases that either we had never heard of, or that nobody knew the names of in English. Like the preservatives, we would have to bring back samples and instructions on all of them, and send them off to a laboratory somewhere. Or better still, a lot of different laboratories everywhere. Rather than inundating one corporation's lab, we'd make out better by sending a little off to every one of them. After all, a pharmaceutical company would want a monopoly on a drug before they invested all the money that it took to prove the drug's usefulness, and then five times that amount to get it by the horseshit shoveled out by the FDA. We knew that it would be many years before any approved drug finally made it on the market, and so there would be no quick bucks made here. But money later is okay too, and maybe we could help cure somebody's affliction.

Curiously, none of the long list of medicines were for use against pain. Since Adam had recently been treated to the delightful pastime of having five bones set without an anesthetic, he just naturally had to ask Master Miamonides about this strange lack.

"We used to have a number of pain removing drugs, but some two hundred years ago, people got to growing them and using them for pleasure," the chief gardener said. "It seems they got drunk on them, or something similar to that. Furthermore, it was a kind of drunkenness where the victim soon cared about little else besides getting drunk again. Men stopped supporting their families and women forgot their proper duties. And it wasn't just a few fools, either, but a fair part of the population that was doing it. Punishing them was to no avail. They were soon back at their old habits, no matter what was done. Nothing seemed to work, save killing them, of course, and that seemed a bit extreme. All sorts of things were tried, but none of them worked. In the end, the duke of the time—I misremember his name—had every single plant that produced a drug of that type destroyed, along with every single seed. A draconian measure, to be sure, but the only one that finally proved effectual."

"We've had that kind of problem back in the outside world," Adam said.

"Indeed? And what did your rulers do about it?"

"They're still at the stage of trying a lot of things that don't work."

"But that means that there is a market here for the pain killers we use in the rest of the world," I said. "If we bring in only refined chemicals, that can't possibly reproduce, and distribute them only through legitimate medical people, it should be safe enough."

"With the duke's permission, of course," Adam said.

"Of course."

Then there were the food plants, and again, there were a lot of them. Even after we were told what they were, I only recognized about two out of five of them. People eat all sorts of things. But there were a few conspicuous plants missing.

"You don't have any rice here," I said.

"True. We have those food sources that were available from Europe, where we started from, and from the Americas, where we explored and traded extensively, but we are sadly lacking in those from Africa, Asia, and the Middle East. Perhaps your coming will help to rectify these faults in our collection."

"Not to mention your diet," Adam said. "You are also missing coffee, tea, and bananas, and you don't have one single kind of pea or bean."

"I thought that beans were known in medieval Europe," I said.

"We do have bananas, but they are the original South American variety, and aren't very popular. We used to have beans, but there was a blight, some forty years ago, when I was still an apprentice. We worked for years, trying to stop it, but we failed. In the end, we lost every single legume in the world."

"In *your* world, maybe," Adam said. "We brought a few tons of them with us on *The Brick Royal*. They were our emergency food supply."

"So I had heard. But after they went through that

*canning* process of yours, well, they would be useless to us here."

"No. They were just dried beans. You could plant
them if you wanted to. There's no reason why they
shouldn't grow."

"And I could have samples of these?" The old guy
was suddenly excited.

"You can take every bag of the things we got. It
was probably a dumb idea to bring them along in
the first place. Give what you don't need to the
farmers here, or eat them yourself, for all I care,"
Adam said.

"My lord, you are a true Christian!"

"Thank you. Send a crew around first thing in the
morning and pick them up. Sorry that we can't help
you with the rice, but all we got is milled white rice,
and it wouldn't grow."

With a bit of a flourish, we were shown the island's
pride and joy, their indestructible high-strength fiber,
or rather the hemp plant it came from.

"They tell the story of the discovery of this strain
to every new class of gardeners," the chief gardener
said. "It was in the fall of 1477, when a poor widow,
Mrs. Eileen Tittle, was harvesting her hemp. Like all
trained gardeners, she had always been taught to look
for anything unusual in the plants she tended, but
to the eye, this one was absolutely normal. It looked
not a bit different from any of the hundreds of hemp
plants growing around it. The hemp fields were much
larger then, since with the way everything wore out
so quickly, they had to plant many acres of hemp
to clothe themselves, and still they could do but a
poor job of it. Many of the poor went cold in the
winter.

"So nothing was known to be different until she
went to harvest her field. It was late in the day, and
she was tired, when the strange thing happened. She
grabbed the top of the plant with her hand and struck

the base of it with her sickle, just as she had done a thousand times that day. But to her great surprise, the sickle bounced right off! What's more, the plant had pulled a bit in her hand, and when it did, it cut her, straight across the palm.

"Now, someone else might have run off and tended her wounded hand. Or another person might have just run off in a fright, with such strange things happening, but Eileen Tittle was made of better stuff than that. She lay right down on the dirt and examined this strange thing. She looked it up and down and all over, but there was nothing to see but a perfectly ordinary hemp plant, although it was now a bit bruised. The only thing the least bit unusual about it was that there was only a single bud left growing on it, and that bud was not yet ripe. She knew that that bud was important, so she went straightaway and brought back sticks with which to build a bit of a basket around the plant, to protect it from the winds and the animals, for in those days there were still small wild animals on the island. That night she sent her only son out to sleep by the plant, to guard it, and the next day she watched it all the day long, while she tended her fields.

"They did this every day and every night for two weeks, until the single bud matured. Then, and only then, did she pull up the plant to find out just why her sickle had bounced off. Oh, it was eleven more years of selective breeding and propagation before the first good crop came in and old Eileen Tittle became the wealthiest woman on the islands, but if she hadn't kept her wits about her in that first moment, the only mutant hemp plant in God's universe would have been lost forever."

"Quite a story," Adam said. "You know, had she been harvesting with the kind of machinery we use in America, the plant would have been lost and the machine wrecked."

"That is probably true, my lord. It goes to show that sometimes the old ways are the best."

We were shown the plant that they made paper out of, with its large, smooth, and veinless leaves, but we saw no commercial use for it. At best, it made only small, single sheets of paper, and modern printing practice demands huge, seamless rolls of the stuff. The same interesting-but-useless label was put on the gourds that were ground up and made into a sort of plaster. It was needed on the islands, but not needed in the outside world.

The plant that made the rubber paint that they put on their floors and the bottom of their shoes was near the top of our need list, however. If a coat of paint would wear on your shoes for a year, and on the floor indefinitely, think of what it could do for rubber tires! Or for the highways they rode on!

It was getting late in the afternoon when we finally left Master Maimonides. He had promised to have his people collect samples of everything that we felt would be commercially interesting, along with instructions, in standard English, on how to use each one. We planned to carry only extracts of each plant back with us, and never a viable plant or seed. We were after trade, after all, not charity.

If any of these plants were to be grown elsewhere, we'd lose a bloody fortune, and so would everyone else on the islands.

# TWENTY-NINE

Since Adam and I had a full day planned for repairing the boat, we agreed to having our guide make a quick trip through the animal caves, rather than putting it off for a day.

There were flocks of ducks and geese that lived off the plant life in the waterways around the islands. These were privately owned, though licensed, to keep their numbers from overgrazing. As far as we could see, they were no different from any other aquatic birds, and Judah confirmed this. Breeding them into something better had been difficult because they sometimes mated with wild birds, which upset things considerably.

We were on the largest and most populous of the five islands, and the caves we were led to contained half of all of the beasts raised in the entire duchy. Whereas plants were grown by half the people on the islands, animal husbandry was kept as a monopoly by the wizard's guild. It was one of their major sources of income. We weren't farm boys but, to us, there didn't seem to be enough animals here to feed a thousand people, let alone six thousand.

"In part, my lords, it is because we get much of our protein from the sea," the head keeper, Master Azzo d'Este, told us. "For feed, we have little else but those parts of the plants that people cannot eat, and indeed, our laws forbid the feeding of an animal with anything that a human could use for food, table scraps excepted. That does not permit the vast herds that I have heard your people possess. Also, it is my understanding that our animals are more productive than yours."

He then went ahead and proved his statements. There were two flocks of chickens in the complex of caves, one for eggs and one for early eating, just as is the practice in the rest of the world. The difference was that the eating chickens were full grown in three weeks flat, compared with the outside record of five weeks. Also, they managed this without using growth hormones, and without feeding the birds anything more than what amounted to being hay. The egg layers were averaging four eggs per day per hen, and again, doing it on waste vegetable matter. Compare that with the grain-fed chickens back home that put out one egg a day.

There were rabbits that grew about as fast as the eating chickens, but whether that was superlative or not, we didn't know. They had just one single mature sow and her sixteen offspring. Being omnivores, just like people, pigs have a diet that competes with ours. The small herd was fed on the table scraps collected from all over the island, and ate them all. Pork was in short supply, and sold for astoundingly high prices. Perhaps this accounted for the popularity of Spam. Or perhaps it was the scarcity of fats in their diet. Chickens, rabbits and fish are fairly fat free. In any event, I saw us importing a lot of canned ham. Then came the real surprise.

"That is the strangest looking creature I've ever seen," I said.

"I think it's a cow," Adam said. "But I wouldn't bet serious money on it."

It was standing upright, but those spindly limbs

couldn't possibly have moved it very far. Judging from its legs and neck, the animal looked to be in the final stages of death by starvation. Yet there was a full manger of greens in front of it and a tub of water nearby, so it wasn't being maltreated. It was only when we stepped back and saw it from the side that we realized that the animal was mostly udder. The huge milk gland ran from just behind the forelegs and all the way back to the tail. It was wider than the rest of the beast, and the teats actually hung down into a hole in the floor dug to accommodate them. They milked the critter from the floor below!

"We milk her every two hours, day and night," Master d'Este said. "She produces some four hundred of your gallons of milk a day, and her three sisters each do about as well."

"Unbelievable," I said.

"You don't believe me? You call me a liar?"

"No! Please! I'm sorry. My command of your language is still poor. You must forgive me."

"Well, I suppose, if I must."

"I meant to say that I couldn't believe my own eyes. Your accomplishment is astounding, an amazing scientific achievement."

"Oh. Well, that's different. Thank you."

"How large is your total herd?" Adam asked.

"Two. Plus the other two on the other islands. Or six, if you want to count the new heifer and the bull as well. We generally have him rented out for plowing and suchlike work."

"And four cows produce enough milk to satisfy twelve thousand people?"

"We make all we can sell, and even have some left over for making butter and cheese."

We bid Master d'Este good-bye, and started back.

"They satisfy the dairy needs of twelve thousand people with only four cows. Adam, there's a fortune to be made here."

"How? I don't see any way to do it. No matter how productive each cow is, we can't feed them here on imported grain and ship fresh milk back to the world outside. If we take something as strange-looking as that animal back to the States, she's going to be noticed in no time flat, and if she is as valuable as we both know she is, somebody is going to steal her. Or kill her just to prevent the competition."

"You're right, I suppose. Anyway, it would be a very long-term project. As slow as cows reproduce, it would take thirty years to build a big herd. What's more, most of your arguments apply to the rest of these animals, too."

"I'm not so sure. I think something could be done with chicken eggs, but we won't have time for it on the first trip," he said.

"Yeah. Maybe, someday, we can sell some of these animals to breeders back in the States for good prices, but that's not going to be for a long while. It's a pity. Well, it's getting late and I'm getting hungry. The girls won't be expecting us for a while, so let's go find a restaurant with a good bar."

"Moved, seconded, and passed by general acclaim," Adam said.

Our guide, Judah, told us of a small, unpretentious men's club deep in the bowels of the island. We'd been following his lead all day long, and we saw no good reason to stop now.

Oil lamps were few in the tunnels getting there, and Adam had to light our way with the penlight he always carried. For a while, the way was so long and dark that I thought that Judah was pulling our leg, but when we finally got there, the place was as advertised. It was a quiet, all-male sort of establishment, except for the help, who were mostly attractive young ladies, and naked at that. A single dancer undulated on a small stage, to the music of a drum and a single flute. The decor, except for the women, was nonexistent, and our waitress started out by offering us a menu, a beer and wine list, and herself.

We took the first two, and said that we wouldn't be needing any additional company. She acted only politely disappointed, and the service remained good throughout our stay there. It was a vast improvement on the only other brothel I'd ever been taken to, years before. I suppose that prostitution was unavoidable on the islands. There was no venereal disease, and they had an effective birth control method. With easygoing morals and a percentage of the population facing mandatory permanent sterilization if they had to spend too many generations being poor, perhaps it was inevitable. But like everything else around here, when these people did a thing, they did it right.

There's something very relaxing about having a surplus of naked ladies about. It tends to eliminate a certain sexual tension that nags you from back in your subconscious and gets in the way of your thinking. Or perhaps it's that it gives the sexual part of your mind full reign, so that your libido in turn lets the rest of you get on with what you really wanted to do. In any event, I liked the establishment, and I didn't hear Adam making any complaints, either. The food was good and the beer outstanding, even though, like all the beer on the island, it was flat. With Judah's help, we started outlining just what would go into our first cargo back to the real world.

The real world. I'd actually gotten to thinking about it that way. These islands, and to a certain extent the yearlong trip getting here, had sort of a dreamy quality to them that was pleasant enough, but was somehow unreal. A part of me was ready to go back to Bay City, and open up a new machinery factory. But that wouldn't happen for a while. If ever. Anyway, we had an important job to do right here.

After a half dozen beers, each, we had our supper

digesting and the program worked out. It was time
to go. Our ladies would be waiting for us back home,
and we called for the check. Fumbling for our money,
we found that neither Adam nor I had anything
smaller than a silver quarter, which was a huge sum
on these islands.

"My lords." The waitress stared at the coin in her
hand and flushed, and being naked, she did it with
a ripple that started from her forehead and went all
the way on down to her toes. "This is a hundred
times too much. I can't make change for such a coin.
There isn't that much money in the whole place!"

In truth, it was the first time that either of us had
actually been asked to pay for anything since we had
been shipwrecked, the custom being for the women
to take care of that sort of thing when they were
around. Our guide offered to pick up the tab, but we
refused him. After all, we were far more wealthy than
he was, and he had spent the entire day doing us
a favor.

"Adam, it's only a quarter," I said, turning to the
waitress. "Miss, please take this anyway. Pay the bill,
give yourself a tip of equal size, and have the manager
put the rest on a tab for Adam and me. I think that
we'll become regular customers here, in time."

The size of the tip delighted her. She squealed pleas-
antly and ran for the back room. Shortly, the manager came out to meet us, a big man with a limp
and a scarred face. He introduced himself as Chevalier
Iwo, confirmed with us what we had told the waitress, and offered us another round, on the house. We
thanked him, said that our ladies were waiting, and
declined the round. We started to leave. Iwo then
became more persistent, insisting that we stay longer.
We, in turn, insisted on leaving. Adam, in fact, even
got a bit rude about it. As we left, I saw there was
a certain look of sadness in the big chevalier's eye.

# THIRTY

"When I took the Oath of Absolute Obedience, I never thought that I would ever be involved in something like this," Brother Bartholomew said.

"Nor did I, but our orders come directly from the archbishop, himself, and he is having us do this to ease the burdens on the duke."

"But if brutal things must be done, why can't they be done by men trained for brutality? Why can't the duke do his own dirty work himself? And if this is really God's work, why can't we don our cassocks?"

"That was all covered in the archbishop's speech. Weren't you listening? Now, hush. Here they come."

Once outside the door, Judah ben Salomon asked if it would be all right if he left us there, since he lived in the opposite direction from where we were going.

"Certainly, but how do we find our way home?"

There were no street signs on the island, no street or tunnel names, and no house or apartment numbering system. Since the island was mobile, even directions were hard to give. Designations like East, North, and South were meaningless. To make matters worse, few tunnels were straight. Dug over the centuries, they met each other at odd angles, most of them curved, and they were as apt to slant up or down as they were to go left or right. Some tunnels managed to do all four. Everybody on the island except us had lived there all their lives and already knew where everything was.

"Simply follow this tunnel until it comes to a split. Take the left-hand branch. When it comes to a crossing, turn left, and you are three steps from your doorway," Judah said.

"That's easy enough, but how do we get there in the dark? My penlight won't last forever," Adam said.

"The manager will sell you a lantern. The taverns all have them for sale."

Adam stepped back in and came out with something similar to a Japanese paper lantern on a long, thin bamboo stick. We bid our guide good night and headed out on our way.

"That didn't feel right," Adam said.

"What didn't feel right?"

"The way our guide took off. That innkeeper knew something we don't, too. Something's wrong."

"It's late and he's been drinking. Probably, he was just in a hurry to get home to his girl. A lot of us are," I said.

Adam was shifting his glance, trying to cover both directions of the long dark tunnel. "I'm serious, Treet. Keep your eyes open."

"You're getting paranoid. Anyway, there's nothing to see," I said, looking often over my shoulder. I like to argue with Adam, but I'm smart enough to take his advice.

"Look, you didn't grow up in the slums of Detroit the way I did."

"I thought you grew up in Hamtramck."

"I lived in Hamtramck. I grew up two blocks away, in Detroit, if you get my meaning. On the streets, you get a kind of feeling about when trouble is coming."

"Maybe I wasn't raised in Detroit, but everybody has trouble growing up."

Maybe Bay City was a lot less violent than Detroit, but I grew up as the only Oriental kid in my class, and I was always much smaller than the rest of the guys, besides. After being pounded a few times by the local hoodlums, I suppose that I overcompensated the way any other boy would. With the shining example of those Bruce Lee movies they were showing back then, I studied the martial arts all through high school under a Korean Tae Kwan Do master. After a while, the bullies learned to stay away from me.

Just after my high-school graduation, my problems with religion in general and the Catholic Church in particular came to a head. I had a row with my parents that got me thoroughly disowned. I was out on the street and absolutely penniless. Karate really came in handy then. Teaching it paid for most of my college expenses.

After I got my sheepskin, I grew up some, and have never needed to resort to violence since. I had been twenty years without even seeing a fight, let alone having to get involved in one.

Until that night with Adam in the tunnel.

I first noticed that something was definitely wrong when somebody hit me in the back of the head with a club.

I went flying down on my knees and elbows, but fighting is a lot like riding a bicycle. Once you learn, your head might forget how it's done, but your body remembers just exactly what to do. I slapped the ground, yelled, and came up on the bounce, smashing someone's testicles in the process.

A whole platoon of thugs was pouring out of a small doorway in the side of the tunnel. I caught a flash of Adam propping his lantern against the tunnel wall with one hand while swinging with the other, and then there were other things to do. It seemed like I was surrounded by dozens of the bastards!

In the movies, the hero can take on vast numbers of bad guys because the stunt men have the courtesy to come at him one at a time. That way, he only has to fight one opponent at a time, ten times in a row. If your enemies have any brains and coordination at all, they will mob you, all of them at once, and then you will go down, no matter how good you are. At best, you might take out one or two before you are deleted.

My opponents seemed to have neither brains nor coordination, but they did have enthusiasm, and there were an awful lot of them. Also, even waiting in line takes a certain amount of coordination, and for these idiots, fighting seemed to be a series of random events. Once, apparently by accident, four of them came at me at once, and I had to drop and roll. Fortunately, they weren't bright enough to know what to do to me once I was down. I was up again in a hurry, and dancing around.

I swear that there were at least fifteen of them on me alone. Against odds like that, you fight to win, without thinking about the damage, jail time, or lawsuits you might be generating. The places you go for are right down the center, the weak "seam" where the two halves of the body seem to join together. Eyes, noses, throats, solar plexi, guts and testicles. That and the knees, and I've always been partial to knees. Knees are low and easy to get to without the flashy, dangerous, high kicks that some of the other good targets require. Also, knees break easily, they put your opponent down fast, and barring modern surgery, they generally don't heal properly for years, if they heal at all.

I guess I broke a lot of knees that night. Six or eight, at least. In a while, the still-vertical portion of the crowd had thinned out quite a bit, and it was actually starting to get fun when a shot rang out loud in the stone corridor, and everything stopped.

"Figure it out, you bastards! I got five shots left and there are eight of you!" Adam said with a gun in his hand and blood running down his face. "All you need are five heroes who want to die, and the rest of you can get me! Okay! Step right up! What? No heroes? Okay, I'll pick 'em myself. How 'bout you, ugly? Want to impress your girlfriend with your heroic dead body?"

As Adam pointed the pistol at him, the fellow who had been singled out froze, then broke and ran. That started the the rest of our playmates running for home, limping, bleeding, and dragging some of their friends behind. In a few moments we were alone, except for nine would-be muggers who were out cold on the floor. A few of them were groaning a bit, but none of them looked ready to get up.

Especially the one with the bullet hole through his throat.

"You okay, Treet?" Adam said, leaning wearily against the wall.

"A bump on the back of the head and a few bruises, but I'll live. Your face is bleeding."

"Face wounds bleed a lot, but they heal fast, too. See if you can get a bandage or a handkerchief or something on it, would you?"

I stepped over a few enemy casualties as I went over to him. I stood on top of one to get a better view of Adam's head. That still left me shorter than Adam, and the cut was near the top of his head. I stepped down, piled two more muggers on top of the first, and then stepped up to the top of the heap. Better.

"I didn't know you were carrying a six-gun," I said as I worked.

The wound was a laceration, a tear in the skin. I

cleaned it a bit with my handkerchief, and Adam handed me his own from his pouch as well.

"I wasn't. That was my penlight."

"Your *penlight*? Then what about the bullet I heard go through that guy's throat?"

"It wasn't exactly a bullet. It was a fifty caliber Gyro-Jet."

"I haven't heard of one of those things in twenty-five years."

"That's when I built one into the bottom of my penlight. Back when I was in high school. It seemed like a good idea at the time. Ouch!"

"Well, hold still. I'm surprised that it did as much damage as it did. I'd always thought of those little rockets as being one of those neat ideas that didn't quite work out. They were too inaccurate to hit anything at a distance and too slow-moving up close to make much of a hole."

I used my handkerchief as a compress and Adam's, which was bigger, to wrap around his head to hold the compress in place.

"Yeah, well, I had some ideas about that. I figured that if I could grip the rocket tight for a while, until it built up some pressure behind it, it would come out of the barrel fast enough to do you some good without giving the gun too much of a kick."

"There, that should do it, at least until we get home. So your idea worked. But I don't see how you could do that with the other five rounds."

"What other five rounds? How much room do you think there is in a penlight? It was a single shot. All that talk about the other shots was just showmanship."

"Adam, if it works, it's sound engineering. Do you need help getting home?"

"Nah, I can walk okay."

"Good. Then how about you helping me?"

I was beginning to realize that I was more bashed up than I had thought.

"All right. I'll carry you if you carry the lantern."

"Deal."

I counted eight of them still on the floor as we limped home. One must have snuck out.

"Treet, I think somebody around here doesn't like us anymore."

"You think that this was a hit of some kind? Bullshit! It was a mugging. Our sin was *hubris*. We deserved worse than we got. We've been strutting around these islands with two-hundred-year's pay in our pouches like a couple of oil-fed Arab assholes. With that kind of money on us, we were sure to get mugged. Maybe most of the people here are peaceful, but every place in the world has an underworld, and you know it!"

"Bullshit right back at you. Those guys weren't thugs. Their clothes were too clean, and they didn't have any calluses on their hands. They were students or office workers or some such. What's more, they didn't know jack shit about fighting, or a couple of old farts like us couldn't have taken out so many of them like that."

"Maybe you're right. They could have been young priests or something. Anyway, it was kind of fun, towards the end, there. Thugs or not."

"You got some strange ideas about fun, Treet. They had to be part of some kind of a political outfit. The islands don't have an underworld," Adam said, shaking the blood out of his eyes.

"How do you know that?"

"Because nobody in this whole place puts locks on their front doors. They mostly don't even have front doors," Adam said.

"You've got a point there."

"Did you notice that all those guys used clubs, instead of knives or guns like hoods in the States would use?"

"It figures, considering the way everybody here always wears what amounts to bulletproof clothing," I said. "Then there's the fact that I've seen darn few decent knives since I got here, and no firearms but our own."

"Yeah. Just another case of technology modifying human behavior," Adam said as he staggered home.

We got to my place, pushed aside the heavy curtains that did duty for a door, and got through the zigzag hallway that gave some additional privacy before Roxanna caught sight of us.

She stared at the two of us for a second and then screamed, and I mean the full-lunged, movie-heroine-being-eaten-again-by-the-monster, 130 dB ear bone smashing air-raid siren variety of *noise*.

Painful. My ears hurt worse than the rest of me.

Adam's women were still at my place, and they came running. Once assembled, all of them, servants included, promptly went into hysterics right along with Roxanna. You'd think that they'd never seen someone come home bloody before.

I don't know. Maybe they hadn't.

"Roxanna!" I shouted above their noise, "Stop acting like a silly little girl! It doesn't suit you, and anyway, I thought you were made of better stuff than that! Get hold of yourself!"

Adam wearily put me down and we stood there bleeding while they took a few more minutes to calm themselves down. Finally, they managed it, and the decibel level dropped below 110.

"Better," I said. "It's pretty sad when the injured have to tend to the healthy before they can get any help themselves. Now, Roxanna, send someone out for whatever passes for a doctor around here. And send somebody else for the police. I want to report an assault with the intent to murder."

That last statement of mine got them all to screaming again. We continued with our standing and bleeding for a while longer, and I added shaking my head to our repertoire. These people were so admirable in so many ways, but they were just not the sorts you wanted on your team when you had an emergency going on.

Eventually, the same lady doctor who patched us up last time arrived. Adam's head was sewn up, this time with the aid of some novocaine from our first-aid kit, and then she went over both of us, tending to dozens of abrasions, lacerations, and contusions. We were even more bashed up than I had thought.

I got my nose reset, and was given something that was supposed to save the teeth that had loosened up during the ruckus. There was a bump on the back of my head the size of half a grapefruit. It was so big that when I put my hand on it, my fingertips couldn't reach my skull. We both got rubbed down with something that was supposed to help bruises, and towards dawn, we were finally permitted to go to bed.

I had to be led there, since by that time, both of my eyes had swollen shut.

# THIRTY-ONE

Our much-needed rest lasted for about eleven minutes, at which time the duke arrived, with two sleepy guards in tow.

"I'm sorry to have to get you both out of bed, but then your actions have forced me to be up for hours, so I'm probably being more than fair. Now then, we'll have a formal hearing, and quite possibly several full legal trials before this mess is settled, but for now I want to hear your versions of what happened this night."

Adam gave him a straightforward explanation of what had happened, and I confirmed his statement.

"So you say that you were attacked without provocation, you admit to carrying and using concealed firearms, and you admit to leaving dead and wounded men in a public walkway without even attempting to render them any medical assistance?"

"Yes, Your Grace. As to the wounded, well, please remember that we were badly wounded ourselves, and that their friends who had run off had to be close by. We assumed that as soon as we were gone, they would obtain the necessary help," Adam said.

"True enough, to the extent that they got their associates to a medical woman as soon as the two of you had left. That doesn't excuse you from your legal duties, however. But then you don't know your legal obligations here, do you?"

"I suppose not, Your Grace. But please consider that *they* also left the scene without rendering aid to us," Adam said.

"That has already been made self-evident. Well. I think that I can tell you that you needn't worry overmuch about the upcoming trial. Even though you were responsible for at least four deaths, the evidence is pretty clear that you were deliberately attacked. Your other crimes were, at worst, misdemeanors which will probably be payable with fines that you can easily afford."

"Thank you, Your Grace," Adam said. "We are much relieved."

"You may be, but I am not! I am not used to this sort of crime in my domains. I am profoundly embarrassed that my subjects should behave in this manner. It is unconscionable, that nineteen healthy young athletes should, with weapons in their hands, feloniously fall on two middle-aged foreigners who were in poor physical condition, and who had only recently gotten out of their sickbeds after very serious injuries.

"And it is infuriating, that my young athletes should then have the incredible effrontery to lose the bloody bedamned fight! They had four of their number killed outright, and at least nine others crippled or maimed, probably for life, some of whom may yet die!"

"It doesn't say much for your selective-breeding program, does it, Your Grace," Adam said.

"No it doesn't, dammit! In fact, it calls into question the efficacy and morality of over fifteen hundred years of controlled marriages, of which, up until now, we were so proud!

"Don't you realize that our athletes, drawn from a population of only twelve thousand, regularly outperform the records of your Olympic champions?

They do it in track and field, where things are easily measurable. Physically, we are a superior people! And mentally, why, you yourself, Treet, have commented about how intelligent our people are! Yet the two of you made hash out of the best we breed!

"Surely, there is nothing physically outstanding about either of you two. Quite to the contrary, I should say, judging by your appearances. Yet you won when you had no chance of winning! I mean, that gun of yours only killed one man. You smashed all the others, almost ripped them apart, with your bare hands!"

"And feet, Your Grace," Adam said. I heard his bed creak and guessed he was propping himself up. "It's much easier to kill a man with your feet. The big difference is that I grew up in Detroit, and Treet wasn't too far away from there. Your people grew up in what amounts to a safe little small town where nobody ever thought much about fighting."

"Physical condition is only a small part of combat effectiveness," I said from flat on my back. "Knowledge of the warrior's arts is equally necessary, and the most important thing of all is the martial spirit. The killer instinct. The eagerness to kill and the willingness to die."

"The martial spirit? The willingness to die?"

"Yes, Your Grace. The true warrior lives every minute of his life ready to die at that instant, if need be." Between the antipain drugs we'd been given and the glorious high of knowing that we had won a rough fight over impossible odds, I suppose I was getting insufferably pompous. Then again, I was just quoting my old Karate master.

"Hmmm. Would you teach us these arts?"

"Are you really sure that's a good idea, Your Grace?" Adam asked.

"No. No, I'm not."

"Neither am I."

❖     ❖     ❖

A week went by before I felt like moving around and getting busy again, and Adam took four days longer than me to get himself mobile. Somehow, big people always seem to take longer to heal than us little guys do. Maybe it's simply that there is more body tissue on them in need of fixing, or maybe it's that when somebody Adam's size falls down, he falls a lot harder than ordinary people do.

Or maybe Adam just likes being waited on hand and foot by two lovely women.

I split my time between getting the boat fixed, and helping out with the island-scraping project. We only had the one diesel powered compressor, and it did double duty. During evenings and lunchtime, it filled the compressed-air bottles that the two "deep" workers used, the ones who went down to a hundred feet or so, and worked their way up, decompressing as they went.

For use during mornings and afternoons, we had cobbled up a whiffletree of hoses that went to the mouthpieces of the snorkel rigs and, at low pressure, the pump could handle the needs of a dozen men. We didn't have the pressure regulators needed to give each man an independent air supply, so the workers had to stay in a row, and maintain exactly the same depth to breathe. You breathed in turn, rose a bit in order to inhale, and kept your tongue on the pipe at all other times.

The workers got used to it quickly enough, and before long were trading jobs with the SCUBA twins, for fun, the experience, and to even out the risk of the bends. Eventually, we got two complete fourteen-man teams trained, and work went on even on Sundays, once we had the bishop's written permission.

We had some two thousand gallons of diesel fuel on *The Brick Royal*, in four integral fuel tanks built into the ferrocrete hull, enough to keep the compressor going for many months.

The problem was getting it out. With the ship on her side, draining out fuel to serve the compressor and occasionally the genset was not a simple task. We spilled a fair amount of the smelly stuff on the floor of the warehouse until we worked out a safe way to do it. Once we had the fuel out of one of the big tanks we were forced to store most of what we had removed in plastic containers. Not what an American Fire Safety Board would approve of, but like the song goes, it's what you do with what you got that counts. Anyway, we figured that diesel fuel has a fairly high flash point, and that the risk of fire wasn't all that great.

With the ship itself, we had the damage cut away, and the metal reinforcement sewn in by the time Adam was up and about. I had held off with doing the concrete replacement work myself, since Adam had supervised the original construction and, for the most part, I hadn't even been there. I'd been out playing salesman, and it's always best to put the most experienced man in charge. It was just as well that I'd waited for him, since, as it turns out, I would have screwed it up if I had started out alone.

It seems that new concrete doesn't stick at all well to old concrete, but not to worry. Adam had brought along a can of incredibly expensive epoxy that was guaranteed to glue old concrete to wet cement. Now, the very thought of gluing something to a semiliquid like wet cement confused me, to say the very least. How can you glue a solid to a liquid?

Hell, how can anyone possibly glue *anything* to a liquid?

When I start hearing something like that, all of my "bullshit" indicators let loose. Inside my head, the lights start flashing, the fireworks go off, and the little American flags come out from the back of the machine and start waving.

"Naw," I said. "Absolutely no way possible."

"You're just not thinking about it right," Adam said. "A liquid is a liquid because the molecules in it don't stick to each other in a permanent way, they just sort of slide around, right? In a setting liquid, like concrete or epoxy, the molecules attach themselves to each other either chemically or mechanically or both. The molecules of this particular epoxy can attach themselves to the molecules of both wet concrete and hardened concrete. What's so hard to believe about that?"

"Somehow, it just doesn't ring right."

"It's the truth," Adam said. "I have it on the advice of four—count 'em, four—separate, independent experts that this stuff works, and that it's well worth the ridiculous price you incidentally paid for it."

"I paid for it? I don't remember any such thing on any bill of materials."

"Of course not. Who could possibly remember the technical, chemical name of any complex epoxy? Some of those words run to maybe forty, fifty letters. It's easier to remember the names of some of those ancient Mexican gods. I just slipped it in with some of the paints and lubricants we also needed for the boat, and you signed it."

"Adam, you shouldn't do that sort of thing to your boss."

"Yeah, but I'm your partner now. Don't it make you feel glad?"

"I'll feel gladder if the stuff actually works. Have you ever used it before?"

"Nope. But then I never had to fix a broken concrete boat before, either. Relax, Treet. Uncle Adam will make it all better."

The actual cementing was done in a day, and then Adam got busy with the rest of the boat. The engine had to be drained, flushed out, and cleaned, and everything that salt water had touched had to be inspected, thoroughly cleaned and often repaired. We

planned to convert *The Brick Royal* from a rather
spacious motor sailer to a tiny cargo ship of the same
size, and that involved removing a lot of furniture,
bulkheads, and decking inside.

I let Adam handle it while I set about getting our
cargo together. The most exciting product the Westronese had was their high-strength fiber, Super-Hemp,
we'd decided to call it. I'd hoped to be able to buy
a few tons of the stuff, but no such luck. The clothing, fishnets, and other fabrics made from Super-Hemp
were so indestructible that very little replacement was
required. This meant that very little hemp needed to
be grown, and so very little of it was on the market. Even less than usual, since a lot of it had been
bought up to make Adam's drift net.

I ended up touring every market square on the
Islands, offering twice the going price, and still coming
home with only a few hundred pounds of the stuff.
Then I went out buying finished thread, finished cloth,
and was eventually reduced to buying used clothing
before I had enough to fill the smallest forward hold
in *The Brick Royal*.

I got home one day to find that a delivery had been
made to me there rather than to the warehouse, probably by mistake. The chief gardener, Master Maimonides ibn Tibbon, had come through on his
promise of samples of all the other products that we'd
agreed might have some commercial value in the
outside world.

There were three crates of the stuff, each product
in its own numbered envelope or cloth bag. Four
handwritten books came with them, describing each
product in English, telling how it was used, and what
the approximate costs of production were. Judging
from the different handwritings involved, at least
twenty different experts had been involved in preparing the notes on the various sorts of vegetable products. It was a remarkable effort, and showed that they

were giving us all the support they could. Somebody out there didn't like us, and it was good to know that we had some friends as well.

In return, we gave Maimonides some one thousand nine hundred pounds of various kinds of plant seeds, mostly peas and beans, everything we had that was growable from Adam's emergency food supplies. Each side went away convinced that they had come out far ahead of the other side. To put it another way, a good deal was had by all.

# THIRTY-TWO

One of the duke's couriers came by and delivered a formal proclamation concerning the upcoming court case of those people who had attacked us. Since neither Adam nor I had as yet any command of written Westronese, we had Roxanna read it to the group.

It seems that for some unexplained reason, there wasn't going to be any trial. It seems that those men who had been killed while attacking us were now dead, and thus were outside the duke's jurisdiction. Those of our opponents who had survived were sufficiently maimed and crippled that additional punishment was deemed unnecessary. Indeed, they had already been punished far worse than the law would normally allow. No mention was made of the six attackers who were not seriously injured.

The crimes that Adam and I had committed, carrying and using a concealed weapon, and the failure to give aid to the wounded, would be fined at the rate of two pounds of silver each, but since we had already gifted the crown by this amount, the debt would be considered paid.

"It looks like a standard coverup job," I said. "Everything is left just where it stands, and the courts put their stamp on it."

"Yeah. That business of fining us an amount equal

to the amount we'd already given says something, though," Adam said.

"Like what?"

"The duke is letting us off, but he's saying that he doesn't owe us any more favors."

"Wonderful. A score of hoodlums tries to kill us, and we're supposed to be grateful for being let off. Not that the same sort of horseshit hasn't happened often enough in the States. Anyway, we gave the duke a lot more than just the four pounds of silver," I said. "He got a couple of pounds of gold, and three or four big boxes of other things."

"Around here, silver is money. The gold and the rest of that stuff isn't. People think differently about social gifts as opposed to money. Gifts are friendly. Money is serious."

Roxanna had followed our conversation in English fairly well. She was picking up my language far faster than I had learned Westronese. In a mixture of broken English expanded with Westronese where necessary, she explained her views on the subject, which were that the duke was a fine man, and that by eliminating the trial, and thus not wasting our valuable time, he was doing us a great favor.

The Pelitier sisters agreed with her completely, saying that we should be thankful to the duke for the courtesies shown us.

Roxanna was a fine and intelligent person in many ways, and Adam's ladies were stamped from the same cookie cutter, but they all were incredibly naive. They'd never heard of power politics, or of the innate sneakiness of governments in general. The duke might be a fine man personally, but as soon as he acted as a head of state, he naturally became a conniving bastard. It had to be that way, if he was going to continue being the man in charge. Wimps don't last long in this world, unless they are content to live near the bottom of the pecking order.

"Eliminating the trial does something definite for the local powers-that-be," I said. "Officially, it renders mute the question of just who attacked us, and far more importantly, *why* they did it. I mean, just what is their bitch against us? Is it open to discussion? Or negotiation? Do we have something that they want? I'm not talking about the individuals involved, since I don't much care who they are. We gave them a licking that they won't forget, and they're not likely to try the same thing again. What I would like to know for sure is just what *organization* wanted us to be damaged or dead. I mean, I'm pretty sure it's some of the archbishop's boys, but I'd like to really *know*."

"There's no possible way that the archbishop could be behind it, Treet. You've never met the man," Adam said. "But, yeah, I would truly like to know who it is that has it in for us. More importantly, are whoever they are still out to get us, and what are they going to try next time? I'm beginning to wish that we hadn't donated my arsenal to the duke for his royal safekeeping. I wish we had those guns still hidden in the bottom of the boat."

"I'm starting to feel the same way. The problem is that if you're right about the need for protection, we won't get the guns back no matter what we do. And if you're wrong, and we don't need the damned things, we can probably have them returned to us anytime."

The women were shocked at our words and thoughts, that we could say that someone as noble as the duke would actually try to protect some criminal element within his realm, or that any of the great organizations of their islands could conceivably stoop to violence to attain their ends.

Adam and I looked at them, looked at each other, and shook our heads. There was nothing that we could say. We'd known all along that we'd come from a totally different world than they did.

We loved these island women, but we were both beginning to develop a lot more respect for the sort of American woman who can stand up to adversity, and who can think things out for herself!

We tried to find those attackers who had survived the encounter, just to talk to them, but no luck. The medical people said that they never kept such records, and had forgotten who they had worked on.

When we applied to the keeper of the royal arsenal for the return of our weapons, we were told that citizens were not permitted to have offensive weapons in their possession. When we objected that we weren't citizens, we were told that foreigners weren't allowed them, either.

The duke and his noble subordinates couldn't quite find the time to see us. The press of important business, we were told.

There was a local baron who functioned like a neighborhood cop. We went to see him and explained our problem. He said that he was sure that there could be no possible repeat of the fighting incident, since violence was so rare on the islands. In any event, the duke had taken the matter into his own hands, and thus it was no longer the concern of the baron.

The islands had nothing like a press corps. There were no muckraking reporters who knew how to dig into a story and get the facts out. All they had were some bulletin boards. We put up a series of posters, eventually offering very considerable awards for information, but we got no takers.

The owner of the men's club acted very glad to see us, and eagerly got every detail of the fight from us, but he steadfastly claimed to have no knowledge of our assailants. The girls there were of no help, either, even when we offered to make anyone who helped us rich.

Judah ben Salomon was missing. He hadn't been seen since the night of the fight.

There was no such thing as a lawyer on the Western Islands. When I first learned this fact, months before, I'd claimed that it proved that these people were totally civilized. Now that I wanted to sue somebody, my opinions were a lot different.

Adam tried to see the archbishop, but was unable to get an appointment.

I was able to see the warlock, but he maintained that he was as mystified by the situation as we were.

Even the priest who was still giving Adam lessons in the local religion couldn't or wouldn't answer his questions about who our adversaries were, or why they were out to do us damage. After a while, Adam stopped going to the classes.

"There is only one way that a blanket of silence this thick can be held down this tight," I told Adam one night. "It has to be all three of the high muckety-mucks working together."

"Yah. I'll be a whole lot happier when we get *The Brick Royal* in the water."

"Me, too. I think I'll start lending you a hand, tomorrow morning."

A week later, in the short grey dawn of the tropics, we were all awakened by shouts of "FIRE!"

I dressed as quickly as possible, but even so, I was the last one out of the house and into the hallway. Buckets in hand, hundreds of people were streaming by, so I followed along with the hurrying crowd. The people here all had various civic duties to perform when an emergency occurred, and helping to fight a fire was one of them. I didn't have a bucket, and I wasn't sure where one was stored, but everyone on the island took their duties very seriously. I dared not appear to be a shirking coward because of going back to the house and searching for a fire bucket.

One wouldn't have thought that a fire would be a great danger on the Western Isles, since the houses, hallways, and businesses were all carved out of the living rock, and thus should be fireproof. The furnishings were spare, and normally kept too far apart for a flame to propagate between them. All that I could imagine was that a warehouse somewhere was going up, and, most unfortunately, I turned out to be right.

In a few minutes, I got to a place where I could smell smoke, and I realized that the all-too-familiar smell was that of burning fuel oil. Suddenly, I knew that *The Brick Royal* was burning, and all our property, all our plans, and all our hopes were burning with her.

A bucket brigade was already set up, and sea water was already being energetically thrown on the blaze. The people were remarkably efficient, except that what they were doing was exactly the wrong thing to do with an oil fire!

Adam was already on the scene, and trying to take over command from the local equivalent of a fire chief. Nobody would listen to him, or to us, when I added my shouts to Adam's. The Westronese volunteers with the buckets were all well trained for the emergency, and they didn't need any damn foreigners trying to interfere with their noble rescue efforts.

Volunteer rescue people are like that everywhere. They train and train, working long, hard, and thankless hours, all in the hopes of one day being in the position of doing something heroic, something meaningful, something that can justify their otherwise humdrum lives. When that once in a lifetime chance finally comes, they are not about to waste it just because somebody they never met before is shouting at them. They want the shouter to get out of the way so that they can continue being heroic.

Adam went on trying to explain to them the dangers

of throwing water on an oil fire, but I knew that it was hopeless. In calmer times, they would be glad to hear from him about the three classes of fires, and what to do about each of them, but not now.

I sadly shook my head and walked away. I went to a place where I could see inside the mouth of the warehouse-cave that we had rented months ago.

Everything was burning. The boat. The electronic equipment. The life raft with all its emergency stuff. The cargo that I had been purchasing. It obviously could be nothing but a total loss. I could see fuel oil spilling in flames out of the ruptured tanks in the hull, running on the floor, and being spread further by the water that the fools were throwing at it.

I saw the cathode ray tube in the old-style television implode, blowing shattered glass and burning plastic around the huge room, and out on the people who were still throwing in buckets of water. Cans and jars of food were exploding as well, with some pickles quenching a bit of the fire, and the ubiquitous cans of Spam adding their grease to the flames.

As things got hotter, I saw bits of cement crumble and fall from the glowing steel ribs of our once-magnificent ship. It was gone.

It was all gone, and there was no hope left for us at all. I sat down on the ground, with my arms on my knees and my head on my arms, and I cried.


Later that day, as Adam and I were going through the mess, seeing what, if anything, there was that could be salvaged, the warlock came by.

"I was devastated to hear about all this," he said. "I came as soon as I could. Can you save anything?"

"Not much," I said. "The gold and silver coins were in fireproof strongboxes, but just about everything else is gone. Great, huh? The only things that couldn't be hurt by the fire were the only things protected from it."

"The air compressor was out on the shore near the SCUBA equipment and the snorkeling stuff, so it's okay, but there isn't enough diesel fuel left out there to run the compressor for more than a day or two. I'm afraid that we won't be able to stop your island from sinking after all," Adam said.

"Couldn't we operate the compressor manually?" the warlock asked. "Or better still, we've still got those solar cells of yours, and that windcharger you two set up for us. Perhaps we could run it electrically."

"Maybe," Adam said. "But we don't have any batteries anymore, and we don't have an electric motor left of any description, let alone one big enough. That diesel engine on the compressor may not look like much, but it puts out five brake horsepower. A fit human being can put out maybe a tenth of a horsepower on a continuous basis. Do you see a way to connect fifty people to the shaft of the compressor? Well, I don't, not with what we have available."

"What about the windcharger, mate?"

"That thing might be able to generate one horsepower, if the wind is perfect," I said.

"But you two are so resourceful, I'm sure that you could come up with something."

"There's a certain problem of motivation," Adam said. "This fire didn't just happen, you know. The lighting here was electric, and there weren't any open flames. Even if something started leaking by itself, diesel fuel isn't that easy to start on fire. It's fairly safe stuff, and that's the main reason why we powered the boat with a diesel engine, rather than with a smaller and lighter-weight gasoline motor."

"What Adam's saying is that somebody on this island started the fire, deliberately. I'd be convinced of it even if we hadn't been assaulted a few weeks ago, but now the pattern is all too clear. Somebody here doesn't want us around."

"Yeah," Adam said. "First they tried to kill us, and

now they've burned almost everything we had. Now, I've got a question for you, Mister Warlock. One of your men was supposed to have been on guard here last night. We were paying for three guards to be on duty at all times, following the same pattern that you people set up when we first got here. One from the church, one from the duke, and one from you wizards. Now we can't find any of the guys who were supposed to be here. Somehow, they are all gone, and there weren't any dead bodies in the ashes."

"Surely, you're not suggesting that *I* had anything to do with these problems that you've been having!"

"It was one of your people, Judah ben Salomon, who set us up for the beating we got a few weeks ago," I said. "And nobody seems to have seen anything of *him* since."

"And we're not *suggesting* anything," Adam said. "We're *saying* that this is one tightly controlled little island, and if anything major is going down out here, it's being done by you or the duke."

"Or more likely yet, by the archbishop," I added.

"But can't you understand?" The warlock said, "I'm your friend! I'm on your side. I'm one of the good guys!"

"Then why aren't you doing something about stopping the bad guys?" I asked.

I didn't get an answer.

# THIRTY-THREE

*"So, Brother Bartholomew, is all in readiness?" the arch-bishop said.*

*"If you mean, have I done your dirty deed, the answer is yes, Your Excellency."*

*"Good, good, my son. Consider that on this occasion, all you have done is to have some of the outsiders' stolen property returned to them. If your soul still troubles you, go to confession when you are done here. Only, please go to the cathedral confessor, rather than the one in your order."*

*"So that word of your deeds will not be bandied about the church? And if you must make me kill, why must you make me kill in such a long, drawn out, and painful manner?"*

*"Because it will be better if the deed takes place off our island. Bartholomew, you are becoming rude, undisciplined, and impertinent! Any more of that and you will be in line for some serious disciplining, boy! Now, be off with you!"*

It was grey dawn again, twenty-four hours after the fire that killed *The Brick Royal*. Our ladies were lined up on the shore of the island, surrounded by their servants and employees, all of them looking tired. Getting ready to go had cost us all a night's sleep.

The small sails of *The Concrete Canoe* were drawing well, and Adam and I were at sea once more.

We weren't exactly running away between two days, but early dawn was close enough. We were waving good-bye to our women on shore. All three of them had wanted to come with us, but that was plainly impossible. For one thing, there wasn't much room on *The Concrete Canoe*, and most of what there was was taken up by food, three barrels of water, and the three crates of agricultural oddities that the chief gardener had given us. For another, well, they were all good, warm, and tolerant women. They were intelligent, learned, and competent. They were beautiful, loving, and sexy. But they weren't *tough* women, and we had one hell of a tough trip ahead of us.

Because of good luck and absentmindedness, I had never gotten around to having the agricultural crates sent down to our warehouse, and thus they were saved from the disastrous fire. We'd managed to scrounge up a few pounds of Super-Hemp thread, and along with several changes of clothing and the strong nets that our fishermen had used; well, it would have to do. The huge drift net that Adam had ordered months before wouldn't be done for weeks, and had to be left behind. Making a fuss and taking delivery before it was completed might have tipped our hand.

We were bugging out, and neither of us liked it. It isn't easy to leave a fight unfought, and it isn't easy to leave a woman you love behind, but it had to be done, so we were doing it.

Whoever the bastards were, they had tried to kill us, but they had failed, and they hadn't stopped us from going ahead with our plans. Then they tried arson, and while that had worked all too well, they still hadn't stopped us, although they sure had slowed us down. We were worried that their next attempt

would have something to do with our ladies, a
kidnaping attempt or some such, and we couldn't let
that happen. Our women were just too fragile, too
naive, and too trusting of their world. Being exposed
to reality's raw side would be a soul-shattering experience for them.

We could see no practical way to guard and protect our ladies, not while we were there on the
Western Islands, and the targets of some unknown
organization's hate. We were vastly outnumbered, and
while they knew who and where we were, we knew
absolutely nothing about them.

However, without us, the girls should be perfectly
safe. We ourselves had to be the threat that the bad
guys were reacting against. Nobody would have any
reason to touch our ladies once we were gone. Still,
just to be on the safe side, we had retained the
services of the fishermen and of Adam's porters, we
had paid them each three years in advance, and we
had made them each swear to defend Roxanna and
the Pelitier sisters with their lives.

We'd left all the silver we had with the girls, which
was enough to make them independently wealthy for
life, even though it really wasn't worth much to the
two of us out in the real world. The gold we took
back with us, since we'd need it in the weeks to
come. Depending on the market, it was worth something like a hundred seventy-five thousand dollars,
money that we'd need to prepare the way for our
return.

Because we most definitely intended to return, even
if we did have to sail across the Pacific Ocean in a
twenty-foot open boat.

Once, before the fire, we'd owned a complete set
of navigational charts, showing every square foot of
salt water in the world. What with our electronic gear,
we'd never used anything so crude as paper charts,
except a few times to show people where we'd been

and where we were going. Now that we really needed them, they were gone. Murphy's Law still rules.

Our electronic navigation gear was gone, along with all of the radios, telephones, and faxes. We had no sonar, no radar, and no satellite weather hookups. Hell, we didn't even have running lights!

We lacked even a pocket calculator, and the sole bit of electronics available to us was my wristwatch. Adam had lost his in the fire. We had debated fastening my watch to the binnacle, but we finally decided that leaving it on my wrist would keep its temperature more stable, and thus help maintain its accuracy. We did have a compass, mounted on the binnacle, and Adam's antique brass sextant had survived the fire, though its mirrors were a bit scorched. Most importantly, the one man on the island that we were sure that we could trust, the chief gardener, Master Maimonides ibn Tibbon, had managed to obtain a Westronese ocean navigational chart for us, and he was able to give us a fix on our position. Thus, we knew where we were, and from that, we could figure out how to get to where we wanted to be.

Or perhaps I should say, we thought we knew where we were. The Western Islands drifted around one of the loneliest areas in all of the oceans, not too far from the equator and a few thousand miles west of South America. Get a globe, find the place where the manufacturer has chosen to put his company logo, and you're likely to be near the spot where the Western Isles are.

Not that we had a globe. We had a strange, handdrawn chart. The Westronese did not use degrees North and South for latitude, or East and West for longitude. They used hours west of a reference point (the original location of the islands off the coast of France), for longitude. If noon at your present location happened eleven and a half hours later than noon happened at the original location of the Western Isles, then your longitude was eleven and a half hours.

The distance from the North Pole to the South Pole was divided into twelve latitude hours, which were just a tiny bit shorter than the hours of longitude. This difference in length was due to the way that the spin of the Earth bulges the equator and flattens out the Earth at the poles, changing it from a perfect sphere into an oblate spheroid. Theirs was as rational a system as any, I suppose, except for the way that their fixed reference point no longer existed.

In medieval fashion, the world map that we were given had East at the top, at zero hours, and Europe at the bottom. What wasn't medieval was that the rest of the world was now charted out in between.

The North Pole was stretched out to a vertical line on the left, while the South Pole was another line to the right. Their arrangement greatly distorted the areas around the poles, but then the Westronese never went near the Arctic or the Antarctic, so to them it didn't matter. Theirs was a very pragmatic technology, with little foundation in the way of theoretical science. For the tropical waters that they were interested in, their maps were more than adequate.

Their system put the latitude numbers across the top of the sheet, going from zero to twelve hours, left to right, and the longitude, going from zero to twenty-four, top to bottom. Which, I suppose, seemed normal enough to them. To us, it was turned sideways. Furthermore, it was written in Westronese, and the spelling and phonic value of the letters in Westronese are at least as random as they are in English.

Another peculiarity of the map, to our eyes, anyway, was that the land masses were almost blank, while the oceans were thoroughly charted. The notations on ocean currents were particularly extensive. Still, we knew vaguely where we were, and once we turned the map sideways, the coastlines of North and South America were easily recognizable.

When we started doing the math to translate the Westronese system into something that we could think in, we discovered that we did not have a single writing instrument aboard. Not a pen, not a pencil, not a piece of burned stick. Not an auspicious beginning.

"Well, we left in an awful hurry," Adam said. "I just wonder what else we forgot to remember."

Still, we were engineers, and nobody gets good with machinery without having a good sense of visualization. We sat down and worked it out in our heads. After a few hours, we both actually managed to come up with the same answers.

"About twenty-two hundred miles west of the Galapagos Islands, and about three hundred north of the Equator," I said.

"Yeah. That puts us just about due south of San Diego," Adam said, "but I don't think that we should try for it. It's too far away. Actually, the islands of French Polynesia are our closest landfall, but we're in the Equatorial Counter Current, and getting there might be rough."

"Not to mention the problems of hitting a small island in a big ocean. I don't have that much faith in our navigation. The same argument holds for trying for the Galapagos Islands."

"Nah, I could do it. I can come to within a couple of minutes of the right latitude easy enough with the sextant, and then we could just drive along that line of latitude until we got there. You can watch for land birds, too, and the skies above an island are supposed to look greener than those above the ocean."

"You've got to be pulling my leg. You don't know a land bird from a penguin, and the only green thing I'm likely to see will be your throat if the weather gets rough."

"You have very little faith, Treet."

"I have none at all, as you've often noted. No, we have to make for the nearest large body of dirt we can find, namely the coast of Mexico, and our course is due northeast. That keeps everything easy."

"Or as easy as a twenty-three hundred mile long trip in an open boat is likely to be."

I said, "At our best speed, say maybe three miles an hour in this tubby boat with its little sails, we might be able to do that in a month or so. We've got all of five weeks worth of supplies aboard, so what's to worry about? Have faith, my friend. Trust in God."

Adam was looking for something that he could throw at me, something that we could afford to lose. He couldn't find anything in that category, and eventually he gave up on it.

A little before noon by my watch, I handed Adam his sextant, and we went through the drill of shooting a noon sighting.

After twenty minutes of fiddling with the ancient contraption, and another hour of doing arithmetic in our heads, we decided that our latitude seemed to be about right, from what we remembered of what the sun should be doing at this time of the year. We could check it with greater accuracy at night, assuming that we could find the North Star.

The big problem was with the longitude. After much mental juggling with numbers, we came to the annoying conclusion that either we had been given a longitude reading that was four hundred seventy-one miles off, or that my wristwatch was wrong by twenty-seven minutes, or that our math was screwed up something fierce. We both did the math all over again, and we both came up with the same bad answer.

"Screw it!" I finally said. "It doesn't really matter

where we actually are! Knowing precisely where we
are won't change our actual arrival time one bit. If
we just keep going northeast, we'll hit land eventually."

"Yeah, but will we still both be reasonably alive
when we hit it?"

"If we're going to die, do you really want to know
about it in advance?"

"Yes, actually, I certainly do. I, at least, have a soul,
and it would be nice to have the time to get it in
order," Adam said.

Adam seemed to prefer conning the boat, and since
it didn't make much difference to me, I let him do
it. I was content to trim the jib, bail the bilge, and
break out stores as required. I took over and manned
the tiller when Adam got sleepy, but that didn't
happen in the first three days. Neither of us could
sleep for the first seventy-two hours, what with the
way a small boat bounces around on the Pacific
ocean.

Even when the weather is nice.

# THIRTY-FOUR

"There are some dark clouds there on the horizon," I said.

"I saw 'em. More important is the fact that they are to windward. Not that we can do anything about it. Everything that can be tied down already is, and we can take the mast down in a few minutes if we have to. So take the Chinaman's advice, and relax."

"Right. You know, Adam, I've been thinking about something you said once on the island, about how it didn't matter if you called something magic or technology. I think you were wrong."

"Three days in the sun is getting to your brain. You should put your hat on."

"I don't need one. Unlike certain others, I still have all my hair. I meant what I said. Technology is something that you understand, or at least something that you *could* understand if you wanted to spend the time studying it. Magic is something that is inherently not understandable, but works on rules of its own. It is a phony alternative to the laws of physics."

"If you want to define your terms that way, fine. I can't see where it makes any difference. We form concepts as a first step in comprehending the varied universe around us. Names are merely the arbitrary labels we put on those concepts, handles that make for easy carrying. As long as we agree on which concept is attached to which label, we can communicate with each other. It doesn't matter if the label is pink or blue."

"But it does make a difference. A big one. All the horse shit going around about politically correct speech is happening because the annoying people pushing it believe in magic."

"Bullshit."

"I'm serious. One of the big rules of magic is that anything may be substituted for its symbol. If you want to manipulate something or someone, you make or get a symbol for that thing or person, and then you manipulate the symbol. You'll find the same rule in European Witchcraft, African Voodoo, and even in the various forms of American Indian, India Indian, and Oriental magic."

"So? All that proves is that crazy people think alike. Or, if you want to state it in a politically correct fashion, it undeniably substantiates the postulation that certain mental aberrations tend to be predominately species specific rather than being substantially culturally engendered. Not that that's a particularly politically correct thought. The people biggest on political correctness are the schoolteachers who want politicians to pay them to make the world bright, beautiful, and suitably respectful of schoolteachers and politicians. Therefore, people of all flavors have to be amenable to education, indoctrination, and persuasion. Strange ideas like inherited intelligence and innate ability must therefore be condemned as basically wrong, if not downright evil."

"You figured all that out for yourself, eh? That might be *why* certain feeders from the public trough push political correctness, but not why it is there in the first place," I said.

Adam moved us a half point farther off the wind, and said, "Personally, I think that political correctness

has a lot to do with the art of memorizing meaningless or at least inane phrases so as to keep your
lungs and vocal cords in operation while your dis-
engaged brain tries to think its way out of the dumb
shit question that some pushy person with a micro-
phone just asked you, hopefully while offending as
few *politically active* people as possible. In American
politics, of course, people who are not politically active
simply don't count, and the only important point for
a politician is to not offend inactive people enough
to make them active for the other side.

"Political correctness is a mixture of mental judo,
verbose blandness, and yoga, and is very useful for
politicians who are trying to convince the voters that
they are the least obnoxious of the various assholes
currently running for office."

"Adam, you are becoming a lot more wordy than
you used to be. You're swearing more, too."

"Current circumstances have deprived me of anything better to do with my time than to spend it on
furthering your sadly neglected education. The minor
profanity simply enhances the descriptive accuracy."

The wind picked up a bit, and Adam adjusted the
rudder and stern sheets, while I decided that the jib
was okay for now.

"The subject of this conversation was magic, not
the speech patterns of assholes," I said. "Now then,
the symbol involved may be a physical object, like
the wax doll used in so many kinds of magic, but
the most powerful symbols we humans use are words.
We communicate in words, we think in words, we
perceive the whole universe filtered through our
words. And the people who believe in magic believe
that if you can change the word, the symbol for a
thing, you can change the thing itself."

"Talk about being wordy . . ."

"Take a neutral example, a group of people that
nobody hates, like handicapped kids. Sometimes,

because of some chemical screwup in a kid's DNA, or something going wrong while the fetus was in the womb, a kid is born wrong. It's usually nobody's fault, and certainly the kid didn't do anything wrong, but there it is. And in a lot of cases, there isn't anything we can do about it. Someday, maybe, the medical types will learn enough about the process and we can fix it. Or maybe not. We all feel bad about it, but what to do? The politically correct have an answer. They say that if we can't fix the kid, we can at least try to make him happy, and the place to start is to be less rude about what we call him. We won't call him 'handicapped' any more. We'll call him 'special,' and that will make it all better. In one swell foop, the whole problem of handicapped children is solved, and we don't have any of them to worry about any more.

"Of course, we now have a problem with all these 'special' kids hanging around, but we can forget about that since nobody will start an Association for the Advancement of Special Kids for a while. If sometime later somebody does get bitchy about it, we can always solve the problem again by calling the little gimps 'challenged.' The fact that the kids involved still can't play like the other children doesn't bother them, but the kids themselves are not that stupid. What they know is that 'special' is now just another word for 'handicapped,' and nothing else has changed. What the kid never knew was that 'handicapped' started out as a politically correct word for 'crippled,' and 'crippled' was once the politically correct way of saying 'gimpy.'

"I could give you dozens of examples of how these people are trying to make things go away by changing the symbols we use on them. Leman. Whore. Prostitute. Lady of the Night. Hooker. Each word was supposed to correct the problem, and if you didn't use the currently correct term, you were not only inhumane and insensitive, you were downright nasty and wicked. However, the change in wording hasn't eliminated the problem of women selling sex on a short-term basis, and those women who sell it on a long-term basis, called wives, are still horribly offended by the ladies who are still taking it in lying down. But don't give up hope, since I have no doubt that they'll be coming up with another new word soon."

"Working girl."

"Eh?"

"Working girl. That's the new word for hooker. The good General Hooker's descendants can now rest easier, because of the kind ministrations of the politically correct," Adam said.

"Thank you. As I was saying. Moor. Blackamoor. Nigger. Negro. Colored. Black. Afro-American. It's the same story again exactly. What should be perfectly obvious is that reality is not about to change just because we changed the symbols we used on it."

"I think I see what you mean," Adam said. "Like the only way that you can get a dinosaur to move is to get another dinosaur to kick it. But don't badmouth these word switchers too much, Treet. Think about it. The entire United States Army Corps of Engineers worked their balls off for two hundred years, attempting to drain the filthy, disease ridden swamps in the U.S., trying hard to turn them into useful farmland, and they only got about twenty percent of the job done. Then the politically correct came along, and bam! There suddenly isn't a swamp left in the whole country!"

"Yeah, but the mosquitoes are still a nuisance in the 'wetlands,' and malaria is on the rise."

"Details."

"All this playing with word games takes the emphasis off working on the problems themselves. If we spent as much time and energy working on engineering solutions to some of these problems as we do on half-baked social 'solutions,' we'd be a lot better off."

The wind freshened up again, veering a bit more from the south. Adam played with the rudder and the main sheet while I tightened up on the jib.

Adam said, "Most folks don't know how to work on engineering solutions. The people you're bitching about don't know how to do much of anything except walk around with signs designed to attract airtime on the news shows, and free airtime just naturally attracts politicians the way shit attracts flies. The people you hear making all the noise are the people who don't count. It doesn't matter what they do, since all of their time is always wasted anyway. The productive people in this world are already doing all they can. I mean, personally, I don't know of any really good engineers who are out of work. Most of us are working longer hours than we want to. Getting uptight about what the useless people do with their time is just being neurotic. Treet, your problem is that you don't have any sense of humor."

"I don't think malaria is funny, so therefore I don't have a sense of humor. Remarkable."

"Sure. You don't seem to understand that laughter is the normal human reaction to pain. Preferably, someone else's pain, but pain none the less. Think about it. Think about any joke that you thought was funny, and you'll end up with somebody having to endure pain."

I said, "I don't feel like thinking about anything just now."

"Then chew on this for a while. Consider the fact that we human beings are members of the only species on earth that expresses pleasure by exposing our fangs."

The wind came in hard, and for a minute I thought that the back stay would part. It held, and then we were busy furling the sails, taking down the mast, and stowing it all as best we could.

The waves were getting huge, taller than five-story buildings, and every time we went over the top of one it seemed like we were airborne for an inordinate amount of time. I was getting worried about something being thrown out of the boat (like me, for instance) when Adam broke out the boat cover and we both got busy fastening it down. This cover wasn't part of the boat's original equipment, since *The Concrete Canoe* had not been mounted on *The Brick Royal*'s deck, but was rather in its own special, covered compartment. It was something the fishermen, or maybe Roxanna, had seen the need for and had had made. It was made of Super-Hemp, and we were very glad to have it. Once it was on, the boat might be upside down, but at least it would be floating and all in one piece. Having it on meant that we had to crawl around the bottom of the crowded boat in a few inches of water, but I got to bailing again while Adam took the anchor off its rope, replaced it with the fishing net the fishermen had left aboard, and trailed the net and about a hundred yards of the rope off our stern.

"The wind's blowing from the southwest," he shouted. "We're heading in about the right direction, and I figure that a little drag on the stern should keep us pointing in the right direction."

"I bow to your wisdom," I shouted back as I continued bailing.

In a while, I could switch from a bucket to a can, and then to a sponge. Within a quarter of an hour, the interior of the boat was fairly dry, despite the torrential rain and spray coming down hard on the boat cover, inches above our heads.

"We're not getting stuffy in here," Adam said, "but we're staying dry. There must be some kind of semipermeable coating on the boat cover. Do you know anything about it?"

"No, but I have looked on it and I have found it to be good."

"Just another piece of amazing Westronese technology. I hope we have a sample of whatever it is in the crates the chief gardener sent us," Adam said, hunkering down on the floorboards and getting as comfortable as things permitted. "Your last statement was almost biblical. Could it be that this storm is finally leading you to religion?"

"Not a chance. If I've got to die, I'd rather do it as an honest man, not as a wimp groveling on my knees in front of a spook."

Adam just shook his head, unwilling to open up on an argument we'd been through a dozen times.

I said, "I have read the Bible, though, something that you Catholics never do. At least it was something I never did until I quit being a Christian, and then only because I needed all the ammunition that I could get."

"Right," Adam said. "In grade school, I asked a nun, one of my teachers, about the Bible, and she said that I shouldn't read it. She said that it was dirty, so, being basically a good kid, I left it alone."

"Reasonable. It really is a dirty book. Look at what Abraham did to poor Hagar."

"I don't want to hear about them."

The storm showed no signs of lightening up, so I crawled forward, dug out the sleeping bags and air mattresses, and tried to make us as comfortable as possible for the duration.

# THIRTY-FIVE

Three days later, I awoke bleary eyed in what I was sure was early morning. Adam was still asleep. There wasn't anything that we could do except wait for the storm to go away. There hadn't seemed to be much sense in keeping one man awake, on watch, since we had already done what little there was to do. Everything that could be tied down, sealed up, or otherwise secured already was. If the sea and storm were going to kill us, they would do so without our permission whether we were asleep or not.

Lying awake there, I suddenly realized that something was strange. The incessant, joint-wrenching pitching of the waves had stopped, but the noise of the storm, which we were sure by then was a full-blown hurricane, was as loud as ever. But the weirdest thing was the way that the bow of the boat was at least five feet lower than the stern. I reached over and shook Adam awake.

"Yeah? What's wrong?"

"I don't know, but I think maybe we're sinking. The bow is low in the water."

Adam was nearest to the tiller, and he started undoing the lacing that held the boat cover in place.

"Treet, wiggle your way forward and see how much water we've taken on."

"Right."

It made sense. Small people are better at crawling through tight places than big people. I slithered downward on my belly, headfirst over lashed down crates and barrels, all the way down to the bow to find that everything there was still reasonably dry. I could feel the boat moving. We weren't on shore and hung up on something. Mystified, I crawled back up to the stern.

"It's dry!" I shouted. "Could something have grabbed us and be pulling us down?"

By this time, Adam had enough of the boat cover off to stick his head out into the air above the boat.

He pulled back his head and said, "Nope. Partner mine, we are surfing! We are on the side of one bodacious wave, and if we aren't doing thirty miles an hour, I'm a German's uncle!"

I had to pull him down, shove him away from the hole, and stick my head out, before I dared believe what he was telling me.

It was awesome! Not three feet behind us, the huge wave was breaking, spraying frothing white water all about us. In front, I looked down into a massive trough at least a hundred and fifty feet ahead of the bow of our little boat, and then the water heaped up, and up, I don't know how high. The scale of things was simply beyond the range of my ordinary thinking. To left and right, the wave seemed to go off into infinity, and to do it in an almost straight line. The wind was strong in my face as I looked forward, which was the opposite of what one would ordinarily expect. I was a while thinking about how the wind pushes the waves forward, and how, just below the crest of a wave on the leeward side, there has to be a barrel rolling counterwind going. It was a while before I finally brought my head back in, to let Adam have another look.

"Amazing, isn't it?" Adam said, his head stretching

against the boat cover so he could look at the compass on the binnacle. "Even wilder is the way we're still going northeast! I think that we oughta tell the people at Guiness about this, 'cause we must be setting a world speed record for surface travel in a tubby lifeboat! Our prayers are answered, or mine are anyway, since yours wouldn't count. Another day or two of this, and we'll be on the beach in sunny Acapulco!"

I was so stunned by what I had just seen that I couldn't think of a suitably cutting rejoinder to Adam's digs. But such is the transience of human nature that even the most incredible spectacle eventually gets boring, and in a few hours we laced the boat cover back down and broke out breakfast, cold Spam and colder creamed corn that Roxanna had once appropriated from the warehouse to her own pantry, thus saving it for our current epicurean repast.

For the last few days, we had been spending most of our time swapping old jokes, and since Adam had a better memory for such things than I did, I was forced to invent some to keep even with him.

"You heard the one about Jack and Jill?" I asked, knowing that he couldn't have since I had just thought of it.

"Do you mean the clean poem, the dirty poem, or the children's poem with all the gratuitous violence?"

"None of the above, but remember the dirty one for when it's your turn. No, Jack and Jill were two young people who hired into a production shop on the same day. For a few months, everything went well for them, since they were both cheerful, energetic types, and everybody around the shop liked them.

"Then word came down to their foreman that new orders to the shop were slowing down, and that it would be necessary for him to lay off one worker. The problem was that it was a union shop, and the rules required him to lay people off by seniority, in reverse order of that in which they were hired, and regardless of their value as workers. Since Jack and Jill both had the same low seniority date, this meant that he was going to have to lay off either Jack or Jill.

"The trouble was that he didn't want to do it. They were both very hardworking kids, and what's more, he really *liked* both of them. So naturally, he procrastinated. A week went by, and then two, and he still hadn't laid either of them off. Finally, the plant superintendent called the foreman up to the head office and chastised him for his blatant dereliction.

"'I know that you like both of those kids, but you have to lay one of them off. Which one is up to you, but either Jack or Jill has got to be laid off.'

"'You're right,' said the foreman. 'It's my job, and I'll do it. I'll tell you what. It's lunchtime now, and they're both out, but the first one of them to come back, well, I'll take him or her to my office and explain the facts to 'em.'

"It turned out that Jill was the first one back, so the foreman called her to his office.

"'Jill, I'm sorry, but, you see, well, it's come to the point where I've either got to lay you or Jack off.'

"And Jill said, 'Well, I'm sorry too, boss, but I've got a headache, and so I'm afraid you'll just have to jack off.'"

Adam laughed politely as we went surfing into the evening. He launched into a long and improbable tale about how his grandfather got robbed on his first day in New York City, but I can't relate it since I fell asleep in the middle of the story.

The boat pitched and crashed, and again I woke up knowing that something was very strange. The noise outside was still loud, but different, somehow. I was surprised to find that the bow of the boat was no longer five feet lower than the stern. It was four feet higher. My first thought was that we were somehow going backward.

Adam was quickly unlacing the boat cover as I said, "How can your sea anchor possibly be in front of us?"

"It can't."

"Then how can we be surfing on the 'up' side of a wave?"

"We can't. Look, stupid, we're not surfing any more. We're not even floating. We have arrived. We have landed. This is a beached boat! What part of that don't you understand?"

Adam crawled out of *The Concrete Canoe* and I followed. We were not on the rocky beach that I had envisioned, but rather in the shambles of a once-impressive building, a hotel, by the look of it. The bow of our boat was propped up on the copper top of a full-service bar. The wave that we had been riding for three days had driven our boat right through a set of boarded-up picture windows that had once looked out onto the beach. Water was still receding out of the hole we'd made, taking various tables, chairs, and other fixtures with it out into the blustery night.

The bartender, two attractive (if wet and bedraggled) waitresses, and four drunken customers were staring at us in disbelief.

Adam turned to them and said, "Are we too late for last call?"

We had not made landfall at Acapulco, as Adam had predicted, but at Zihuetanejo, just over a hundred miles west of it. All things considered, it would have been a remarkably good piece of navigation if it hadn't been such an incredible load of blind luck.

"Luck, hell!" Adam said, "Why can't you believe that I have God on my side?"

*This time*, I let it go, and ordered another round for all present. We had no Mexican money, but my credit cards worked. One of the waitresses, using her limited English rather than my nonexistent Spanish, eventually got around to asking about our strange clothing. I told her that we had been acting in an amateur Shakespearian comedy when we had been shipwrecked, and the story was believed. Buying new clothes was the first item on our agenda in the morning. Adam had to settle for some strange-looking beachwear until a specially made suit, shirt, and even necktie could be tailored for him, but then people his size always have a problem with buying clothes.

The Mexican police took only three days to decide that we were victims of the storm, rather than vandals intent on wrecking the best bar in town. The fact that Adam's insurance policy on *The Brick Royal* covered the damage that its tender, *The Concrete Canoe*, caused when it penetrated the hotel didn't hurt matters a bit. I hadn't even known that we had insurance on our ship. Or perhaps I should say on Adam's ship, since as it turned out, I never had gotten around to putting the thing back into my name. Also, the boat itself, completely unscathed despite all the rigors of the trip and the hole punched in the side of a major hotel, was graciously donated by the two of us to the local lifesaving society, which pleased the local mayor and his cousin, the chief of police, as well. It seems that they both enjoyed deep-sea fishing, and hinted that *The Concrete Canoe* was remarkably well suited for such a noble occupation. And since they were president and treasurer, respectively, of the lifesaving society, well, we took the hint.

It certainly beat the heck out of having them decide

that we had stolen the forty-two pounds of gold we had on board, and retaining it for evidence.

I was about to reset my watch to local time when Adam stopped me. At his insistence, we carefully checked its time against the time given us by the phone company. It was only a cheap electronic watch made by an unknown outfit called "Innovative Time," but the thing proved to be dead nuts accurate. With this information, and a book of navigation tables, we were able to calculate our true position at the time of the first fix we took after leaving the Western Isles. Then, given satellite weather photos, and modern charts of ocean currents, we figured that we would be able to make a good guess at the approximate location of the Western Islands for the next few months.

The Westronese agricultural samples were shipped along with everything we had made out of Super-Hemp via UPS to Adam's mother in Bay City. It had taken me fifteen hours to fill out the paperwork on it to get it through customs, and unless the U.S. Drug Enforcement Agency decided that we were small-time drug runners, there wouldn't be a hangup.

My credit cards stopped working. It seems that the bank in the States hadn't heard from me for over a year, and had put a stop on the account. Adam had never used a personal credit card once in his life, since they were issued by bankers and other unsavory people that he preferred not to associate with. His old company credit card was, of course, as defunct as his old company.

We bundled up all of our insurance forms along with our claims on the policies to send them off to our lawyer, Alan Greenberg, back home. I phoned him to tell him what was coming, and he just said, "Come home, both of you. Bring the papers with you. Do it now."

So we gave away the rest of the food, supplies, and

other gear that we had on the boat, mostly to the hotel bartender in thanks for his forbearance. We both thought that serving us politely showed a lot of class, considering the way we'd just demolished his bar. After we'd given it away, we discovered that both of our unopened water barrels were still filled with some of the rum we'd bought back in Puerto Rico. Had the trip lasted much longer, and with us trying to survive on rum instead of water, Adam and I could have died of dehydration, a nasty death.

"Adam, do you think that the rum could have been a third try at doing us in?"

"Nah. It was just some stupid mistake. We was real rushed, that morning, and tired, too. Anyway, nobody would be so rotten as to make you die of thirst with sixty gallons of booze right next to you."

"No. Think about it. We bought four barrels in Puerto Rico. We pretty much killed one of them by the time we hit the island. Then we took another barrel from the warehouse to Roxanna's place, for that party. That left two barrels still in the warehouse during the fire. These have to be the same ones, because the islanders don't distill liquor."

"Damn. You've got to be right. So whoever started the fire, stole the booze before they did it. Then they somehow switched these rum barrels for two of our water barrels. We are dealing with some nasty sons of bitches, there. And if they're that bad, are they going to hurt our ladies when we're not there? Even when it can't do them any good?"

"Adam? Would you pray for our women?"

And such was our distress that neither one of us thought my request unusual.

The barrels never had any markings on them, since the rum was probably bootlegged in the first place. But studying the three barrels we had aboard, these two were obviously machine made, and the almost empty water barrel was just as obviously made on the island. Still, we had no use for them, and in fact we had already given them to the bartender.

The bartender was delighted to have the rum, and presumably put it to various good and profitable uses. At least, rum drinks were on special for the rest of our stay in Mexico, and presumably for a long while after we left.

We paid off our hotel bill with my credit card (which, after my third begging and pleading session with the bank, was again working), rented an old but well-cared-for car, and picked up Adam's newly tailored clothes, so he had something to wear besides tights, a terry cloth *serape*, and a loud bathing suit. We bought two small carry-on suitcases to hold a change of underwear, a few trinkets, and twenty-one pounds of gold each, and we caught a plane that morning out of Acapulco for Detroit.

# THIRTY-SIX

We were in Bay City that night, and in Alan's office the next morning. After a minimum of social pleasantries, Greenberg pulled out a yellow legal pad and started right in.

"I know that the two of you have a year and a half's worth of stories to tell, but we have to spend the afternoon in court, and what we're seeing the judge about concerns the two of you. Now then, pursuant to your instructions, as implied by the powers of attorney that you gave me, I have looked into the strange circumstances surrounding the demise of your fortune, your company, and your marriage, Treet."

"What strange circumstances?"

"The fact that it all took place at the same time, and entirely too quickly, for starters. Normally, a company bankruptcy will drag out for a year or so, and a personal bankruptcy takes at least half of that. And no way does Michigan law allow a divorce to be granted in three weeks flat!"

"Then how did the judge allow it?"

"The judge didn't *allow* it. He *caused* it. He was conspiring with that carnivorous ex-wife of yours. Together, they came up with a plan that gave her not half of your wealth, but all of it."

"But why would he do such a thing?"

"Why? That's usually a hard one to answer, but in this case, it's fairly clear. Exactly one week after the two of you left town, your ex-wife married the judge, but they had been working on the plan for a long time.

"Fact one. The Brazilian company that you were dealing with never did go bankrupt. They mailed you a check on time and for the full amount owed, some seventeen point three million and change. But they mailed it to a post office box number here in Bay City at what they thought was your request. That is to say, your wife and the judge stole some of your company letterhead, typed up a letter to the effect that you were now using the P.O. Box number, and forged your name to it. After you were out of town, they cashed the check."

"But, we got Brazilian bankruptcy forms, and letters from Brazilian lawyers," I said.

"They were forged, and drop mailed through Brazil from here. Look in the back of *Popular Mechanics* for a listing of foreign companies that do drop mailings and that sort of thing. It usually costs a couple of bucks to get a foreign stamp put on your letter and to get it dropped off at a foreign post office. Deadbeats use the system all of the time.

"Fact two. Your company's bankruptcy sale was never properly advertised. No legitimate buyers showed up for it, and everything was sold to one bidder at less that five cents on the dollar. Needless to say, this bidder was working with the judge and your ex-wife.

"Fact three. Or maybe this isn't a fact, since I can't prove it, but it appears that an attempt was to be made on your life, while you sailed through the Panama Canal, but apparently it misfired."

"Dere was somebody dat was supposed to shoot him?" Adam asked. His phony accent had come back the moment he stepped off the plane in Bay City.

"Yes, that's what I heard, from another client of mine who's presently in jail."

"Well, dey did shoot somebody on our boat back den. A young girl named Dawn Daleki. She was maybe tree feet from Treet when dey killed her wit a long shot from a rifle."

Greenberg wrote the name down, and said, "Shit. Murder One. That opens another can of worms. But let's finish up with what I was saying, before we get into this murder case. I'll go through all the details and show you the file on your case later, before you get my bill for all of this work, but the short of it was that the judge deposited your Brazilian check in his trust account, but was hesitant about disbursing the money while you were still alive. I brought considerable pressure on him, which eventually got him disbarred and impeached, and seventeen point three million of your money is now in *my* client trust account, awaiting your pleasure.

"The machinery dealer who made such a nice profit on the resale of your equipment, faced with things like Conspiracy to Defraud, Purchasing and Possession of Stolen Goods, and Grand Larceny saw fit to pay you the full replacement cost of the machinery that had been in your plant. That is to say, what it would cost you to go out and buy all new stuff. It came to eight point eight million, and it too is currently drawing interest in my client trust account, less the two point one million that it took to satisfy your legitimate creditors. Incidentally, I had your bankruptcy overturned, and your good credit standing has been restored.

"Now then, the public humiliation of all of this proved to be too much for the judge, and he committed suicide twelve days ago. Any animosity you might have for him is now moot, but there is still your ex-wife. What do you want me to try to do about her? The terms of your divorce settlement have

also been overturned, and she got absolutely nothing out of it except for some personal property and
the bill from her lawyer. She has already been stripped
of most or perhaps all of the financial gains she'd
hoped to make, but we can still see that criminal
action is taken against the woman."

I was stunned by all of this. It was a few moments
before I said, "I don't know. This is all coming too
quickly at me, and I just don't know what to do."
I paused for a while, thinking. "No. I don't hate
Helen. I know it sounds crazy, but I think that some
part of me still loves her. I don't want to hurt her.
I just don't want to ever see her or hear from her
again."

Alan was taking copious notes.

"Dat sounds just fine, Treet. But what about Dawn?
Don't we owe her sumptin? I mean, she was wit us,
and we let her get killed."

"True. Alan, just what can we do concerning
Dawn's death?"

"Thinking about it, probably not much. She was
apparently accidentally murdered in a foreign country by a foreign hired assassin, who won't be easy
to find. I didn't hear whether or not your ex-wife
had anything to do with it. It's possible that it was
totally the judge's doing. The information that I got
on it was from a multiple felon, who claimed to have
heard about it from another prison inmate who has
since died. I really don't see how the prosecutor could
put together a case out of it, even if he did have
jurisdiction. I'll look into it for you, but don't expect
too much."

Greenberg looked at his watch and said that he
was going to have to leave in order to get to court
on time. He said that since I didn't want to continue any further legal actions against my ex-wife,
and didn't want to see her, it wouldn't be necessary for me to show up personally in court. His

legal secretary could take care of the insurance claims forms for us.

He was halfway out the door when Adam yelled, "Hey, you want dinner wit us tonight? Dat place at da river, Knot's Landing? I'm buying!"

"You're on. Seven." And Alan was gone.

I said, "Adam, your Hamtramck accent is back."

"Natch. I'm back in Bay City, ain't I."

We took over Alan's office, since we had a lot of planning to do. The claims on *The Brick Royal* came first. Adam had it insured for almost three million dollars, with lots of documentation and photos in a safe-deposit box to back up his claims. Rather than trying to explain a case of arson on a mysterious floating island, which the insurance company wouldn't have believed, and which would have kicked off a round of lawsuits and countersuits that would have dragged on for years, he just put it down as sunk in the storm that blew us into Mexico. Officially, it was his ship and his insurance policy, so I just kept my mouth shut.

One of the big advantages to being a Christian is that you can confess your sins, say a few prayers, and your sins are all gone. Us Atheists know that the universe has a way of getting back at you for all your transgressions. It keeps us a good deal more ethical than most Christians tend to be.

Once the insurance claims were attended to, the secretary tried gently to get us out of there.

Adam said, "Come on, Sarah, we got work to do. You guys is makin' probably a coupla million bucks off us, so can't you let your best customers borrow an empty office for a coupla hours?"

She allowed that put that way, it seemed reasonable.

As she left the room, I said, "We have a lot more money going for us than I thought. That means that we can start our project in a lot bigger way than what we had originally planned."

"Yeah, but you keep sayin 'we' and 'us.' Dis is mostly *your* money, ain't it? I mean, except maybe for da boat. Maybe it would be fair to call da boat 'ours,' and I did pay for dat insurance myself, you know."

"Didn't we agree to be partners? 'Retroactive back to the beginning of time'? You can't wiggle out of it now, Adam."

"But you're bein' way too generous wit dis ting."

"Nope, it's going to cost you, maybe more than you'll want to pay."

"Like what?"

"Like if you want in, you've got to stop using that God damned *phony Hamtramck accent*! The damned thing drives me crazy! From now on, you've got to speak like a normal human being, or our whole deal is off!"

"Oh. Well, if you feel that strongly about it, okay, I'll speak Midwest Standard whenever I'm around you. But if it bothered you so much, why didn't you ever say anything?"

The next two months were "interesting times."

At our lawyer's urging, we decided that we'd be better off with a corporate form of ownership rather than a simple partnership. Soon, we were The Western Isles, Ltd., with half the stock in each of our names. Adam was chairman of the board and treasurer, while I was president and CEO. I kept a million in my personal account, Adam kept a million in gold, and we threw everything else each of us owned into the corporation treasury.

Our lawyer's bill came to twenty percent of what he'd saved for us, a huge sum, but considering that we wouldn't have gotten anything at all without him, we considered it money well spent. We were both surprised that Greenberg wasn't interested in buying any stock in our new corporation, and being on the board of directors, even after, having sworn him to secrecy, we told him the whole true story.

"You are passing up the opportunity of a lifetime," Adam told him.

"I'm still aghast at your newfound diction, Adam, but no. I work best as an individual, not as a member of a group. But thanks for the offer, anyway."

So, we put him on a retainer as our corporate attorney, and let it go at that. Personally, I think that he thought we were both more than a little crazy, and that no such island could possibly exist.

Shirley, my old office girl, accountant, and receptionist jumped at the chance to come back and work for us. She didn't care whether the islands existed or not, she said, and she claimed that she already knew that we were both crazy. She said she'd known that for years. Mostly, she just wanted to be part of the team again, and was downright antsy to get out of Chrysler Corporation, where she'd been working for the last year or so. Her husband, who also used to work for me, felt the same way, and while we didn't need a machinist just now, you can always use an intelligent and honest man, so we hired him anyway. All this despite the fact that we were moving the office to San Diego, and before we told her that we were doubling her salary.

We gave Shirley a checkbook and told her to rent us a warehouse with a nice office suite near the San Diego docks, and a couple of big apartments near them for Adam and me. She was given a long list of things to buy once we had a place to put them, and was told to look around for a small, used ocean-going freighter, as well. It's great to have people that you trust. It's awkward and then some to have to work with those that you don't dare trust.

When you need to get a lot of things done, you have to start working on your long lead time items first. The thing that we needed to do that would take the most time was to design and build a machine to scrape the coral and waterlogged featherrock from the bottom of the Western Islands. Having such a machine working would show the duke that we were seriously concerned with the long-term welfare of his people.

We spent a week looking for a company that could build us an underwater, remote-controlled, inverted bulldozer, until we finally found the outfit that makes those underwater remote-controlled submarines that are used for deep-sea exploration and salvage. What we wanted was bigger than anything they'd ever built before, but we figured that they knew enough about the special engineering problems that are faced in deep, high-pressure water to handle our job.

We faced a problem in that we couldn't tell them exactly what we wanted to do with the machine we were asking for. We had to keep secret the fact that the Western Isles existed. Public disclosure would be socially, medically, and politically disastrous for the islanders. It would also be financially disastrous for Adam and me, and would destroy any hope we might have of reconciliation with the powers that be on the Western Islands.

The people at Modern Oceanographics couldn't help being curious when all we could tell them was what the dozer had to do, and not where it would be used or why it was needed.

Finally, Adam said, "Look, if you want us to tell you lies, just say so. Otherwise, please shut up about it."

In the end, they agreed to stop asking why, and we agreed to give them the design and build contract for what we needed.

Adam and I are machinery designers, and it would have been fun to do the design job ourselves, but in design work, the fun jobs are those where you are doing something different from what you have done before. That is to say, where you don't quite know what you are doing. Making something that works properly requires that you *do* know what you're doing. Situated between fun and accomplishment is education, and educating yourself with only mother nature for a teacher is always a *very* expensive and time-consuming proposition.

Even so, one of us, usually Adam, flew out to New England about once a week to keep an eye on what was happening, until we were ready to go back to the Western Isles. By then, the design was complete, but the dozer itself wouldn't be completed for another three months. Also, by then the dozer was no longer a dozer. It was now a submarine with caterpillar treads on the roof and a set of vertical milling cutters in front.

As Murphy's Law required, we were three weeks getting our Westronese agricultural samples through customs, and after two weeks we had to put Greenberg on the case, but eventually we were successful.

Shirley and her husband got going on the three crates, the four books, and the electronic version of *Thomas Register*, trying to match each item up with a company or two that might have some use for it. Soon, they were going international in their company search.

We started negotiations with dozens of outfits, and had sent samples to six of them before we shipped out. Not that being on shipboard would stop us from negotiating anything, what with modern communications and all. There was no significant income from all this yet, but it would come.

In the meantime, we amassed canned meat and grains, enough to feed twelve thousand people for a year.

We bought an estimated two-year supply of commercial fertilizers.

We bought samples of small, Japanese-built farm machinery, suitable for working small plots of land.

We bought samples of hand tools and gardening equipment of a hundred different types. Indeed, we bought enough hardware of all kinds to open a fair-sized store, which was just what we planned to do.

We bought lumber, steel, and glass.

When the cost of silver coins proved to be much higher than the cost of silver, we had our own coins made, slugs, really, but in the denominations in use in the Western Isles. Copper pennies, on the other hand, were cheaper than the cost of copper slugs, thanks to the strange ways of the U.S. Government.

We bought diesel generators sufficient to electrify about a quarter of the island, and wiring and lights enough for all the regularly traveled tunnels.

We bought fuel enough to run those generators for a year.

We bought televisions, VCRs, and radios. And a big projection system, for auditorium-style viewing.

We bought compressors, hoses, and SCUBA gear for fifty men.

We bought a small but complete machine shop, with a small electric smelter and a modern forge, to fix anything that broke, and to make anything that we might have forgotten.

We bought a cellular, digital phone system, with two hundred handsets. And a satellite communication system to tie into it.

We bought more navigation, communication, and remote sensing equipment than we had on the old *Brick Royal*.

The biggest, long lead time items like generators and machine tools were often bought secondhand, but most of the rest was new, with factory warranties.

And we had a ball doing it, spending much of our newfound wealth.

We found and hired a medical doctor and her nurse, two women with experience in mass immunizations in faraway lands. We were vague about where we told them we were going, but we let them buy what they felt they needed to take care of twelve thousand people.

Finding the freighter to haul all of this out to the Western Islands wouldn't be difficult. There were lots of them on the market. Hiring a captain and crew that we could trust was another problem entirely. They had to know where we were going, or we obviously wouldn't get there. Once we were there, they would know what we had found. We needed people who were either absolutely honest or absolutely loyal to us, because they would be in a position to screw us royally, while making themselves a fortune doing it.

"Dare we try to run the ship ourselves?" I said.

"If it was in good enough shape to begin with, and not likely to break down, I don't see why not. Navigating a big ship is no different than navigating a rowboat," Adam said. "Except for the fact that it would be against the law. It takes all kinds of licences and permits before they let you run a commercial, oceangoing freighter."

"Well, what if we buy a boat registered in Nigeria or Ecuador or something. Doesn't that get us around the law?" I asked.

"Maybe, I'm not sure. But I still don't like it. There's a lot more to running a ship than a sailboat. If we blow it, we could get a lot of people killed. Including us. Tell you what. Let's go talk to a bonding company. They sell a sort of insurance on people, where if somebody cheats on us, or gives away company secrets like the Western Isles, we get paid a lot, and the crook gets shafted properly."

So that's what we did. We got recommendations on a captain, and had the bonding company check him out. Then we told him exactly what we were doing, paid him half again what was usual, and had him check out and recommend the ship to buy. We even let him hire his own, minimal crew, although they also had to pass the bonding company's muster.

We used the same approach on our security team. Soon, we had our own, well-paid, twelve-man police force. Their leader was Colonel Jezowski, and Major Perkins was his executive officer. Of the other ten, some of them were ex-SEALs, and the rest were ex-Special Forces. They were all retired sergeants or navy chiefs, and all had some civilian police training. And yeah, they were expensive, but this time, Adam and I weren't going to be beat up, burned out, and chased out of town.

# THIRTY-SEVEN

We set sail on a fine morning, under a clear blue sky, which was ordinary enough for San Diego, but a special delight for a couple of men born and raised under the often grey skies of Michigan. With Shirley and her husband holding down the office in San Diego, Adam and I were returning to the Western Islands, and to our ladies fair.

Our ship was fueled, loaded and crewed. Captain Cyrus Johnson was the sort of man who exuded trust and confidence, almost too much of it, with his close-clipped white hair, his ramrod-straight posture, and his impeccably tailored uniforms. He was an Annapolis graduate, had been a career U.S. Navy man, and had spent the last ten years as a merchant captain before he had been forcibly retired at seventy-one. He was physically healthy, mentally alert, and wanted to stay at sea. If some idiot shipping company insisted on letting him go, that was their sad problem. Adam and I figured that we would have been fools to pass him by.

The members of his seven-man crew had similar backgrounds, and they always saluted him in military fashion. It just came natural around the man. Even Adam and I had to restrain ourselves from saluting, genuflecting or kowtowing in some manner.

Here he was, working for us, and there we were, working hard at not subordinating ourselves to him. But I could hardly criticize a man for being too much of what we had asked for in the first place. We figured that if we ever needed someone to stare down his grace Duke Guilhem Alberigo XXI, Captain Johnson was our man.

The ship, the *James Crawford*, was old but well kept. We got it for a lot less than I thought we'd have to spend. Small freighters like ours were no longer economical. They couldn't begin to compete with the big, fast container ships, but for what we had in mind, it was perfect.

Adam and I toyed with changing the name, since nobody had the slightest idea who James Crawford was or had been. But the captain wasn't enthusiastic about it, so we let the matter lie.

Our Chief of Police, or perhaps I should call him our Guard Captain, Colonel Jezowski, had a fair amount in common with Captain Johnson. A West Point graduate, with a distinguished career in the U.S. Army, he had been a police chief in a middle-sized Oregon town until he too had been forcibly retired.

This business of hiring retirees wasn't accidental. We wanted steady, calm, and experienced men, not fire breathers. We wanted to keep the peace, not win a war.

Our police force was fit and well armed. Although we hadn't seen the need for any heavy weaponry, or explosives, we were strong on detection equipment, bugging devices, and surveillance cameras. Since our enemies on the island were not likely to know of the existence of such things, we resolved to use them discreet©ly, and to mention them not at all.

Our new CD library was well stocked in most areas, but not in spy movies and police melodramas. Oh, the islanders would be able to pick up just about anything off the satellite hookup, but having them learn later rather than sooner was all for the better.

Except for the captain and the colonel, we had kept our mission destination a secret from our newly hired people, just saying that it was a remote but healthy place with friendly people. Once at sea, we gathered them together, and Adam, having lost the toss, swore them to secrecy and then told them the whole, true story.

I don't think one person in ten completely believed us, but via the internet, they'd seen that their pay was being deposited into their bank accounts in San Diego, and that's enough for most people.

We had Captain Johnson check out our calculations, guesses really, as to the position of the Western Islands. We showed him Adam's antique sextant, which he found to be quaint, but accurate, and told him how we checked out my watch, a week or so after the sighting. The captain had us shoot a noon fix, and he couldn't fault our equipment, our technique, or our calculations.

It wasn't until we showed him the map we'd gotten on the island that he really perked up. He asked all sorts of questions about it, and even about the "paper" it was drawn on. Eventually, I got the feeling that the good captain was starting to believe that we were telling the truth about the islands.

Maybe we should have showed everybody the crates of agricultural products we'd brought back, instead of keeping everything as secret as possible. Some of the stuff, like Super-Hemp, was as impressive as all hell. The simple fact was that I had never had trouble making people believe me before, and neither had Adam. We had thought that our problem would be to keep the place secret, to keep the profits up, and to keep our promises to the duke. That everybody would think we were liars had simply never occurred

# 300

to us. If we hadn't had enough money to convince people to come along even if we were crazy, the whole project would have ended in that smashed-up Mexican hotel bar.

We had some island clothing with us, saved for our grand entrance there, and one day I showed a group of security people my gorgeously embroidered jacket. When they looked unimpressed, I challenged them to rip it up, and once they saw I was serious, five big men gave it their best shot. Not so much as a wrinkle! One of them had a fighting knife at his belt, and I told him to go ahead and cut it up. He tried, without doing anything but dulling his knife.

"So," I said at last. "Have I made believers out of you?"

A huge ex-SEAL said, "I don't know, sir, but that's the prettiest piece of Kevlar I ever saw!"

I picked up my jacket and walked away, my head hung low. Somehow, I'd make them believe.

We started giving a series of talks and seminars about the Western Islands, explaining their history, their technology, and their customs. We even tried to teach our new employees a bit of the language, simple stuff like "Hello," "Thank You," and "Take Me To My Leader, Since I'm Lost." Attendance was dismal, even when we told people that attending was part of their job.

We got more excuses than warm bodies. Part of the reason for the seminars was to convince people that the islands really existed, but we still hadn't made believers out of them.

It took us just over a week to arrive at our estimated position for the island. We were on deck, along with most of our people, but there was nothing to look at but an empty ocean. The island wasn't there, but we weren't worried. Even though it was statistically the most likely place for the Western Isles to be, we had calculated that there was only about a one in twenty chance that we could see them from where we were. The islands moved, after all, with the winds and the currents.

We started in on a standard search pattern, spiraling outward from our point of origin. Besides having at least two men on lookout at all times, we had both radar and sonar going continuously as well. We'd find it.

Adam and I continued working, checking on the progress of our submarine milling robot, encouraging the negotiations on the island's products, and generally keeping busy. The truth was that we both had first-rate cases of nerves. We each found excuses at least six times a day to go up on deck, have a look around, and see nothing but the empty sea.

Adam came to me one morning, looking excited.

"Treet! You heard the news?"

"We found the island?"

"No. That lab got back to Shirley about what Super-Hemp is made out of."

"The chemical formula? So?" I said.

"It's polyethylene. Super-high molecular weight polyethylene."

"Bullshit. Polyethylene is the cheapest plastic around, and it was almost the first one invented. If it could be made that strong, somebody would have done it years ago."

"I'm serious! Ordinary, commercial polyethylene is weak because the molecules are short, they slide against each other, and slip apart. Super-Hemp has molecules three feet long! To break it, you have to break a covalent bond, and that's not an easy thing to do."

I said, "It still doesn't make sense. The molecules would have to be thousands of times longer than the cells of the plant they were formed in. How could that be?"

"So maybe they stick out a hole in the cell wall. Did I say I was a botanical cytologist? All I know is that we are dealing with a high-molecular-weight plastic."

"Interesting, but I don't see where it changes anything. No news on the island, huh?"

"No."

The ship's crew and our police, who were standing deck watch, were doing their duty in a calm, professional manner, but I had the feeling that they didn't really expect to find anything, much less a fabulous floating island. Several times, we heard laughing from the crew's quarters, and we were pretty sure that they were making jokes about us.

Four days later, Adam and I were still less confident. In fact, it was getting downright nervewracking. What if everybody else was right and we were wrong? People have gone crazy before. Good, sane men have had hallucinations. I had been hit on the head on three separate occasions. Could I have imagined Roxanna? Was it all just a fantasy trip indulged in by two horny, middle-aged men? These were not pleasant thoughts to dwell on.

"We're now circling our starting point at a radius of four hundred and thirty miles," Adam said.

"We've been gone from the islands for over a hundred days," I said. "At one mile an hour, which is slow for an ocean current, that gives them time to go two thousand four hundred miles."

"I know. And if we go on circling and searching for another hundred days, our radius will be only twenty-two hundred miles, while they could easily have gone a total of forty-eight hundred miles by then. What it adds up to is that if they want to run and hide in some other area of the ocean, we can't catch them by searching, even though we're twenty times faster than they are," Adam said.

"So we have to go on the assumption that they aren't deliberately running from us. Let's continue using the present search pattern two more days, and see what turns up."

"Okay. For now, I'm going to see if I remember how to do a Drunkard's Walk analysis."

"You do that," I said. "I'm going down to the mess to do some empirical tests on the same problem."

"You're going to get drunk and then try to walk."

"Right."

Being drunk does not make your problems go away, but it does make enduring them seem to take less time. When the two days had gone by without incident, we went to the captain and asked him to return to our original position and to try the search pattern again, only running it clockwise this time. After all, a standard search pattern can be guaranteed to work only if the target stays in one place, and ours was obviously not doing that.

Captain Johnson agreed to follow our instructions, mentioning that we had fuel and supplies aboard for another two months. Adam prayed that it wouldn't take that long, and I almost wished that I could do that with him.

At three the next morning, I was beating on Adam's cabin door.

"Adam, wake up. Tell me, how would the Western Islands show up looking from a geosynchronous weather satellite?"

"We checked that out once," he said groggily. "An area the size of the islands is just on the edge of detectability from a weather satellite. It would appear to be about the size of a single pixel. A spy satellite can read the headlines on a newspaper, but they have to be pointed at what you want to see, like the telescopes they are, and nobody much cares about this part of the ocean."

"Right. So what we need is the raw data from

several months of weather satellite observations. We look for anomalies, glitches and noise right on the edge of detectability that are close to other glitches that showed up on the previous day's photo. When we have a string of glitches in a row, we know the position of the islands!"

By this time, Adam was fully awake.

"It's easier than that," he said. "We know the starting position, the date and place of our first sighting on the *Concrete Canoe*. We need some computer programmers, and there's an outfit I know of in New Dehli that works cheap. Also, they'll be awake right now."

"But, we can't tell them about the islands!"

"Right, but not because they'd believe us. Nobody believes us about the islands! We need a story that they *will* believe. How about we lost a huge drift net that got tangled up with a lot of flotsam at a certain time and place, and the ship that left it there had to run from a storm. Now we need to find it to stop it from causing further ecological damage."

"Sounds good to me, except that it wasn't us who were using the thing, but some bad guys we heard about," I said.

"Good point. That way they'll know that we were using it and want to get it back before we're caught."

I said, "Then you are letting them think that we committed a crime!"

"True. That way they'll keep it quiet, since if we get arrested and our accounts are frozen by the courts, the programmers won't get paid."

"Adam, you have a devious mind."

"Don't it make you feel proud?" Adam almost slipped back into his Hamtramck accent, caught himself, and continued on in English. "Come on, let's put in a call to New Dehli!"

❖   ❖   ❖

Captain Johnson continued our search pattern for five more gut-wrenching days before the Indian programmers finally got back to us. They had a definite fix on the islands, and a chart showing where they had been almost every day for the last four months.

As it turned out, we had been within a hundred miles of the islands on three separate occasions since the search began, but had just missed them each time. I razzed Adam about his "God's on my side" statements, and he didn't even get decently mad at me.

We "wired" the programmers a check for their services, along with a nice bonus, with the understanding that they were to destroy their files on the job and tell no one about the work they'd done for us.

This they promised to do, thanking us for the prompt payment and the gratuity. We were confident that they would keep it all quiet, since they thought that they had participated in an international crime, using a drift net on the open ocean.

We changed course for the island's present position, and our captain said that we would be there by the next afternoon.

The captain soon had the crew cleaning and polishing the ship, and our police promptly joined in. The next morning was spent cleaning ourselves, since a mostly male group can get pretty rank at sea.

Men who openly scoffed at our search were suddenly transformed into true believers. Adam and I were mobbed by crewmen and guards who were suddenly eager to learn everything they could about the Western Islands. Those few people who had attended our seminars regularly were also in demand. Our men were vastly interested to see if the island women were as warm and as loving as we had promised.

A crate of old signal flags had been among the extra equipment we'd inherited when we bought the ship, and I told the captain that I wanted them flying when we reached the island. When he asked what I wanted them to say, I said that the ones in front should read, "Roxanna, I'm back!"

Our ship had every flag on board flying and we were all in our best, as first the radar, then sonar and finally the watch on the bridge sighted the impossible floating islands.

Adam and I were in our fanciest, festive island clothing, brought along and saved for the occasion, when we finally saw our home again with our own eyes.

A huge crowd of islanders was waiting for us at the entrance to the island's central lagoon, the Llyr. They all seemed to be happy to see us, and nowhere was there the angry face of someone who wished us ill.

The duke was in the forefront, smiling and waving, and beside him stood the warlock. Adam searched the crowd carefully with binoculars, and said that the archbishop was conspicuously absent.

We spotted the Pelitier sisters, and standing next to them, laughing and cheering us in, was my own true love, Roxanna.

# THIRTY-EIGHT

Sitting in front of the full Grand Council, the duke leaned heavily on the arms of his massive chair.

"So. It's them? There can be no mistake?"

"No, Your Grace. I could read the signal flags they are flying. Treet calls Roxanna by name, and tells her that he's returned," the warlock said.

"Then there is little more to say. If we oppose them further, we shall lose everything. The only sane thing to do is to admit defeat, and offer our services as administrators to our conquerors. That way, we can at least protect our people and maintain our crown."

"That would be a dastardly thing, a cowardly thing to do!" shouted the archbishop. "Your forefathers were made of better stuff! Has your line become nothing but the trail of slime-covered slugs? Fight them! Your people would follow you to the death, if you but asked them!"

"Yes, they would, because they love me and trust me, just as I love and trust them. How then could I lead them into certain destruction? No. We are beaten, but we can still put a good face on things. We will all give them a cheerful welcome into the harbor, we will invite them to a feast, and we will do everything that they ask, to prove to them that we will be good and faithful servants to them. They, being *as intelligent as we are, will know that we will be able to serve them well only if the people see us still as their leaders. In name at least, I will still be duke, and you will still be my noblemen, my churchmen, and my wizards.*

"*Then, one day, who knows? We of the Western Islands are accustomed to thinking in the long term, working in generations and centuries when lesser breeds think in days and years. These two men will not live forever, and one day we may well be masters of our own souls again.*

"*But for now, our path is clear. We must be united in welcoming our new masters to power.*"

*The archbishop stood, shaking with defiance. "And I swear to all of you that I will never do such a foul thing!"*

*The duke looked at him for a full minute, while all in the room sat silent, half afraid to breathe. Finally, he said, "Very well, you need not join us. Indeed, it is only fitting, since it was due to your advice, and your covert actions, that we find ourselves in this sorry condition. Uncle Felix, take the good Archbishop out and kill him. Make it look like an accident.*"

*At the top of an open-centered spiral staircase that seemed to go down into infinity, Earl Felix and the archbishop were approached by a tall young man in a monk's cassock.*

"*Bartholomew!*" *the Archbishop cried. "Thank God it's you! Help me! Save me from this man, who means to kill me!*"

*The monk stepped closer, but Earl Felix raised one hand and said, "Stop! This man has offended the Duke, who has ordered his death.*"

*The monk stopped, saying, "I am relieved, my lord, for the Duke's word takes precedence over even a Vow of Absolute Obedience. You may proceed with my blessings, for this man has dirtied my very soul. With your permission, my lord, may I watch?*"

*The earl nodded.*

*"Thank you, my lord. Then again, may I do the job for you?"*

The water by the stone wharf proved to be deep enough so that we could tie the ship up without difficulty. The ancient dockage at the mouth of the Llyr could not have been built for ships as large as ours, and most harbors in the world are gradually silting up, getting shallower unless they are regularly dredged out. However, since the Western Isles were sinking, its harbor was actually getting deeper. We'd have to watch the situation carefully, once we got to scraping the bottom of the island, to make sure that we didn't beach our ship.

Adam was the first one ashore, and I was inches behind him going down the gangplank, eager to give Roxanna a proper hug and a kiss.

After allowing us a few minutes with our ladies, the duke himself came up to greet us. He made a short speech, first in Westronese and then in English, welcoming us back, and granting all the men on the ship visas to stay on the islands for as long as they wished. He even threw in a line to the young ladies of his realm, asking that they give his new guests a warm welcome. He acted as though we had left and had returned with his understanding and permission, rather than having been beat up, burned out, and then forced to sneak away in the early dawn with only a third of the water we'd need to survive the trip.

Adam glanced at me, I nodded, and wordlessly we decided that if the duke wanted to put the best face possible on the situation, we would let him do it. *We* had the power, now, and we could afford to be generous. When the colonel stationed armed guards around our ship, most of them standing on the

sovereign territory of the Western Islands, the duke
said not a word about it.

Adam handled the formalities, introducing everybody to everybody else, while I stood back, wondering
why, when we had that machinery company, I hadn't
put Adam in charge of sales instead of trying to
handle it myself. He was much better with people
than I was.

Adam and I, along with the captain, the colonel,
the doctor, and our ladies, were invited to a royal
feast that afternoon. Within minutes, we received
formal written invitations, with the ink still wet on
them.

We only had about two hours before we would have
to leave for the palace, a place that Adam and I had
never been to before. Our group broke up, the nobles
to the palace, our officers to get into their best dress
uniforms, Adam and his ladies to their place for a
quick sprucing up.

Walking to Roxanna's to change into clothing that
would be appropriate for a royal banquet, I was
stopped by the warlock.

"Well, Treet, you seem to have done everything
properly."

"Properly?"

"Yes. You've arranged matters such that the duke's
only option is to act as though none of the unpleas-
antries of the past ever happened, and that you went
away and came back entirely with his permission. He
knows that if you and Adam, drunk and just out of
your sickbeds, could wipe out a score of his top
athletes, the trained fighting men you've brought with
you could easily conquer the entire island, if it came
to that. His grace's best hope is therefore that it will
be more convenient for you to rule through him,
rather than trying to do it yourselves, directly."

My head was spinning. These people actually
thought this way? That under the bland, civilized

exterior, we and they had been playing some sort of game of power politics all along?

All I could think of to say was, "How did he know that I would bring back a sufficient military force?"

"Simple. He knows that you would not dare to return without one. Since you have returned, the force must be there."

"His Grace is doubtless correct." Again, it was all I could think of to say.

"Of course. Trying to manage an unruly population would be expensive and bloody. The duke's presence can do you a great deal of good. So, to put it simply, you've won. You know you've won, and the duke knows that you've won. He knows that all that he can do now is to aid in making the transition as painless as possible."

"Good," I said, feeling I was in way over my head. "I'm glad that's all cleared up. But for now, the less said, the better."

"Of course. I only wanted to add that if there is anything that I or my people can do, you have only to ask."

"Good. Uh, it might be nice if the archbishop would stop trying to stir up trouble," I said, taking a stab in the dark.

"That matter has already been taken care of. Our good archbishop suffered an unfortunate fall on a long stairway only an hour ago. We'll all go to his funeral in a few days. You'll get an invitation. Until the banquet, then."

And then he left.

Roxanna seemed to be in shock after hearing the warlock talk, and said not a word during the rest of the walk home. An hour later, she was back to normal. Later, when I asked her for her thoughts about what the warlock had said, she claimed that he had said nothing, that the warlock had never spoken to me at all!

My only conclusion is that her mind was made up of little boxes, and that like all Christians, there were areas that contained things that she simply wasn't able to think about at all.

I was happy to meet Adam on the way to the palace. I waved the women on ahead of us and then told him word for word what the warlock had said.

"It's a real pity, about the archbishop, but I guess it had to happen," Adam said. "But about everything else, it's wonderful! Success in our own time! Victory! Our plan couldn't possibly have worked out better! It'll be clean sailing from here out."

"Plan?" I said, "What plan? We never had a plan! And since when were we playing power politics on that level?"

"Since we left with our tails between our legs, survived the trip back, set up our trading company exactly like we told the people here we were going to do, and came back with a small, but very competent army to back us up. I mean, why else did we hire those ex-SEALs and the ex-Special Forces types? Rent-A-Cops would have been a whole lot cheaper. I was real impressed with your style all the way along there."

"But I never really had a plan, Adam. I was just doing what seemed right at the time, making sure that we could get back here to the girls, and making sure that we could protect them."

"And now they will be perfectly safe. You planned this outcome right from the beginning. Without a well thought out plan, it never could have worked out this perfectly."

"I tell you, Adam, I never had a plan!"

"Yes, you did, even if maybe you didn't know about it. You see, Treet, you have one of those 'compartmentalized' minds, the kind that can be totally rational in most things, but with some areas that are sort of like a computer in 'protect' mode, where you aren't allowed to think about what's in there. I mean, how else could you be such a good engineer, and still believe in that Atheism shit you're always spouting? Anyway, we gotta get going, or we'll be late to our own victory celebration, that the duke's throwing for us."

I stood there speechless, with my mouth open, until Roxanna took my arm and dragged me after the others.

# The End

## AUTHOR'S NOTES

This book had its start in a couple of failed projects. There was a ferrocrete boat that I planned to build, but was never quite able to get going on. The culture of the island came about when I was trying to form up a variation of the SCA that nobody wanted to join. I guess if you can't do it, you might as well write about it.

The rest was the result of noticing, in the course of my usual random reading, that there were these insistent references to the Western Islands. One legend had the apostle, Doubting Thomas, going to spend his days on the Western Islands. The Arthurian legends have Uther Pendragon, King Arthur's father, coming from the Western Islands. Medieval maps clearly show islands off the west coast of France. Irish legends repeatedly talk about floating islands off their western shore.

And there is this floating volcanic rock in Hawaii.

Given the above, well, what's a novelist to do?

Leo Frankowski
January 9, 1999
Sterling Heights, MI